Presents

R.K. Byers'
UPTOWN HEADS

Published by
THE X PRESS, 55 BROADWAY MARKET, LONDON E8 4PH.
TEL: 0171 729 1199   FAX: 0171 729 1771

© R.K. Byers 1995.

Distributed by Turnaround, 27 Horsell Road, London N5 1XL
Tel: 0171 609 7836

Printed by BPC Paperbacks Ltd, Aylesbury, Bucks.

ISBN   1-874509-30-1

To Bevelyn J. Byers
And all the other revolutionary mother/sistas who make
guys like R.K. Byers virtually, it would seem, by themselves.

SUPREMACY

Harlem has changed, we often hear and we probably believe it. We see the new cars, new clothes and the occasional new building and ignore the same old filth in those new trash cans, the same old sins from those new sinners, and the same old mentalities underneath those brand new hats. We see that the vendors are gone off One Hundred and Twenty Fifth Street, a directive of the new mayor, who replaced the black new mayor in the same old government. And that the Nubian Islamic Hebrews have replaced the Nation of Islam on the soap boxes— the Nation of Islam having now gone mainstream, no longer needing to scream to get the attention of the masses, while the Nubians, in their 'straight-off-a-Funkadelic-album-cover' costumes have not gotten that message yet. Oh, you'll still find a hypodermic needle or two, but where have you been if you're looking for the golden days of 'smack' on every corner, cause now there's crack on every corner. As George Jackson would say, a psychic adjustment at best. And if you're wondering whatever happened to Nicky Barnes, the baddest Uptown player depending on who you ask in history, he got Fed time, Son, back in the seventies when it seemed that President Carter himself couldn't deal with the notion of a nigga having the reputation of being that big time. Can't be going out in grander style than the mob now, can you? Yeah, there was another big time brotha with a name like dog food, but nobody seems to know exactly what happened to him. Still, we can say that things have changed because you no longer see brothas gather on corners trying to be the new Dells, or new Platters, or new Temptations, crooning, harmonising and trying to get their collective sound just right before they approach somebody's uncle's cousin about getting their foot in the door at the local radio station or going on the Apollo amateur night. Now, brothas are standing on those corners trying to be the new Mobb Deep, or new Wu Tang Clan, attempting to finish a rhyme where they killed enough niggas and smoked enough blunts to be believably 'hard' despite the fact that most of them can't even fist fight, trying to get their demos in the doors of a record company using somebody's uncle's cousin. New parks and projects and hangouts have replaced the old parks and projects and hangouts. The big timers don't drive Caddys anymore, they drive BMWs. Striver's Row is still where the rich niggas live and everywhere else is where everybody else lives, and if you look around and make changes, not big ones, but small, subtle changes, you'll notice something that'll blow your mind. Date all the cars back a decade, or two, or four. Take the brothas outta dreads and bald heads, Tommy Hilfiger and Karl Kani boots, and put them in Afros and dashikis, or zoot suits and conks. Take all the sistas out of box weaves and bobs, knit summer one-pieces and polyesters. Don't do **anything** with the rats, the roaches, the crime, the grime, the pimps, the players, the numbers to be run, the tenements and brownstones—in no particular order—the unpaid rents and undisguised rent parties, the pickpockets

1

*and idiots who still put their wallets in their back pockets, the big-legged girls,
the peddlers of dope, skin, and religion, the juke joints and joy houses, the
churches and the mosques, gentrification and back to Africa, the holly rollers and
the bootleggers, the believers in a new Harlem renaissance and the remnants of
the first one, the cheap bottles of bum wine, and is it my imagination, or is
everybody smoking weed again? And think about it. I mean really think about
it. But there has to have been some kinda change, we say to ourselves, as the old
folks shake their heads solemnly back and forth at us as if we don't, couldn't, and
will never understand. And it's when we finally look into their eyes and away
from all the superficial 'newness' of these old things that we begin to get the message. That we begin finally to understand. What we understand is that this is
Harlem. And nothing has changed, or ever will change. But what we still don't
understand, what perhaps we'll never understand, is why we love it so.*

Tyrone and Tony were making their way through the haze of another
Friday night. They had started at Tony's building, on the corner of One
Hundred and Eleventh Street and Lenox Avenue. They were late.
Knowing this seemed to put them in no particular hurry. As opposed to
walking up St Nicholas, which would have brought them closer to their
destination, they walked all the way up Lenox Avenue past One
Hundred and Twenty Sixth Street, and to the basketball courts further on
the east side in the mid One Hundred and Thirties. There were always
people out there in the summer playing ball, and Tyrone was hoping to
get chosen in a pick-up game. Neither he nor Tony was surprised when
he wasn't. Steve wasn't with them. Neither of them ever got picked
unless Steve was with them. Still, Tyrone needed something to work off
the nervous energy he felt because of the announcement he was about to
make. He and Tony crossed back over to Lenox, and walked down to
One Hundred and Twenty Fifth, and took a right. There were a lot of people out, Tyrone noticed. But anybody not hip enough to already be where
he and Tony were going, he didn't wanna be bothered with. They
stopped at the corner of St Nicholas Avenue at the liquor store. Bumpy
was there, probably taking a break, and soon to be on his way back to
their final destination. They tried to con him into buying them beers that
they were too young to buy for themselves. After a few choice profani-
ties and some, "I knew ya Daddies," Bumpy finally agreed. Outside the
store, Tyrone and Tony listened as some old niggas told lies about places
they'd been, people they'd seen and things they'd supposedly done.
Beer, in brown paper bags, in hand, Tyrone and Tony walked up a block
then made a right. Passing a group of girls who only talked to brothas
with money—a category that neither of them fitted into—they made
obscene gestures, thinking, as every man does that, deep down, that
kinda shit really turns a woman on! The nervous energy was getting to

2

Tyrone again. He felt like doing something, he said to Tony. Tony didn't understand. They were about to go to the Uptown Heads barbershop; as far as Tony was concerned, that was doing something. Tyrone didn't feel like explaining.

The Uptown Heads barbershop had come on the scene five years earlier like a dynamo, putting every other barbershop in the area out of business. The cornerstone of a block that was only known for being the block behind the world's most famous theatre. The Uptown Heads barbershop had always been as much a hangout spot as a place of business. But unlike any other hangout spot, the rules of conduct were strictly adhered to because anyone caught in violation would be banished, or have to deal with Riff. And while some could take or leave banishment, nobody wanted to deal with Riff. Riff was one of the barbers. There were only three. Riff, Mike, and Supreme. Their skills were legendary. Riff was what the old heads liked to call a 'professional'. He got the job done. There were no tricks or gimmicks in his approach. He simply gave what was asked for, no more, no less. Older men loved him because he could make them look like they had back in their younger days from just a photograph, or give them a modified, more mature version of a current style. Women bringing their children in for a cut loved him because the kid would be sure to leave with a 'safe' haircut. He also attracted a large number of the young clientele who thought Supreme was plain crazy, and Mike was a little too flamboyant for their taste. Riff remained busy. Very busy.

Who the best barber was, was debated between everyone except the barbers themselves. If asked individually who was the best barber among them, each one would simply reply himself, and not be surprised or offended when the others answered the same way.

The customers who preferred Mike didn't have an exact idea of what kind of haircut they wanted, all they knew was that they wanted to look good. They would sit in Mike's chair and give a vague description of what they thought they wanted with phrases like 'sorta like' and 'kinda like'. What they got was a masterpiece. Mike had a way of making a cut look like it was a natural part of the head; like the customer had been born with it. The angles and dimensions of Mike's cuts all blended in perfectly with the customer's head, and even complexion. The customer would leave speechless, never having known that he could look that good.

Supreme's customers knew exactly what they wanted the minute they sat in the chair. They barked orders with explicit detail and exact specification. What they got was what they asked for, and a little more. Supreme had a certain signature technique. Everybody knew when you had a Supreme haircut, and other people who had one smiled and nodded when they encountered someone else with one. It was like a membership to an elite social group, and once you were in, you refused to join any other. The customer left unable to do anything but talk; talk about the pleasure of, for once, getting exactly what he wanted.

Tyrone and Tony burst through the door of Uptown Heads in the middle of one of the shop's big laughs. The place went dead silent. All eyes went to Supreme.

Supreme glanced up briefly from the head he was cutting to see who had just entered, then resumed his work.

Steve had been waiting for his two friends. He looked first at them, then at Supreme. "Just remember," he reminded the barber, "I was on time."

Supreme breathed a silent chuckle. Tyrone, Tony and Steve had a regular seven o'clock appointment for a haircut every Friday. It was now eight-fifteen. When you missed your slot at Uptown Heads there was always someone else to take your place in the barber's chair.

Tony eased warily into a seat next to Steve, but Tyrone remained standing. It was time.

"Got a letter today," he told Supreme proudly.

Supreme didn't bother to look up.

"Gonna ask me who from?"

Silence.

"From Garvey X University," he continued anyway. "You know, the Mecca of Black Education." Supreme remained silent, but a few impressed eyebrows raised throughout the shop. Tyrone frowned, waiting for a response, a facial expression, something from Supreme. Nothing came.

"You know," he began again, using this time what he knew was sure to provoke a response from Supreme—an insult. "The place that brothas like you woulda tried to go if they'd let niggas in with just a G.E.D."

The barbershop exploded with laughter and "ooohs," the biggest "oooh" coming from Supreme himself.

"That why you late?" Supreme asked.

"Nope." Tyrone reached into his bag and pulled out three forty-ounce bottles of beer. "This is why I'm late!"

"No drinkin' in the shop." Supreme sounded like a teacher reciting an often violated rule. Three old-timers sitting in the corner with brown paper bags to their lips lowered them half an inch and eyed Supreme like he was crazy.

"I mean," he continued, noticing their expressions, "no under-age drinking in the shop."

The old-timers nodded in agreement before continuing to indulge

4

themselves. Tyrone went to the refrigerator to store the beer.

"So, whatcha gonna major in?" Supreme asked, as if only half-interested.

"Engineering," Tyrone proudly announced.

"Yeah? Whatcha gonna engineer?"

There were a few expectant chuckles.

"Nothin'," Tyrone answered, a little offended. "I'm gonna be a builder."

Supreme glanced at Mike so quickly that no one else noticed, then scratched his head through his hat—Supreme always wore a hat. Mike smiled.

The barbershop was now on edge. Tyrone sat down casually next to Tony and Steve. Tyrone seemed to have forgotten that Supreme had been up to his usual antics before he and Tony walked in, but everyone knew what was coming next. Now *his* time had come.

"You know something, Tyrone," Supreme began in a loud voice. Tyrone's jaw dropped. Uptown Heads was famous for two things: its haircuts—which were the best in the city—and its humour, which was the funniest. Friday nights were special because there was always a personal war of words between Supreme and Tyrone. "I like you," Supreme continued with a smile. Smiles and chuckles of anticipation had already begun to break out. "I like you 'cause you ignorant." People in the shop readied themselves for a big laugh. Most of them wanted to laugh at the last comment, but they were afraid if they did they'd miss the big joke. "You so ignorant," Supreme continued, "that when your pops toldcha that he was in Seoul during the Korean war, you asked him if he met Aretha Franklin, 'cause you heard she was the queen!" The shop exploded in laughter. Tyrone frowned bitterly. That shit wasn't even funny.

Uptown Heads was more like a theatre than a barbershop, with the barbers' chairs elevated on a platform in the middle of the floor like a stage, surrounded by chairs arranged in a broken circle for the audience which always seemed to be in attendance. Supreme's workstation was nearest the door, Riff's was in the middle, and Mike's was at the far end. The place had space. It had once been a burned-out disco. There were mirrors everywhere except the far wall, where hundreds of autographed pictures of some of their famous patrons were displayed.

Supreme managed Uptown Heads but there was much speculation as to who the owner was. Right then, he was in control.

Supreme loved his role as Uptown Heads' comedy king, and welcomed challengers to the throne; after all, it made the night more fun. His humour was almost Southern—in the sense that it was personal. Every joke was like an inside joke, and *everybody* was inside. In a thick Harlem accent, he would insult people all night long until they had no choice but to respond, but they would almost always regret that. By eleven it would be time to close, with the few heads still left to cut getting priority in the morning.

Once, a TV talent scout came to check Supreme out. He laughed harder than anyone else in the place, and then approached him. "Say," he began. "How would you like to get paid for what you're doing?"

Supreme looked him over once or twice. "What do you think I'm doing now?" he asked, bluntly.

The agent left without another word.

It was just after eight-thirty when Stephanie, Supreme's twenty-one-year-old sister, and Born, his five-year-old son, walked in. For the second time that night, the shop fell dead silent.

"Peace Daddy. Peace Uncle Mike. Peace Riff," Born greeted everyone. Most of the brothas were staring at Stephanie. She was what most of them considered their *future* woman. What they were working for: fine as wine in the sunshine, with a behind *and* a mind. Eventually, each of them believed, he would have enough to get her. Enough of whatever it was they needed. They needed something, though, that much they knew.

"Here's your brat," Stephanie told her brother flatly, as she took a seat.

"Nothin' like the love of your family," Supreme said, with a sardonic smile. He turned to Mike. "See, this is how real families treat each other. Not like you and your people, all concerned about each other, helping out with bills, taking care of bastard nieces and nephews, bailing niggas out of jail and what not."

"Hi, Michael," Stephanie said sweetly.

Mike smiled warmly and nodded. "Little Woman!"

Stephanie looked wounded. He'd been calling her that since she'd entered puberty. He seemed to be the only one who couldn't see how much she had grown. She switched her attention to Supreme.

"Don't you have a baseball game or something to go to?"

"Oh shit!" he gasped.

Born shot him a disapproving look. "Daddy!"

Supreme covered his mouth. "Sorry, it slipped. Yo, look everyone, I gotta be out."

His customers began to grumble.

Supreme shrugged. "My fault, fellas, but once you get in the habit of breakin' promises, you stay in the habit."

"Come on, man!" pleaded a customer requiring immediate and intensive barbering.

"Look," Supreme shot back, "just 'cause most of you knuckleheads is bullshit fathers don't mean I gotta be!"

"But whaddabout me?" Tyrone asked, as if his haircut was more

6

important than anyone else's.

Supreme looked him up and down. "Fuck you!" The barbershop roared.

"Daddy!"

He covered his mouth again quickly. "I'm sorry." Supreme turned back to Tyrone again and mouthed another silent 'Fuck you!' giving him yet another big laugh as an exit cue.

Supreme scooped his son up and headed for the door. Most of his customers followed right behind, for they would allow no one else to cut their hair. Tyrone stayed, waiting for Steve, who was Mike's customer. Tony also stayed. He was the only one of the shop's customers prepared to get his hair cut by any of its three barbers.

Mike glanced over at Tyrone, Tony and Steve. He remembered that he, Supreme, and Vince had each had their favourites between them. Supreme's favourite was Tyrone. Tyrone was a young angel-faced, coolly dressed, criminal-minded smart ass. For fun, he used to think of new ways to get in and out of trouble. The people who liked him loved him— the people who didn't were few. Supreme, Mike thought, must have seen a lot of himself in Tyrone.

Steve was the basketball player of the bunch. He was Mike's favourite not only because Mike was a ball player himself, but also because Mike loved the way Steve played. Steve was very tall for his seventeen years. However, unlike most tall young men he wasn't awkward. On the basketball court, he was incredible. Steve's coaches often criticised him because they didn't believe he worked hard enough. The never realised that, to Steve, basketball was anything but work. It was very important to him, but also something natural; something he could do to express himself, work off some tension, and take a few brothas to the hole in the meantime. Steve already had a variety of scholarship offers, as well as reports that he would be taken in the first round if he turned pro right out of high school.

Tony was a wanderer. He didn't have many friends because he didn't look for them. He didn't excel in anything because he didn't try anything. He seemed to just muddle through life in a state of complete indifference. He was drawn to Tyrone and Steve when he first saw them. Steve was teaching Tyrone how to dribble between his legs. Tyrone was laughing at the absurdity of ever needing to dribble through his legs and kept suggesting that he teach Steve how to roll dice instead.

"That," Tyrone suggested, "will come in handy Uptown." They were seven years old at the time. The simplicity of the two boys at play had fascinated Tony. He was so used to seeing children like himself—dull and uninterested in anything—that to see two boys actually enjoying themselves appealed to him. He walked over to them and just stared.

7

Steve didn't understand why the strange kid with the wide eyes and open mouth was staring at him and Tyrone. Tyrone smiled at him. "C'mon," he said, motioning for Tony to follow him, "I'll teach you how to roll dice." Tony smiled. Steve shrugged his shoulders and joined them. They had been friends ever since. Tony had been Vince's favourite. Vince always loved the underdog.

Supreme was mad and uncomfortable. Or maybe he was *mad* uncomfortable. The fact that he was uncomfortable made him mad, and the fact the he was mad made him more uncomfortable. It was one of those nights. As he lay across his bed, he wished he was a smoker. Smoking seemed like the thing to be doing. Anything seemed like the thing to be doing except what he was doing—nothing. He got up. He laid back down. He got back up. He went to the air conditioner and turned it on, then off, then on, then off again. He wasn't hot or cold, just uncomfortable. He went to the kitchen and poured a tall glass of lemonade. He sat it on the table and looked at it long and hard. He wasn't thirsty. He drank it anyway. He rubbed his hands together. He went to the window, opened it, then closed it again. He walked to Born's room and looked in on him. Born was asleep. He looked at the smaller, younger version of his own face and the extra curly hair. He loved Born so much. Sometimes it was difficult not to show just how happy he was because of his son. He couldn't baby the boy, though. He had to make him a man. Let him become a man, he reminded himself. Born. If Supreme was Uptown's king, then Born was without question its prince. The son of Supreme. *Born* Supreme.

He left the room, closing the door gently behind him. He went back to his room and stretched out on the bed to rest his troubled mind. He tried to go to sleep again, but failed. Nothing was helping. It was one of those nights.

In the five years since Born's birth, Supreme had been celibate. Well, almost. Sometimes the desire to be with somebody became so unbearable that all he could think about was finding somebody somewhere. It didn't matter who, it didn't matter where. All that mattered was that she was black and consenting. This was one of those times. It was one of those nights!

He leaned across to the bedside table and flicked the radio on. Someone was huggin' and kissin' and missin' and blissin', and all kindsa things on the late night jam. "Damn!" He hit the dial and changed the station to a news broadcast: "*...and on Wall Street today Rhineholt Dunn III...*" Frustrated, he flicked the radio off and reached for the remote control beside it to turn the television on. The news was on: "*Once again the elusive Rhineholt Dunn III managed to avoid our cameras and any inter-*"

views..." He hit the remote button again to switch off. None of this was helping. It was definitely one of those nights!

An hour later, he was sitting on the edge of the bed thumbing through the long list of names with coded letters beside them in his address book. 'NC' were women whose numbers had yet to be called; 'JF' were 'just friends'; 'OR' were the 'old reliables', and 'NA' were women he would never be calling again. He had had that same address book since he was fourteen. Since then, many of the 'OR' women had become 'JF' or 'NA', but there were still plenty left. He flipped through the pages until he came to the name of a girl whose presence wouldn't be difficult to deal with after the fact. His mind returned briefly to Vince, as it always did on nights like these.

"You need to stop sleeping around so much," Vince had told Supreme about a year before Born was born.

"I know, right? I need to start sleepin' in one place." Supreme had nudged Mike playfully in the ribs. Mike shook his head. That wasn't one of his friend's better jokes.

"You know that's not what I mean."

"Vince," said Supreme tiredly, "not now, all right. I mean, you read all those black history and psychology books and you think you're Malcolm Freud or somebody! Don't start with that shit, all right!"

"I'm not gonna start. I was just wondering..."

"What?"

"Do you realise that you're dissing yourself every time you sleep with a woman you don't love?"

Supreme turned to Mike. "His mother taught him that. That was some straight up 'Mommy says' shit."

"Would you let me finish?" Vince sounded annoyed.

Supreme turned to Mike in disbelief.

Mike shrugged. "Let him finish."

"Brotha, you can *always* finish," Supreme said mockingly.

"How do you feel about a woman while you're sleeping with her?"

"During the entire time we're sleeping together, or while we're actually fuckin'?"

Vince's face soured. "Why you gotta be 'fuckin'' the woman? How can you talk about sistas like that?"

"Vince, get off it!" Supreme said flatly. "I'm not talking about your mother! I'm talking about *girls.* Now what was your question? How do I feel about a woman while I'm fuckin' her?"

Vince's face soured again. "Yeah," he said, apparently ready to leave the issue.

"I like her," Supreme said smiling. "I like her a *lot.* And when I'm about to come, I love her!"

He and Mike laughed.

"And what about after you come?"

"She gotta go, she gotta go, she gotta go! No standing around. I'm not the line for free cheese. She don't hafta go home, but she gotta get the hell away from me. That is, unless she can cook."

Vince remained serious. "See, you just dissed yourself. You played yourself, brotha. When you sleep with a woman you don't love you feel disgusted, don't you? You want her out 'cause you think *she's* why you feel that way. Fact is, you're disgusted with yourself; the satisfaction you expected wasn't all that, so now you want no trace of her 'til the next time you feel horny. You don't want her to call. Don't want to see her in public. All you want to do is tell the fellas you 'fucked' her in the hope that bragging will help you feel satisfied. But it won't. Nothing will. You tell yourself you're just out for physical pleasure, but if you really were you wouldn't feel so damned disgusted every time you got it."

Supreme looked at Mike, then back at Vince. "I don't know if I'd call it *disgust*," he said wryly.

"What would you call it then?"

"I call it, 'already bust a nut and I need to get some sleep'."

"But if you cared about her, wouldn't you want her to stay?"

Supreme shrugged. "Don't know. Haven't been there yet."

"But don't you think you're dissing black women?"

Supreme thought, *first I was dissing myself, now I'm dissing black women*, but shrugged it off. "How?" he asked.

"By..." Vince cleared his throat to say a difficult word, "fucking them and not loving them. Treating them like the slave master did."

The words hit Supreme hard. "Wait a minute," he said hotly, looking at Mike. "He ain't saying what I think he's saying, is he?"

"Sounded like that to me, yo!"

"Naah, couldn't have."

"Maybe you weren't listening," Mike said, holding back a smile. A fight between Supreme and Vince would be some funny shit. He'd break it up of course—*eventually*.

"I'm not gonna let you call me no fuckin' slave master just 'cause I fuck around a little somethin'."

"What would you call yourself then?" Vince asked calmly.

"Supreme!"

"They called themselves by their first names too," Vince said, off-handedly.

Supreme turned back to Mike. "Are you listening to this?"

"The question is, are *you*?" Mike asked, his lips trembling from suppressed laughter.

10

Supreme looked back and forth between his two best friends. He wasn't sure, but he felt they were standing against him. He hated to be alone in an argument, unless he was right—but in this case, he wasn't sure if he was. Slowly, he began to nod. So Vince was right on that point—but only that point. Supreme planned a new attack.

"All right," he began. "But if I was a slave master, I'd hafta force myself on girls."

"True," Vince agreed.

"Then whaddaya call what I do?" Supreme asked.

"What do you call it?"

"Fuckin'!" Supreme said emphatically. *Damn it Vince, hasn't the whole conversation been about that?*

Vince shook his head. "See what I mean. How can you fuck somebody you love?"

"Who said anything about *love?*" Supreme asked.

"Not the slave master," Vince said evenly.

"Look," Supreme was becoming frustrated. "you don't have to love a girl to wanna fuck her."

"Then why do it?" Vince asked bluntly.

"Because pussy is pussy. You don't have to love her to want it."

"So you'll take the pussy with or without the woman?" Vince's tone was mocking and the tone of finality and triumph in Mike's laughter told Supreme that the argument was over.

"Look," he began. "Right now I'm not looking for a wife. I'm young and I got a hard dick, that's a fucked-up combination. I gotta have some fun. All that shit you said is well and good for when I get older, but right now I'm not even thinking along those lines."

"You're not thinking at all," Vince said. "I mean, what would you do if you got Denise pregnant?"

Supreme winced. Denise was his current 'fuck' interest.

"Call Greyhound and see when their next bus was leaving for Africa or some shit."

"That's foul, yo," Vince said. "Then you'd be no better than your pops who you hate."

"Yes I would, man. My pops is still around, getting laid off every other week, eating up food that could be goin' to either my moms or my sister, and just being an overall pain in my ass in particular. At least your pops died before you were born, yo. You never had to go through any of that bullshit."

"I'd like to try it though..." Vince said evenly, "...some of that bullshit—even if it was only for seven years like Mike."

Supreme felt bad. He knew he had touched a nerve. Vince had always been sensitive about never having known his father.

11

"Hey, my pops was the man when he was alive," Mike said, sounding riled. "I didn't get no bullshit."

"Naah, he gets that now," Supreme said, attempting a joke.

"Just think about what I said, Supreme," Vince began again, serious. "I mean, you're my man. I hate to see you play yourself. And really, it's not like the sistas that sleep with you actually dig you or anything."

Supreme frowned.

"How you figure that?"

"Most of them do it because you're Supreme. You've got a rep, you should know that—you worked hard enough to establish it. Those sistas don't love you. They don't even care about you. All they want is a piece of you. The same piece all the other sistas are talking about."

"Yeah?" Supreme said, grinning and becoming himself again. "Have you really heard 'em talkin?"

"Have you?" Vince asked simply.

Supreme's grin faded. He never asked Vince what he meant by that; he thought it was better that he didn't know.

Supreme was thinking of Vince tonight. The brotha had known so much at such a young age and knew right from wrong before any of the brothas his age. Or maybe he didn't. Vince made his own choice. So it wasn't a tragedy. And you could only mourn for a nigga if it was a tragedy.

Slowly, a familiar sensation crept back over him. It was still one of those nights. He had had enough. He looked at the clock. It was a quarter to one. He picked up his address book again, studied one of the last names he'd checked before finally deciding to call the number.

"Hello." Her voice sounded almost feline.

"Valerie!" Supreme began. "What's up baby? This is Supreme—you miss me?"

Every Saturday morning, Supreme would leave home early and take a slow walk down Lenox Avenue to see if he could run any errands for the old-timers in the neighbourhood before going to work, or maybe buy breakfast for some of the hungry-looking kids he came across. He'd take Born along because he wanted his son to get a real perspective on Harlem and catch the latest word they were bound to hear from the brothas kickin' it on the street corners. See, Supreme knew that Born needed to see that the neighbourhood wasn't just about poverty and crime, as those in other parts of the city believed. And it wasn't just about history and heritage either. Harlem was about its people. That's what made this part of the city special—more than its once-elegant brownstones or the beautiful view of Manhattan from up on the hill. The people today—as much as when James Baldwin, Langston Hughes, Countee Cullen, Zora Neale Hurston, Jean Toomer, Count Basie, Duke Ellington, Charlie Parker, Joe Louis, Dizzy Gillespie, Cab Calloway and Malcolm X had walked the same avenue. But great people hadn't been the only people to walk up and down Lenox, Supreme wanted to show his son. And regular people could become great just by knowing and being known in their own community.

Saturday morning was kids' time at Uptown Heads. Most of the children from the neighbourhood came to the barbershop to play. This had been Mike's idea. He had built a playground out of scrap metal in the barbershop's backyard; he'd made the backyard by having the asphalt of the old disco's parking lot dug up and the ground planted with grass seeds. The kids took over the barbershop's back room. No one interfered with what they did back there. No grown-ups were allowed. The kids ranged in age from two to thirteen and the older kids watched over the younger ones. Sometimes there would be disagreements and even a few brief fist fights. The offended kid would go away vowing never to return, and he wouldn't... until about fifteen minutes later.

The barbershop wasn't officially open yet, but the kids were allowed in as long as at least one of the barbers was there. The week's check on the communal funds was underway.

"How much extra we got this week Tim?" Born asked.

"Not that much," Tim said, dejected. "We did a little more than break even."

"Enough for candy and soda all week?" Born asked, concerned. This was essential for the group.

"Oh yeah," Tim reassured him. "But no big extras."

"That's all right," Born said, "I wasn't plannin' on gettin' a bike until next week."

Supreme flung open the back room door and found the kids playing innocently. Too innocently. He knew something underhand was going on, and felt that Born had to be partly, if not mostly, responsible. But the kids seemed to be prepared for him every time he tried to catch them off guard.

Supreme went back over to his workstation. He knew that the customers he hadn't got to the night before would be arriving soon. Mike wasn't in yet. Supreme looked at Riff, with his Mike Tyson-like fade, bulging biceps, jeans and a T-shirt that was suffering from being stretched beyond its limits.

He laughed to himself, recalling the first time he had heard of Riff. Supreme had been thirteen and in the ninth grade when Riff was a sixteen-year-old hood, able to beat up grown men, not only one at a time but in groups too. He was from Brooklyn and was dubbed 'Riff' because his fights were over so quick. Riff would swing once—just once—and the guy he hit would wake up the next day.

Riff began cutting hair when he was seventeen and quickly became the best barber in Brooklyn. But the transition from hood to barber was not an easy one. Once, a bunch of brothas that he had beaten up single-handedly in his roughneck days, came to the shop where he worked to get even.

They took a look at the guy whose hair Riff was cutting at the time—then at the line of people waiting exclusively for him—then saw their own uncut dos in the mirror and joined the line. They'd been regular customers ever since.

Before he teamed up with Mike and Supreme, Riff had worked in a shop with four other barbers for two Jewish guys—the Schwartz brothers. They paid him fifty per cent of each head he cut, and business boomed—but after about three years, although his skills were on a steady incline, the number of customers was beginning to decline. He started hearing stories about a newly opened barbershop in Harlem—Uptown Heads. 'Heads' had taken over almost all of Manhattan, most of the Bronx and some of Queens, and was now starting to move in on Brooklyn. He heard the two barbers there were looking for a third, but no one had the style they liked. Riff didn't like the sound of them or their business. He hated niggas from uptown.

Riff continued working for the Schwartz brothers, but times were getting tight and he knew he had to do something. One morning a postcard arrived at his house. On the front was a brilliant logo of an asymmetrical haircut rising over the Manhattan skyline. On the back it said 'We've seen your work, we're impressed. Give us a call.' It was from Uptown Heads. Riff was about to tear it up when he realised that if those Uptown niggas were as *busy* as everyone said, he could make a fortune. And if they were as *good* as everyone said, then they were definitely busy. He made an appointment to meet with them early one Saturday.

When he got there he was shocked at how young the two barbers looked. He was twenty-one, but they looked like they were still in high school. And they had those damn uptown looks on their faces: smug, as if they were so cool that Jesus coming in to get his dreadlocks trimmed wouldn't faze them. The one with the funky haircut asked him to sit down and the one wearing the backwards hat just kept nodding at him as they went about their business. Maybe they were gay. They seemed to be studying him intently.

"You do your own?" the one with the funky haircut asked, referring to the smooth blends and razor sharp edges of Riff's own cut.

"Indeed," Riff said flatly.

The two barbers looked at each other, nodded.

"My name's Supreme, that's Mike. We're not going to waste your time or ours, so lets get down to business."

Riff nodded, impressed. Down to business, huh? Maybe they weren't gay. Mike said:

"We got a lotta new customers that used to be yours."

A lot of brothas would have been offended by his bluntness. Riff wasn't.

"We noticed a pretty funky style to your cuts that lasted after the hair had grown back," Supreme added, "so we was wondering if you'd be interested in working for us?"

"What kinda percentage you talkin' 'bout?" Riff asked, after a long pause.

"Better than fifty-fifty."

Mike nodded. "You get a hundred per cent of what you earn and we get another barber."

Riff was thrown. "What about overheads?"

"Taken care of," Supreme said casually.

"Electricity, operating expenses, rent, shit like that?"

"What about it?" Mike asked.

"I hafta think about this," Riff said, frowning. "OK, I thought about it. I'm with it."

"Cool," Supreme said, and handed Riff a set of clippers. They were double-adjustable for added length and width with front and back removable blades and a tiny, but powerful, light at the head. "Couldya learn to cut with these?"

"I could cut hair with a butter knife." He studied the clippers. "Where'd'ya get these, anyway?"

"Mike designed 'em. We get 'em made by a private company. They're not on the market yet."

It was now Riff's turn to study the two good-looking young brothas who looked uptown but dressed like those niggas from Queens he used to beat up in clubs because they tried to play hardrocks while wearing silk. But these two brothas were different. They had a strictly business attitude about money and thus deserved some respect. But Riff had something to say before he left.

"Let me explain one thing to you brothas. This shit's just temporary. One day, I'ma own my own shop, and that day is on its way."

Supreme looked pleasantly surprised. "More power to ya, kid!" Supreme said, then winked at Mike in a way that said things had gone exactly the way he had expected.

Riff was confused, but if he thought too long about why he was agreeing to work with these two strange-ass niggas, he probably wouldn't do it. So he went straight back to the Schwartz brothers, packed his shit and started work at Uptown Heads the next day.

Supreme was smiling now as he watched Riff and saw the look of contented anger on his face—like he was happy to be angry, but mad that something like anger could make him happy. People who looked at his face and called it ugly were the same kind of people who listened to rap music but couldn't hear poetry. Riff's eyes were so fierce that they intimidated everyone—everyone except Supreme and Mike. That was one of the reasons he had agreed to work for them. They had looked him in the eye from the time he came in until the time he left.

Now Riff was twenty-seven years old, and married. His beautiful wife Stacey was finishing her Masters in psychology. They met when Riff had approached her on the street one day—not as a boy looking for a pussy-handout but as a man, admiring a woman who deserved to be admired. Stacey was used to men approaching her, but not the way Riff had. He never screamed "Yo!" never begged her pardon, didn't even say "scuse me." He just walked up, introduced himself fully and explained that he had seen her walking and thought she was very attractive. He made it clear that although he wasn't in the business of approaching women on the street, he knew that if he didn't say something to her right then, he might never see her again.

Stacey liked his style—and his eyes were as clear as his intentions. They had lunch that afternoon and married a year later—and she had been the perfect wife ever since, giving him love when he needed it and a good ass-kicking when he needed that. Stacey felt he should use his savings to buy a barbershop—so Riff had to practically force her to let him help pay her school fees.

Riff caught Supreme smiling at him. "Why you always lookin' at me like that, yo?" he asked, frowning.

"You..." Supreme shook his head, "...you're just a big ugly mothafucka. Didcha ever think about that? Yo! The fact that you are a big—ugly—mothafucka? You're lucky you're married, 'cause how would you make out on the singles scene?"

Riff raised an eyebrow. "You're just a little pretty mothafucka," he nodded. "Didcha ever think about that? Yo! The fact that you are just a little—pretty—mothafucka? You're lucky you're legit, 'cause how long would your ass last in jail?"

Supreme laughed at his own joke. As usual, Riff didn't find much to laugh at.

Tyrone, Tony and Steve burst through the door, sweaty and out of breath.

Supreme closed his eyes and shook his head.

"How bad this time?" he asked, referring to the basketball 'lesson'

16

Steve had just given the other two.

"Never mind that...just look at this!" Tyrone said, pointing to his uncut hair.

"Whassup?" Supreme began. "If you'da been here on time last night—"

"If you'da been here on time last night..." Tyrone repeated in a nasal imitation of Supreme's voice. "Just cut my hair, barber."

Supreme sighed heavily. "Get in the chair," he said.

Mike walked in. On seeing Tyrone, Tony and Steve, he called out, "What, no hubcaps to steal?"

"Why, that's mighty white of you," Tyrone retorted.

Mike laughed and went over to his chair to prepare his workstation.

With the chairs in the middle of the shop it was inconvenient to stack things on the wall or one of the mirrors. Mike had created barber chairs to his own design. Pockets on both sides and shelves that folded out enabled each barber to do his necessary cleaning and organising right from the chair itself. They were more efficient than anything available on the market.

"Yo, Mike," Supreme called out. "Tyrone and Tony got their ass kicked again!"

Mike shook his head.

"Why you worried about that?" Tyrone asked. "You got hair to cut, barber!"

Supreme ignored him. "What was the score?"

"Twenty one to zip," Steve said casually.

"Y'all couldn't even score?"

"Yo, Steve is nice man," Tony said, containing his own awe at the way Steve had dunked on him.

"Two on one, and no score," Supreme continued, enjoying this opportunity to ridicule Tyrone.

"Look," Tyrone said, "the brotha just got a scholarship offer from Black State. How do you expect me and Tony to be able to fuck with him?"

Tyrone had a point, but Supreme also knew that Tyrone had had the opportunity to be as good a player as his friend. As kids, Steve tried to teach Tyrone to dribble between his legs and Tyrone tried to teach Steve to roll dice.

"This is uptown, Son. We make money. Let them Brooklyn niggas play hoops!" he had advised. By the time Tony moved to the neighbourhood, both Tyrone and Steve were expert gamblers—but Tyrone's basketball had not improved one bit.

"Black State University?" Mike asked with interest. "The defending national champs? They've got the best basketball program in the country!"

"Yeah, they got a little somethin'," Tyrone said with mock humility.

"You gonna go?" Supreme asked.

"Probably. The coach says I could start by my sophomore season, and from what I understand the honeys there are pretty dope."

Supreme nodded. "Yeah, the sistas that go there do look good."

"So whatcha tryin' to do, Steve?" Riff asked. "Play pro ball?"

"I hope," Steve said with characteristic indifference. "If not, I'ma major in accounting anyway, so I'll just get a nine-to-five."

"I like that kinda brotha," Supreme smiled. "I know a few people that could use a good accountant too."

"You don't know nobody but Bill," Tyrone told him. "Rent *bill*, light *bill*, past due *bill*..."

"Accounting runs in my family," Steve continued. "My pops was an accountant and my little brother Tim wants to be one too."

"Speaking of money," Tyrone said. "Did anybody hear about that Wisconsin shit that Rhineholt Dunn III did yesterday?"

"Yeah, whatcha think he's trying to do?" Riff asked.

"Get his name mentioned on TV more," Supreme said flatly.

"Yo, how come whenever anybody mentions that brotha's name you start blaspheming against him?" Tyrone asked.

"He's got his thing and I got mine."

"Yeah, but his thing is worth *mad* more money than yours."

Supreme shrugged.

"I think you're jealous," Tyrone continued.

"One thing I'll never be is jealous of that guy. Hell, we grew up with the mothafucka."

Tyrone looked sceptical. "Who did?"

"Me and Mike."

"For real, Mike?"

Mike nodded.

"So why the beef? What, he take your girl or somethin'?"

Supreme held his gaze.

"Or something..." he answered eventually.

"That explains it then."

"I guess it does."

It was Saturday night, so everyone met up at around nine o'clock at Uptown Heads to discuss their plans for the rest of the night. Stephanie had come earlier and taken Born to the movies and the rest of the kids had gone home. Fat Freddie, the rap star, was drunk and staggering around in the season's newest Karl Kani.

"I'm gonna...go to a club...and get somebody to buy me another

18

drink," Freddie blurted with some effort.

Everyone laughed as he tried to steady himself.

"You need to get somebody to buy your big ass a chair!" Supreme called out.

Freddie turned to face him, looking truly hurt. "Yo, 'Preme. How you gonna play me?"

Supreme grinned broadly. "Like a game of tennis, you fat fuck. Your serve!"

The barbershop rocked with laughter.

"What does my fat have to do with my fuckin'?" Freddie asked earnestly. "After last night, your girl said she wished you'd put on a few pounds." Mixed 'ooohs' and laughter burst from the crowd assembled in the shop.

Supreme was laughing the hardest. He first met Fat Freddie right after Uptown Heads had first opened. Freddie had just cut his debut album and was beginning to gain popularity. He walked in early one morning when Supreme was cutting one customer's hair with two more waiting. Mike was free.

"Yo, which one of y'all is Supreme?" Freddie had asked. Supreme motioned with his head. "How many heads you got waitin'?"

"Two."

Freddie looked at Supreme and then at Mike. "I'll wait."

When he finally sat in Supreme's chair, he described in a thousand words or so what kind of haircut he wanted, and asked:

"Now—do you think you can handle that?"

"If *you* didn't wouldcha even be in my chair, partner?"

Freddie didn't say another word during the cut. When Supreme finished Freddie frowned and nodded in the mirror, moving his head from side-to-side to check it from every angle. He checked the back, and a satisfied smile broke on his face before he finally spoke. "You'll see me again," he assured Supreme. Since then he had become one of Supreme's best customers and closest friends.

No matter where on the planet he was at on Friday, Freddie would be in 'Heads' on Saturday. Now that he was one of the biggest names in rap music, Saturday was the only day he could relax, get a trim and get drunk.

"You know," Freddie once began in a moment of reflection. "I never dreamt of success, I had a vision."

"Don't get deep on me, Fred," Supreme warned to a few chuckles.

"Naah Brah, let me finish."

"All right. So what's the difference between a dream and a vision?"

"A dream is something kinda unconscious like. Something thatcha never really expect to get. A vision is something in sight. Something you just gotta work for."

Supreme understood exactly where Freddie was coming from, and was aware of the Uptown Heads crowd silently waiting for his response.

"I'm glad you feel you know me well enough to share that with me," Supreme had said, in a voice so solemn that people began to laugh. "I'd hate to imagine that you run that kinda shit down on mothafuckas you just met."

The shop exploded, but before Freddie had a chance to become even a little offended Supreme leaned forward and patted him on his shoulder.

"Keep seeing things, Brah. Keep seeing things," the barber whispered in his ear.

Tonight, Freddie was in charge and Supreme was happy for a rare and much-needed break from being the centre of attention.

"Yo, Fred," a young garbage collector called out from the crowd. "Run a funky rhyme for me."

"Come on, Lou," Freddie answered him. "Rapping's what I do for a livin', I get tired of it. Today's my day off. What if I came over to your crib on your day off and said, 'Yo, Lou, take out a load of trash for me!'"

Everybody laughed except Lou.

Supreme was trying to relax. Relax and enjoy the simple fun of the night without thinking or having to come up with joke after joke without a pause between thoughts. Tonight he didn't feel like telling jokes—even to people who only had those jokes to look forward to.

Over in the far corner were a group of brothas who came to Uptown Heads every Saturday to forget. They sat together, a living example of how misery loved company. These brothas had lost the one thing more important than losing everything; they'd lost their essence. See, because everything else is attainable and re-attainable if a nigga's essence is intact. Material shit is replaceable, jobs are switchable, and women are leavable if necessary. But when a nigga's lost that essence—that 'what a motherfucka's made out of'—he's lost more than even a man who's lost his way. He's lost the knowledge that there ever was a way.

There was Davey Dave. The lover. He had five children by four different women. He claimed them all but could support none. He used to have a job, but he quit because he got tired of working for the white man. Now he begged from the black man.

There was Larry. 'Big Money Larry.' He was from a rich family and as a teenager never felt he was sufficiently 'down' with his 'straight off the block' homeboys. So whenever he hung out with them, he made a point of acting the baddest. One night he had accidentally killed an innocent bystander while he was fooling around with a gun. In prison he was raped continuously throughout his seven-year stretch. On release he discovered that his family had disowned him. Now 'Big Money Larry' was a homeless brotha with a limp.

There was Cool Antoine, who had been on his way to college when he got some chick pregnant. Instead of getting an education, he stayed home and got a job at a gas station. He got promoted to manager, and made plans for his family, then discovered that the child he'd raised was not his own. The next day at work he was found getting ready to strike a match, having poured gasoline all over the grounds of the station.

Then there was True Lee. Lee thought with his heart. He was everybody's best friend and everybody's biggest sucker. He never had any money, but he always had a million friends who 'owed him one'. He used to have a nice ride, but a 'friend' needed it one day. He used to have a nice apartment but his girl 'had to get out of her parents' crib and just couldn't live with him'. He wasn't with her any more, and her new boyfriend had moved in. But Lee still paid the rent. The brotha was *true* all right.

There was 'Pretty Ass' Jamal. His face was his claim to fame. He was once the finest nigga out. One night Jamal got real drunk. He could still drive though—at ninety miles an hour; he just couldn't avoid the parked cars in front of his projects. After his plastic surgery—five operations in all—Pretty Ass Jamal had to find a new name.

Strong Stan was his own man. He did his own thing, lived his own life and made his own rules. One day a cop took offense to the strong look in his eye and spat in it. I suppose you could call a nightstick shoved eight inches up a cop's ass assault. The niggas uptown could only call it funny. But unfortunately for Stan, after fifteen years in prison he lost that strong look in his eye.

What could Supreme do for these brothas, he asked himself often? What could he do for anybody? Why did he even feel a desire to do anything? Sometimes he felt like he was on a mission to resurrect uptown and its inhabitants. *Don't get deep,* he would warn himself, but the truth was that he was already below sea level. He turned his gaze from the brothas to the opposite corner—where his eyes rested on a group of sistas with stories that made the brothas' stories sound good. The sistas came to Uptown Heads every Saturday, hoping to find someone to help them remember. Remember that they were women and that they were beautiful—to somebody. Amongst them was Sexy Suzy. Supreme still remembered the song he and the other brothas used to sing about her:

Sexy Suzy,
You gotta be kidding me,
Naah it couldn't be,
Just wouldn't be...

Didn't make any sense—but not much that he and his friends did back in those days did. It had been a long time since the term 'sexy' was used to describe Suzy. In the last five years drugs had ravaged her once-full figure and aged her thirty years. She was one of Vince's first girlfriends, and first 'victims' too.

Next to Suzy was Dolores, the 'one that got away'. Supreme frowned. He could remember he used to plead with her daily to give 'it' to him. Now she was begging him to take it. Her chocolate and Pepsi diet had cost her about ten teeth, half her hair had been eaten by perming cream, and she'd gained forty pounds from fried chicken and forties. She had two kids by a drug dealer named '2 Smooth' who had two kids by everybody—hence the nickname.

Then there was Dee Dee. Damn, what a waste! She didn't do nothin'. Didn't go to college because she couldn't leave home...couldn't leave all her friends. Her friends all left her, though. Some went to college; some just went. Now her favourite pastime was reminiscing over what could have been.

Beside her was Lori. Lori once met a nice guy—a nice guy who beat the shit out of her. Her parents warned her that there was something wrong with him, but she loved him.

"He'll change!" she confidently told anyone who asked. One day he had too much to drink and was beating the shit out of her again. The knife was nearby; she picked it up. Instead of getting charged for manslaughter, Lori did her time in an asylum.

And there was Veronica, who knew the same kind of brotha, except he didn't beat her, he simply warned:

"You ever fuck around on me, I'll kill the mothafucka." Veronica had always smiled when he said that. It proved that he cared. One day, he saw her kissing another man on the cheek, pulled out the pistol he kept for just such occasions, and fired, point blank. So Veronica's family didn't have to figure out how to get all her brother's winter clothes down to Garvey X after all.

That was all the sistas except one. Tears swelled in Supreme's eyes as his eyes rested on a sista sitting perfectly still by herself. Supreme couldn't even understand how she could still manage to be around so many people. Anita had never bothered anybody. She'd had a four-year scholarship to Black State. She was going to be a teacher. Why'd those maggots have to do it? Nobody would ever see any of them again, though; Riff had made a couple of phone calls. Still, that had been just damage control, not prevention. And what Supreme really wanted to know was what makes mothafuckas think they can get away with that in the first place?

As Supreme observed them now, the sistas were mostly smiling and laughing and seemed to be having a good time, because the Uptown Heads barbershop allowed them the opportunity to chill out and think of good things. Supreme wondered jealously why Heads wasn't giving him the same opportunity.

He was almost eighteen, still living at home, and the father of a newborn baby boy with a crazy name when Supreme's pops decided he'd had enough of his shit.

"Get the fuck out!" his father had yelled.

So what; he was paying the rent. Supreme hadn't boasted exactly, just stated a fact—that he should be allowed to come and go as he pleased since he kept a roof over their heads. Stephanie cried and begged her father to let her brother stay. But it was no use and Supreme knew it. His father was adamant. It had been a long time coming.

Supreme gathered up as much money as he had and handed it all to Stephanie, telling her to use it on nothing but food and clothes. When the time was right, he'd help her get her own place. In the meantime, if she needed him, Mike would know where he was. With that he packed only the 'Supremacy' outfit his sister had made for him and took his leave. He didn't know where he was going. All he knew was he felt empty, very empty. It had been a fucked-up year. He had just lost the mother of his child, one of his best friends, and now his home. He knew one thing for sure—he had to get the kid. Having Born would make him feel better, he told himself.

It was a long walk to Denise's house but it seemed to take only seconds. Supreme rang the doorbell. He knew he wouldn't be invited in, because he wasn't shit and because since he had got their daughter pregnant Mr and Mrs Mitchell hadn't been able to stand the sight of him. They weren't in the least bit impressed with all his big talk about all his big plans. Mr Mitchell had seen enough niggas like Supreme in his time.

"You can't do whatcha want in a white man's world, boy," he had once said.

"That's not the kinda world I intend to do it in," he had said simply.

Oh, Supreme would learn, Mr Mitchell had promised him. But not while fucking up his daughter's and grandson's lives.

The look on Supreme's face today frightened Mrs Mitchell when she opened the door. He didn't wait to be welcomed in, walked past her and her husband, through the living room and straight into Denise's room. The 'dead' girl was holding his kid. He snatched Born out of her arms. She looked at him, shocked. He didn't speak. He never wasted time talking to dead people. He walked back through the living room.

By now Mr Mitchell was yelling at him. Supreme could hear the sounds, but not the words. Mr Mitchell hit him. He felt his bottom lip swell with blood, but he kept walking. He was out the door now. He had his son. He heard more screaming, then an explosion. He felt a jolt in his right shoulder, then a burning sensation. It took him a few moments to realise he had been shot, but he kept walking. He didn't know where he was going, all he knew was that he had his baby and now he had to get some money. He went to Mike's house and rang the doorbell.

Mike's aunt opened the door and looked at him in horror. "Michael!" she screamed. "Come here, quick!"

The whole family appeared, to see what the commotion was about. They stood over Supreme, staring in shock.

Each of the late Ron Sr.'s children had acquired certain aspects of his persona. Mike got the look—the look that could be given without as much as an intended-to-be-spoken word. The look that cleared rooms, got dishes and homework done, got trash taken out, and got the channel changed back to the game or the fight. Mike's family saw Ron Sr.'s look on his face as they all stood before his bleeding best friend—gawking at the boy with the baby in his arms like he was a woman with Clyde Frazier sideburns. They saw the look—and gave their youngest member and his bleeding best friend a moment alone.

Mike turned to Supreme. He knew better than to ask what had happened. He knew Supreme would ask for what he needed and tell him all he needed to know.

"I need dough," Supreme managed to say with some difficulty.

"How much?"

"All you got, brotha."

Mike went to his room, returned a few seconds later and handed him some money. It was enough. Not a lot, not a little, just enough.

"You'll get it as soon as I got it," Supreme told him.

Mike nodded.

"I'll letcha know where I am as soon as I get a place to stay."

Mike nodded again. They held each other's gaze briefly, then Supreme left.

Holding his son in his uninjured arm, he walked down Frederick Douglass Boulevard from One Hundred and Forty Second Street, then decided to hit Columbus. Almost an hour later, he had passed Columbus Circle and was heading toward Sixth Avenue. It was then that Supreme began to wonder what the hell he was doing in Midtown. It had started to rain. He pulled Born's hood up onto his head.

Supreme had thought that seeing Born would make him feel better. In some ways it made him feel worse. How was he going to provide for this child? At barely eighteen, how was he going to provide for his damn self? All he wanted was to be a good father. He had seen too many bad fathers and Lord, he wasn't gonna be like his father! He was going to make his son a man. No, the image of Vince was still clear in his head: he was gonna *let* his son *become* a man. He would stand back and let Born develop naturally. He had seen so many parents like Vince's moms, forcing so much down their children's throats that the children regurgitated it. Babies were supposed to become adults. Baby girls became women. Baby boys became men. It was supposed to be that simple. So what went wrong when things went wrong?

"The substitution for truth," Vince had announced once during a discussion of just such a nature. "If you look at it, so many people nowadays tell their kids what they think the kid should know, or what's easier to hear than the truth—and it's messing them up. Kids always wanna know the truth. They see their parents and elders as the source and once they find out they've been lied to they lose trust. Trust in their parents, trust in themselves, trust in the world itself. Truth can't be substituted."

"You finished?" Supreme had asked, before taking over. "I'll tell you what it is; it's standards. Parents try so hard to build their children into some fucked-up preconceived image of what they think the child should be. They never help the kid become himself. They look at people they admire and say 'see, you gotta be more like him'. That automatically tells the kid there's somethin' wrong with him as he is. Then he goes around acting the way everybody else told him to act and hates it, or just fuckin' gives up and becomes a rebel."

Vince wasn't satisfied. "Whadda you think, Mike?"

"I think both of you nuts are too deep and you need to get off that social worker bullshit and start thinkin' 'bout this game comin' on tonight."

"So who's playing? Black State, right?" Supreme asked, in typical 'drop one subject, pick up another' style.

But Vince was still not satisfied. "Naah, Mike, who won the argument?"

For a moment, Mike looked distracted. "Supreme won," he said indifferently. "I don't know what the hell you was talkin' 'bout, Vince."

All three would find out later on that year.

It had begun raining harder. Born was crying. Supreme looked up at the street sign. He was by the A&S Plaza on Thirty Fourth Street and a huddled-over bum was hobbling beside him. He made Supreme nervous. He sped up, but the bum sped up too. He started to run but the bum ran with him. He stopped. The bum stopped. Then he turned to confront the man. The bum seemed familiar. He was carrying a baby too.

Supreme was shocked when he realised that he was the bum. He stared at his reflection, amazed—saw his soaking wet outfit, his dishevelled hair, his bleeding lip and shoulder, and his hollow eyes. *There's no life in them, no fear, nothing.*

Just then a tall, handsome young man wearing an exquisitely tailored business suit and carrying an umbrella slipped up next to him. "You've really fucked up this time haven't you, Supreme?"

Supreme summoned up the last of his pride. "I thought I told you to be out!" he cried out, all bravado, but no substance.

"And what? Watch your son die from a distance?" the young man asked. Supreme blinked wearily. "Why do you insist on playing this 'tough guy' role?' It never got you anywhere. You never think, you just do. Then you come running to me to bail you out. Well I'm tired of that. I'd leave your ass out here to die if it wasn't for your son." He looked at Born and shook his head

"The only thing you did right in your entire life, and even that was by mistake. How many more promises are you going to break?"

Supreme became furious—a spark ignited in his eyes. "I never promised you shit!" he screamed.

The man looked at him wryly. "Oh you didn't? We agreed all that fucking nonsense was your business, but when it came to making babies, the woman would be my call."

"Now how would that have been fair?"

"Well she would at least have been somebody we both agreed on. I told you how I felt about Denise. The girl's head wasn't strong enough for motherhood. Now look at her. You're lucky the baby's healthy!" He paused, and looked long at Born. "Listen, from now on I'm calling the shots. You don't make another important decision, period."

Supreme's face twisted into rage. "You're crazy if you think I'ma let you tell me what to do..."

"Oh really? You *do* like to eat, don't you? And you *do* need shelter, don't you?"

Supreme didn't answer.

"Let's face it, you don't know what to do with your life. If it wasn't for me, you probably wouldn't make it through the week."

"So what am I supposed to do?" Supreme asked, pathetic-ally.

"Cut hair!" the young man said, as if it should have been obvious. "In the meantime, I'll be making some real money. You'll see me around."

Supreme was furious. He could deal with the fact that the man had been right, but he hated his arrogance.

"Oh, yeah," the young man added. "And grow up!" With that he disappeared.

Supreme's chest became heavy and his eyes began to swell. He knew what was about to happen and it made him angry. He tried to fight it, because he knew that if it started, it might never stop. His body tensed.

He began to blink. His shoulders began to shudder. His eyes closed tight. There was no denying it. The first drop in an ocean of tears began to fall. His son joined him.

"Grow up?" Supreme was asking himself now.

"Grow up!" Freddie echoed to the youngsters in the shop.

It was time for Supreme to cheer up. All he needed to do was find some brothas and sistas with a little something going for them and he'd feel better. It wouldn't be hard. This *was* the Uptown Heads barbershop. Right behind Freddie stood five young brothas, all from different walks of life, all doing completely different things in life, yet they were laughing and joking like they had all grown up together. They came to the Uptown Heads every Saturday night for the same reason as Freddie—to relax.

Like Gary, who was laughing and acting stupid. He had graduated from Garvey X University with honours and was now in his senior year at medical school. He planned to become a surgeon and then open his own private hospital.

Next to him was Hot Rod. He was Freddie's producer. Rod had started out with just two record players and a true knowledge of what sounded good. The company he owned—Rough, Rugged & Raw Records—was the largest rap label on the east coast.

Then there was Jungle Jim, who had grown up right next door to Mike. Jim was always talking about how much he hated the way black people were portrayed in movies as 'other'. He figured that was because hardly any black people actually made movies top to bottom. There was always some white person in charge of production, marketing, distribution or finance. He had decided to do something about that. With a video camera he borrowed the money to buy, he made a movie called *Temporary Insanity*, using people from his neighbourhood as actors. The movie was about a young, qualified, black congressman who thinks the country has become colour-blind, runs for president and actually believes he might win. The movie left everyone who saw it—in a special screening at Uptown Heads—laughing, crying and wondering why such beliefs are only held by the insane. Not long afterwards, Jim received a phone call from a group of African-American investors in Hollywood who had just formed their own movie studio. To Jungle Jim's surprise one of the investors had seen the film and loved it. Arrangements were made for him to meet with them, and Jim had come away with a deal to make many more such films.

There was King James also. His real name was James King and his 'down home' style had the media calling him the brightest new comedian in years. He had made movies and records and even given command performances. He told jokes everywhere. Everywhere but Uptown Heads. At Uptown Heads, he left comedy to the experts.

There was 'Slick' Shawn Sanders too. Slick had been all set to inherit his father's auto repair shop. He had a degree in engineering and was a licensed mechanic. One day he was fiddling around with two broken down cars when he realised that neither car was running because of the easy over-accumulation of dirt in their fuel systems. He checked the engines of different makes and models, and discovered that they all had the same problem—they had been built to run, but not to last. Then he hit the text books. He went through car manuals to books on engineering, to books on chemistry and physics. He worked on paper and in junk yards for two years until he devised a motor that would clean its own fuel system. It would have more than three times the life expectancy of an ordinary engine. His prototype 'Slick Silhouette' automobile was due on the road in the fall. Many leading businessmen, including Rhineholt Dunn III, already had one on order.

Supreme glanced over at a group of sistas. He smiled as he looked at a few choice hips and asses, and thanked God for black women. Supreme had grown up with most brothas' preconceived notion that women were idiots: How could they be taken seriously if hair and nails were their first priorities? But the sistas he was looking at now had put to rest such notions. They didn't gossip. They didn't seem to be petty, jealous, or vain. They seemed to be genuinely happy to see each other succeed. These sistas came to Uptown Heads on Saturdays to 'check in' on each other and give praise and sometimes reassurance when necessary.

There was Sharon: the essence of Sistahood, her long tapering legs always on view for brothas to drool over under shorts or summer skirts. She had a model's height, but that's where any similarities between her and those mascara-mad divas ended. She had a short natural, which she let Riff cut because she loved the gentleness of his massive hands against her neck and chin. She and Mike were close. She was going into her senior year at Black State University and majoring in architecture.

While in Africa one semester on an exchange program, Sharon came across an industrial material that many African nations had been using for building for centuries. She had mixed some cement with the material and discovered that the new compound she had come up with was half as heavy, yet twice as durable, as concrete. She had now secured a contract to co-design and partially build office buildings for Rhineholt Dunn III upon her graduation, although she was yet to meet the man himself.

There was Angie. She had been a break dancer, before studying modern dance with Alvin Ailey's Dance Theater of Harlem. But neither form could contain her style and individualism. She caught the attention of the producers of *Soul Train* and was asked to appear as one of the regulars. Even on a show with the best dancers in the country, her uniqueness shone through. Now she was a leading choreographer for television, film and music videos.

There was Natalie. The last of the true singers. Her voice was so beautiful that, when she sang, even Riff's expression softened—for a second. She had started singing in church, but quit because she was broke and needed to earn a living. Her church had lots of money but Reverend Needabuck was very into his Mercedes. Natalie—on the other hand—was into gold. Which was what her last album had gone in less than a week.

Kookin' Keisha hated her nickname and didn't really like to cook. What she liked to do was play around with electronics. She was always wiring or rewiring something. She decided to rewire her microwave so that it seasoned the food while cooking—then experimented for months until she eventually found a way for the seasoning to be dispensed by the microwave. She had no idea that it would be marketable, but it was.

There was Cee Jay, too. Cee Jay used to hate doing her sisters' hair. It was time-consuming and expensive, and she also hated the use of chemicals on hair and preferred more natural products. But there were none that worked right, though. Determined to make her own line, she read the label of every hair care product she normally used, substituting the harsher chemicals with more natural products with the same properties. Now she had her own line of natural hair products.

There was April—who had a knack for words and phrases. At twenty-six she owned her own marketing firm. She had coined such phrases as: *If you ain't wearing Brothas' Pants, you ain't a brotha!*; *Crossroads Sneakers—when you drive in these, you never have to change lanes*; and *If you want it Dunn right first, get it Dunn by Rhineholt Dunn III*. She had also written the line for the Hardrock Athletic Wear commercial, *Whaddaya mean I fouled you? You ain't bleedin'!*

Supreme felt a lot better now. He looked over at Tyrone, Steve and Tony standing by the empty vending machines. Tyrone was talking to the girl of his dreams, Sylvia. She had agreed to go to the movies with him but he didn't have any money so he brought her to Uptown Heads instead. She was laughing and having the time of her life. Tony and Steve were also laughing—but at Tyrone. There were few things as funny as Tyrone trying to be smooth.

More than anything, Supreme hated black people who acted like life was supposed to be fucked-up and never tried to change it. He had always found pain a waste of time. Those old drunks had always represented pain to him, always bragging but never doing anything.

Brutal, accepted pain, that had existed with such frequency in their consciousness that it was expected, even welcomed. The world had told those niggas never to expect things to improve, never to expect to better themselves and never to expect happiness. How could they accept that? It was only natural for a man to seek happiness. For Supreme—who always believed that no matter where he started in life, he would end up on top—those old-timers were a reminder that a black man was more likely than anyone else to be a victim of circumstance.

His opinions of them began to change one particularly sober day when, for some reason, all of them seemed serious. Every time Supreme had seen them before that day, they were drunk and boasting about what they had done with, to, or in some woman. That day they merely sat and talked. A seventeen-year-old Supreme, Mike and Vince had been walking past the 'Get Ripped' liquor store, where the old-timers hung out before the Uptown Heads opened.

There was Willie T. Williams, who had shined shoes for a living for the past fifty years. In the process he had put all four of his children through college. None of them chose to acknowledge him now. After all, they were professional people and he was nothing but a shoeshine man.

There was Bumpy. Bumpy was one of the first Harlem big shots. He used to run an illegal numbers operation and operated a few after-hours bootleg liquor and gambling houses. One day an Italian dude came to visit him with a deal that would 'let him keep' twenty per cent of his own racket. Bumpy and his boys beat the dude bad and sent him back to his boss with a note that read, "Fucka you!" The next day, his three-year-old son was found dead in the trunk of Bumpy's car. Bumpy's note had been stuffed in the child's mouth with the word 'too' added. Bumpy went out of business the next day.

There was Nelson Gibbs. Mr Gibbs was the first black student at Allwhyte University. He was jumped and beaten repeatedly throughout his four years there, sometimes to the point where the injuries he sustained were life-threatening. At the end of his senior year he had more than doubled the standard requirements for graduation but was told he wouldn't graduate because 'no nigger would ever graduate from Allwhyte U'. No wonder Mr Gibbs recommended black colleges!

Dr Charlie Andrews was also there. The doctor had developed a revolutionary surgical technique that helped prevent the loss of brain capacity and death after head injury. His beloved wife died in his car outside a hospital—having been denied admittance—after being hit in the head with a night stick by a white cop. Dr Andrews rarely practiced medicine again; one of the few times he did was when a young man he'd come to know well from Uptown Heads came to him with a bullet lodged in his right shoulder. Luckily for Supreme, Dr Andrews still always carried his medicine bag.

Last there was Crazy Injun. Crazy Injun was half-black, half-Cherokee. He had lived in the deep South until he was twenty-three years old. On his twenty-third birthday he had walked into a segregated restaurant and shot the owner. The authorities searched everywhere for him. Everywhere but on his sofa, at home, where he had been since the crime. When they did catch him, they weren't exactly sure who had been caught; him or them.

"Hi there!" He welcomed the crowd of white men with rifles who burst into his home with a smile.

"You know," he told them. "Taking my life will in no way have the effect on me that losing your friend is having on you." The outraged citizens decided they had to kill him quickly. A lynch mob was formed. They marched Crazy Injun to the most public place in town and in their hurry forgot to go through the customary ritual of beating him half to death. That was their mistake. They sat him on a horse with his neck through a noose, then whipped the horse's behind and made it gallop out from under him. The rope snapped.

In the confusion Crazy Injun seized the the sheriff's shotgun and fired once into the air. The mob fled in terror, and Crazy Injun simply walked away. All the way to New York. To those who knew him, Crazy Injun seemed to be the sanest of all them old-timers.

Supreme was looking at them now and wondering what it must be like to be denied your manhood. To be told "No, you're what I say you are." He had heard that some asshole had once said, "Give me liberty or give me death!" What then was death but life without liberty? How could a black man be considered alive when he was not free to determine the outcome of his own life? Yet white people could say: "And before I'll be a slave I'll be buried in my grave." Had they ever felt the lash of a whip?

Death was not always a simple alternative to life. He realised how, during slavery, black people must have treated life and death with equal indifference; how mothers had to decide whether to kill their newborn babies to protect them from slavery, or let them live their lives in shackles and leg-irons; how slave fathers—separated from their families—had to choose between committing suicide in utter despair, or living in the futile hope that maybe, one day, they would see their wives and children again.

'But enough of this deep shit already. *God*-damn she got a phat ass!' Supreme's mind screamed as his eye caught sight of Angie demonstrating a new dance step.

The last person Supreme looked at in his little visual tour was his brother—the one that flesh and blood hadn't been kind enough to provide, but nature made impossible to deny. He saw Mike's tall figure

31

swaying with laughter from Freddie's last joke. He frowned as if puzzled. He always frowned when he looked at Mike, because it was hard to keep 'looking' at Mike from becoming 'staring' at Mike.

"Mike, how good lookin' do you think you are?" Supreme asked him.

Mike looked embarrassed. He shrugged. "I dunno, but I'm probably cuter than the last chick you slept with!"

Supreme shook his head. "How can you talk about your own mother like that?"

They both laughed. But in truth Supreme knew that Mike, an irresistible cross between Denzel Washington and Michael Jordan, was one of the most heavily sought-after brothas in the city. Women stopped dead in their tracks to gaze at him—even when they were with their husbands. This caused the occasional fist fight. When it came to that, Supreme would try and placate the offended man, "You gotta excuse my partner. He can't help himself. He was born that way," he would explain—making Mike's looks sound like a disfiguring disease.

Mike was also one of Harlem's most creative minds; though to look at him or listen to him one would never be able to tell. He dressed with style, but not with flair, and he talked intelligently but not articulately. "I'll never be satisfied," he had once told Supreme. "I may be happy, but I'll never be satisfied."

"Don't get deep on me, Mike," Supreme warned.

"It's not deep, it's just reality."

"Oh, and reality is some shallow shit?"

Mike looked at him, unblinking. "Yours may be, but let me finish explaining mine."

"Well what does it hafta do with?"

"Satisfaction."

"Then go ahead Aretha!"

"No. She's 'respect'."

Supreme frowned. "Oh yeah, so who's 'satisfaction' again?"

"The white dude with the big lips."

"Oh yeah, Mick Jagger," Supreme said. "So whatcha saying is that you can't get no satisfaction?"

"Not exactly," Mike said casually.

Supreme smiled. The fact that Mike stayed calm and answered all his ridiculous questions rationally—even when Supreme was obviously fucking with him—amazed Supreme time and time again.

"I'm saying I'll never be satisfied. I may be happy but never satisfied," Mike stressed.

"What's the difference?" Supreme asked.

"Happiness is the feeling you get when you accomplish a goal. Like getting the woman of your dreams, buying the house you've always wanted, putting your kids through college, you know, that type of shit. But satisfaction, satisfaction is like saying thatcha fine right where you are in life, you don't want anything more. You can't do no better and you don't wanna do no better. You have no more goals to shoot for 'cause you've accomplished them all. I know for a fact is that if I ever run out of goals, if I ever feel satisfied, I'll die right there on the spot. What else is there to live for?"

Supreme digested Mike's words, then nodded slowly. "Well then I hope you'll never be happy."

"You mean you hope I'll never be satisfied."

Supreme shrugged. "That either."

It was closing time. Freddie was leading a group of cars downtown to Zimbabwe's, New York's hottest night spot. Riff couldn't go because he was taking Stacey to Swahili's for a romantic candle-lit dinner. Supreme couldn't go either, because tomorrow was Sunday, the only full day he got to spend with Born. Mike didn't want to go because...hell he just didn't want to go! They were all exhausted after a long week. The last twelve hours had been particularly tough. They always worked extra-hard on Saturdays because people wanted to look good Saturday night and weren't going to take no 'ifs' or 'buts'. It was decided, then. They were each going their separate ways tonight, so they quickly cleaned up their workstations. Riff was the first to leave.

"Where's your car tonight?" Mike said, as he and Supreme made their way out.

Supreme gasped a sigh as he remembered. "Stephanie and Born had to do some shopping in Jersey," he pointed out. "They've got the car."

"Well, I guess you know what that means."

"We could take the train."

"Let's see, two blocks over to Lenox, a block down to One Hundred and Twenty Fifth and a ten-block train ride, just for one block when you get out and three blocks for me?" Mike asked.

"You're a cheap bastard," Supreme laughed. "Won't even pay for a subway token."

"No, you're just lazy," Mike said. They started walking. It was always tough to walk down One Hundred and Twenty Sixth Street behind the Apollo Theater in the summertime. If a show was on, the temptation to go in the theatre was incredible. You never could tell who you might meet; what you knew for sure was that you would meet somebody. Maybe a bad honey from Queens, upstate, or New Jersey who might not ordinarily be uptown. Maybe some hot new celebrity who was trying to be noticed. Maybe the new drug dealer on the block, or even the old one. Anybody really. Anybody and everybody. Even when there wasn't a

33

show at the Apollo, One Hundred and Twenty Fifth Street was packed on summer nights. The brothas with the cameras and the cloth canvases spray-painted with the current rap stars and sayings were still making money, even though it was almost midnight. Brothas selling T-shirts with ONE TWO FIVE across the chest could still expect a sale. Sistas could be seen moving from car window to car window, giving their phone numbers out to the brothas who were cute enough, and their cousin's numbers to the guys who weren't. Brothas didn't seem to care. Most of them had learned by that point that it wasn't the capture of the booty that was exciting, it was the chase.

Everybody out on the street would be trying hard to look 'uptown', except the brothas and sistas actually from uptown—and they could all tell the fakes. Especially Supreme. When a brotha walked too hard, or tried to stand, talk, or rap to a sista too cool, he wasn't uptown. When a sista threw too much ass in too many directions when she walked, or epitomised the word she'd kill you for calling her, she wasn't uptown. Harlem brothas and sistas didn't ever go to extremes to seem cool. Cool was what they were, just like black was. Of course there were Harlem nerds—Vince had come close to being one at one time. But the difference was, when brothas or sistas from uptown were nerds, they were always nerds. They didn't put on airs for the One Hundred and Twenty Fifth Street imposters. They didn't have to. They were home.

Supreme followed Mike west down One Hundred and Twenty Sixth Street despite the fact that they both lived off of Lenox Avenue—which was past where they were. Supreme realised that this was one of those nights when Mike wanted to check out what was happening on One Hundred and Twenty Fifth. Supreme couldn't blame him.

"Whassup with your finances?" Supreme asked after a pause.

Mike sighed heavily. "Not too good."

"You in trouble?"

"No more than usual, but I'ma look over my bills tomorrow and double-check."

"You know if you need anything..."

Mike looked at him deadpan.

"...I'm talkin' about a loan, not a handout."

"A loan that I won't be able to pay back?"

Supreme smiled. "Who said anything about paying me back?"

"Do you know how much I owe you already?"

Supreme nodded.

"Almost enough to buy a new ride, like a Slick Silhouette when they come out—and as you should know, they ain't gonna be cheap."

"But you saved my life that time, remember?" Supreme said.

"You saved my life a hundred times since. Besides..."

34

They noticed a group of young brothas getting out of a car on the corner of One Hundred and Twenty Fifth Street. Mike's face took on an odd, uneasy look. A tall, nervous looking young brotha was last out of the car.

"Friend of yours?" Supreme asked, although they both knew who it was.

"Well, well, well...!" the young brotha began in a loud voice. "Long time, no see." It was Vince—now the biggest drug dealer above One Hundred and Tenth Street, and below it too for that matter. He looked awful. His clothes were new and expensive, but ill-fitting. He was covered in jewellry. His skin was drawn and his eyes were anxious. The brothas with him looked similar, only worse—more anxious.

"Whassup Vince?" Mike said evenly. Supreme studied Vince and his gang casually, but did not speak. Vince was 'dead' as far as he was concerned. Supreme caught himself thinking, *This can't be the whole clique. I could take on these niggas and their pistols with two bricks!* He knew that there had to be someone, somewhere, who at least looked like a leader. There was. Another car pulled up. The driver was alone. When he got out, Supreme recognised the familiar gash above the eye. It was Breeze. When Breeze saw Supreme across the street, he nodded. Supreme nodded back.

Breeze was Vince's right-hand man. He was nicknamed Breeze because anytime he entered a room, the atmosphere acquired a chill. He had come out of nowhere with nothing and nobody. He seldom smiled, and laughed less. He was tall, slim and good-looking, though his eyes were cold. He got the gash above his left eye when he was twelve, and got kicked by a cop whose gun he had stolen to rob a liquor store. At fourteen he earned his 'rep' with the daylight robbery of an armoured car. Armed with only a brick, he had walked up to two security guards and told them to give him a bag of money. The guards saw this serious-looking black youth with a brick in his hand and laughed. "Is this a hold-up?" one of them mocked.

"It ain't an introduction," Breeze said evenly.

They laughed and turned to go back to their work. That was Breeze's cue to attack them and beat them both savagely with the brick, nearly killing one before walking away calmly with a bag of money.

It was Breeze who had told Vince that Riff would never work for them. Neither of them had ever met Riff, but Breeze knew a little more about his character than Vince. "Our kind of money," Breeze explained, "is not the kind he's tryin' to make."

"That's bullshit!" Vince had told him. "Every nigga's got a price. His may just be a little higher, that's all."

Vince had always been into theatrics. He figured that he needed to have an enforcer who would relieve his constant paranoia, like the white

35

gangsters in old movies. He figured that, with the notorious Riff as his enforcer, he would be feared. He had called Riff and asked him to come to his apartment for a proposal concerning "big money." Riff had been with the Uptown Heads for about a year then, but he always listened to proposals that had to do with money.

As he entered, Riff noticed that Vince's cluttered and dimly-lit apartment was filled with expensive but tacky things. He looked at the young brotha sitting behind the massive desk with the light shining down on him and figured he must be the boss. He had already seen that movie. The young boys surrounding the boss were punks. They posed and acted like tough guys, but avoided direct eye contact with him. All except one. The tall young brotha with the scar above his eye, leaning against the wall, seemed out of place. He held a fixed, but distant stare, as though he knew Riff already. Riff and the brotha exchanged slight nods before he took a seat opposite the brotha behind the desk.

"What's the deal?" Riff asked. No small talk, no greetings.

Vince was caught off guard. He had planned an introduction ceremony that would last at least thirty minutes. That was his hook; intelligence. His was still intact. He could dazzle or daze people with his intellectual light show, but Riff had pulled the plug on it. Instead, Vince talked vaguely about building an empire—taking over this and that part of here and there, eliminating him and her—then offered Riff an extraordinary amount of money; so much that even his boys gasped. Except one.

Riff looked thoughtful. "So you want me to be a drug dealer?" he asked evenly.

Vince laughed. "You must have misunderstood me. I said that you'd be affiliated with..." His mouth caught the back of Riff's hand before he could finish.

Riff understood exactly what Vince said he'd be affiliated with, and he didn't like it, nor the suggestion that he had trouble understanding. He stood to leave. Vince's boys looked on in shock. Except one, who just shook his head and smiled. Riff stood in the centre of the apartment, hands on his hips, looking from face to face, in case Vince's boys tried to retaliate. Fortunately for them, none of them tried anything and he left without having to *really* hurt somebody.

Supreme was staring at the tall scar-eyed brotha now, recalling his first and only conversation with him. It was one of the most amazing conversations he'd ever had; one of the few times he had walked away doubting his own convictions. He had seen Breeze getting out of his car one afternoon while he was on his way to Uptown Heads. He'd heard how Vince was losing props uptown because he was an old face in a profession that thrived on new ones. Vince, always at the top of his game, didn't wait for a new face to challenge him, but put out the most impressive new face he had to work for him.

Everything that Supreme had heard about Breeze up until then had made him sound like a superhero. He was smart and had reorganised the uptown drug trade almost single-handedly; he had expanded Vince's operations as far as Long Island, Westchester County, North Jersey and New Haven, Connecticut; he had personally developed a new method to cut cocaine so that impurities wouldn't weaken the coke itself. And he had set up bullshit-legit businesses throughout Harlem and beyond. Nobody wondered why young boys and girls, some barely sixteen, were minding bodegas, liquor stores, clothing stores, jewellry stores, and supermarkets. Nobody except Supreme.

Supreme had heard that Breeze was tall, had a scar above his eye, and sistas said he was good looking. That day, when he saw the young brotha in a blazer and slacks, he figured that there couldn't be two of them that fitted the description. Supreme walked over to him calmly. This was a brotha he'd hafta know.

Breeze had seemed like he was teaching a lecture to a college campus, as opposed to rapping to some young brothas who were standing around looking like the hoodlums they were. Supreme waited for the other brothas to leave before he approached. Breeze's back was to Supreme, so he shouldn't have noticed Supreme approaching. He seemed to be aware of him though.

"You holdin'?" Supreme asked, trying to sound like a drug customer.

"I'm never holding," Breeze answered, turning slowly, steely eyes sizing up Supreme. "But that's not what *you* wanted to know."

"You're right."

"Then what? You wanna give me a haircut?"

Supreme wondered how the brotha knew he was a barber. But then again, *he* had known Breeze was a drug dealer. "No, I just wanted to see how fuckin' stupid you really are."

Breeze was unruffled. "Now was *that* called for?" he asked calmly.

Composure, Supreme told himself. He was gonna hafta deal with this brotha with intelligence and composure.

"Now what can I help you with?" Breeze asked, obviously eager to send Supreme on his way.

"Why do you sell that shit?" Supreme asked bluntly.

Breeze raised a brow in surprise. "What would you suggest I be doing?" he asked evenly.

Supreme shrugged. "I don't know. What are you good at?"

"What I'm doing," Breeze said, matter-of-factly.

Supreme frowned sourly. He should have seen that one coming.

Composure, composure... "So whatcha wanna be, Vince's bitch for the rest of your life?"

Breeze raised an eyebrow again, this time he looked offended. Supreme knew he'd struck a nerve.

"Brotha," Breeze said hastily, "it's been real, really. I'd love to stay and be insulted by you all day, but I don't have time to waste—I don't cut hair for a living. So if you'll excuse me," he turned to leave. "I've got plans..."

"Oh, the pusherman has plans?" Supreme interrupted with mock surprise.

Breeze stopped to look at him. There was a flicker of life in his eyes as he wondered if he'd have to kill Supreme to get rid of him.

"I didn't know you had plans, Brah," Supreme continued. "That changes the whole shit. A brotha that can plan must be a genius. You a lot smarter than I thought."

Breeze looked more confused than anything. Supreme shook his head. He was disappointed. This nigga wasn't all that after all. Just another wannabe gangsta nobody. He had plans. *Everybody* has plans. Even Vince had plans.

"Why me, man?" Breeze asked. "There's a million brothas on a million street corners in a million cities for you to do your Jessie Jackson on. Why me?"

"I'm starting to wonder about that myself. It's obvious that you ain't sayin' shit." He began to walk away.

"That's good!" Breeze called after him in an even tone. "Believing that will make things a lot easier for you!"

Supreme kept walking.

"You'll be able to say to yourself, 'brothas like me are right and brothas like him are wrong'—period!"

Still Supreme kept walking.

"And you'll be able to keep thinking like the white man you wanna be!" There was a hint of mockery in his voice, and although Breeze had not once raised his voice above a whisper, his last statement entered Supreme's head like a scream.

Supreme stopped dead in his tracks. It took all the effort he could muster to control himself. He turned and walked slowly back to Breeze. "Oh I wanna be a white man? You're the nigga doing his job for him! Selling his drugs, making his money, killin' niggas so he won't have to."

"Oh that's what I'm doing?"

"Yeah, did I miss something?"

"Yeah," Breeze said flatly. "The point."

Supreme looked away incredulous. *What point?*

"You look like the kinda brotha who knows a little bit about history,"

Breeze began in the college lecture tone he'd earlier used on the brothas. "For as long as anyone can remember, white people have been giving coloured people the tools to destroy themselves so that they wouldn't have to. White people pumped opium into the Orient, gave 'fire water' to the Indian, and as for the brothas...?" Breeze shook his head woefully. "The Brothas got *everything*."

Supreme's face evened out, his attention became acute. He knew this, but he was surprised that Breeze did too.

"Opium never held the black man's interest," Breeze continued. "We became immune to alcohol, and marijuana to us was like cigarettes. The problem was, since our systems were stronger, they needed much more to fuck us up. So our friendly neighbourhood white man came out with shit designed specially for us. This way, he kept us not only high, but poor. He made sure that what made us high would make him a profit, and that the profits would never be distributed to the victims."

Where is this all leading?, Supreme wondered. He was uncomfortable with the fact that he was in a socio-political discussion with a drug dealer and was actually agreeing with him!

"So what are you gonna do?" he asked.

Breeze laughed and all of a sudden his face became almost boyish and happy. "Make it a family business," he said after a pause.

"You don't mean...?"

"Black people," Breeze interrupted, "will be making all the money from the drug trade; from the corporate level to the street."

Supreme smiled at the thought. A picture was forming around Breeze's words and for a moment it looked pretty good—but he soon came back to reality. "Not!" he said, shaking his head. "How couldcha even begin to expect to pull off some shit like that?"

The Breeze smirked. "There'll be a series of assassinations in this country and in all the drug-producing countries in the world. The key members of the white mob, as well as the top officials, are history. When everything's taken care of, my clique's gonna take control of all the merchandise coming into this country."

Supreme's face went numb. He blinked slowly.

"You're gonna do this," he asked with difficulty, "with Vince's boys?"

Breeze laughed, the boyish, happy laugh again. "Would you?" he joked. "I got my own brothas; The Black Experience. We're gonna handle this. I personally have contacts with brothas in major cities all across the country. Once we take over, drugs won't be dealt, they'll be distributed."

That brought Supreme back down to earth. Breeze was still a drug dealer, no matter how you sliced it, worded it, phrased it, or said it. Supreme was both relieved and disappointed. Relieved that he was right in his beliefs against drug dealing, but disappointed that Breeze had not given him better ones.

"You make it seem like you're gonna be doing the black man such a big favour, when the fact is, you're gonna be exploiting him just as much as the white man ever did, if not more."

Breeze nodded. "Yeah, I thought about that. That's why I'm making major changes in the way shit is to be conducted. First the concentration of drugs is gonna be moved from the city to the suburbs. There's more money out there and less black people. Second, there will be no sales to black people under eighteen. I figure that's old enough to decide if you wanna fuck up your life. Third, there'll be no more black-on-black blood-shed, which I'm sure you'll agree is killing some of the best young brothas we got. With all the shit that's about to go down, we need every available brotha with a gun. Any troublemaker or loud mouth will be made an example of. But we're all gonna be making so much money, I don't expect much of that."

A professor, Supreme thought. *Breeze had the oratory skills of a professor, but the intellectual simplicity of a pre-school teacher.* But the barber still had one more question to ask.

"Do you think the white man's gonna letcha get away with this?"

"You think I'm waiting for his *permission*?"

Supreme smiled. He loved to hear a brotha talk like that. Any brotha.

"But why dontcha just destroy the drugs when you get 'em?" he asked.

"I thought about that too. But it wouldn't make any sense. It would just leave millions of people in this country with addictions to satisfy, somehow. They'd just invent some new shit to get high on. They always do. Our way, at least we'll be able to control it and all the money will go into black hands. Exclusively black hands!"

Supreme was hanging on to a moral thread. He couldn't accept what Breeze was doing.

"Besides—there's too much money in it," Breeze continued. "Sellin' drugs ain't somethin' you just give up. But I don't plan to waste the money either. Don't tell me you haven't already noticed what I've done in Harlem. Tell me, when we were coming up, was there anywhere near this many jobs available for young brothas and sistas?"

Supreme didn't want to answer. He was sick of agreeing so much with a dealer.

"Once things get rolling the Black Experience is gonna set up schools, poverty relief programs, nursery programs, homeless shelters...everything people have been waiting on the government to do."

Supreme had to leave. He could feel it. If he kept listening to this mothafuckin' Breeze, he'd be asking for an application form next. "Why couldn't you just sell something else?"

40

"Because these days only two things sell. Shit and substance. I ain't got no substance, but I'm full of shit."

Breeze laughed—and slowly, almost against his own will, Supreme joined him. He thought of one last alternative.

"Listen, I know a brotha who's lookin' for intelligent young brothas like you. You could come and work with me."

Breeze looked confused. "In the barbershop?"

"No, not exactly. Look, I can't explain it right now, but I'm sure he could find you a job."

"Oh..." Breeze said, as though he understood more than Supreme believed possible. "I know what you're saying. I'll think about it. I really will."

They punched fists and were about to part. Supreme knew that Breeze wouldn't think about it too hard or too long. And why should he? Barbers and bartenders always *knew* everything, but what did they every actually *do*?

"By the way, my name is Supreme."

"I know who you are. You think you could talk all that shit to me and live if I didn't?"

Supreme turned his head. "When I'm dead, make sure somebody has the decency to *bury* me," he said to Mike, though looking at Vince.

"What's wrong with that nigga?" Vince asked Mike.

The word 'nigga' sounded ugly in Vince's mouth. The kid who used to spend hours lecturing on the evils of the word now used it commonly.

"You know how he feels about you," Mike said. "To him, you're dead."

Vince was offended, but smiled to cover it.

"Good ole Mike," he said. "Always calls it like he sees it."

Mike shrugged. "Ain't no other way to call it, yo."

"Better tell your boy to be careful," Vince announced loudly. "Callin' niggas dead could get him killed."

By a dead man?, Supreme felt like asking, but he wouldn't give Vince the satisfaction. He just started walking in silence, waiting for Mike to catch up. It always took Supreme a while to start talking again after seeing Vince. *Seeing a dead man brings back memories.*

Saturday night studied Supreme with a watchful eye as he and Mike made their way to Lenox Avenue.Only a few heads were on the avenue at that hour, but Supreme and Mike made sure they 'broke-off' the brothas with handshakes and the sistas with light pecks on the cheek.

Supreme had that stupid smile he wore whenever he was about to say something ridiculous.

"You know who'd make a cute couple?" he asked.

41

Oh, this one! Mike frowned. "Don't!" he warned in advance.

But Supreme wouldn't give up so easy. "Mike you know she's always liked you."

"She once had a crush on me. A *crush*, y'know, like something a kid gets. A kid...'cause that's what she always was to me when we were growing up. Why do you imagine some mysterious romance going down between me and the Little Woman? Why can'tcha be like every other black man in America..." he switched to a deep, dumb-sounding voice and pointed a threatening finger in his partner's face, " 'don't fuck wid ma sister, man. I'll fuck ya up!' "

Supreme laughed. "Is that how I should sound?"

Mike nodded vigorously. Supreme shrugged his shoulders.

"I'd just rather see her with you—a brotha I can trust—than with the next man."

Mike could see only one way out of this argument.

"You know, that might not be such a bad idea," he said, assuming a conciliatory tone.

"See!" Supreme cried triumphantly.

"I mean, Steph is kinda dope," Mike continued. "Cute face, thick legs, that big ass, juicy titties, I'll bet the pussy's just—"

"Hey, hey, hey! " Supreme yelled. "What the fuck? Yo! That's my sister!"

"So you should know shit about her," Mike continued. "Like yo, does she suck...?"

"Now look, maybe I was wrong. Maybe she should only mess with people I don't know. I wouldn't wanna hafta kill your ass because she told me you're a freak in bed or something."

Mike laughed. It took Supreme a few seconds to realise that he'd been had. When he figured it out, he had to laugh too.

The two of them walked on into the night. They reached Mike's building three hours after starting their fifteen-minute journey.

"Yo," Supreme began as they touched fists before parting, "whatcha gonna do tomorrow?"

Mike shrugged. "Who knows? Ain't got no money, so it's not like I got a variety of options."

Supreme laughed and walked off. He figured he'd call Stephanie to check on Born once he got back to his place. He always stayed with Stephanie on Saturday nights. Sunday was their father-son day. Supreme really loved their father-son days. He'd take Born out, watch him, laugh and enjoy. *How can you have a child and not enjoy?*

When Supreme unlocked the door of his apartment he was surprised to see Stephanie sitting on the sofa, waiting for him. She had put Born to bed and was skimming though a magazine.

42

"I've got to talk to you," she said.

"No kidding."

"Seriously, Supreme, I'm worried about you."

"The *world*," Supreme said in a tired voice, "is worried about me."

"But I'm your sister and I love you."

"They love me too. Love my looks, love my style, love the funny jokes I tell, love the way I..."

"Supreme! Listen, I'm serious!"

"Maybe that's your problem, Sis. You're too damn serious. You need to lighten up, getcha self a man or somethin'. Be damned if you ain't just like Mom..."

"I am *not*..." she said through gritted teeth, "...like Mom."

"Yeah, you're right," he nodded. "Then again, you haven't had some tired-ass brotha like Dad running you down for the past thirty years. Why dontcha have a man, anyway?"

" 'Cause there's no such thing as a 'man'," Stephanie said evenly.

Supreme smiled and shook his head.

"Don't give me that look, homosapien." Supreme winced. "You know what I'm saying is true. Black males nowadays use every excuse in the book to avoid having to be a man—*the white man has castrated me!—the black woman has castrated me!—I can't find a good job!—I can't find a bad job!—White women are better than black women!—Black men are better than black women!—White men are better than black women!—I can't be a father to a baby if I don't love the mother—I can't be a father to a baby if I do love the mother—I can't be a father, period—I can't deal with all that shit!*"

Supreme had been laughing throughout.

"She's back!" he screamed happily, as if at the return of his favourite soul singer. "And with a new list of put-downs for the male species! Called a nigga a *homosapien!* That's some *new* shit! Glad to see you're always working on your game."

"Can never let it slip for a minute," Stephanie said, accepting the praises.

"So does that little tirade include all of us?"

"Mostly...except maybe..."

"Mike, right?"

"For all the difference it makes—yes. And Riff's kinda cute, but he's married."

"You need to come by Heads on Saturdays and stay a while," Supreme said, seriously. "There's *mad* eligible brothas there."

She frowned. "Like who? Slick and the rest of his 'player's ball'?"

Supreme shook his head. "You just don't know them well enough. That 'player' shit is the same thing they say about me, and you know what my sex life has been like for the past few years.

43

"Anyway this is all beside the point," Stephanie said. "I didn't come here to talk about my love life—"

"Well if you came to talk about mine there's nothing to discuss."

"Well there could be," she said smiling, "I've found the perfect girl for you."

"Where at this time? Burger King?"

"Will you listen? I go to school with her. She's bright, she's attractive, sounds exactly like you when she argues, and her ambition is to be the female Rhineholt Dunn III."

"Then why dontcha introduce her to him?" Supreme said hotly. "You know him as well as I do."

"I just thought you'd like to meet her and at least see what you think."

"Why does what I think matter? If she goes for twenty million dollar suit-wearin' bastards, let him meet her."

"But I thought maybe you'd like her too."

Supreme shook his head. "If she likes *him*," he said slowly, "there's no way in hell I'd like her."

Supreme noticed his sister's pained expression. "Look Sis, I know you think that the solution to all of my problems would be a woman in my life. I agree with you. But you gotta realise that it's my choice. Mine. Not yours. Not anybody else's."

Stephanie shrugged. The only thing that bothered her was that, this time, she was certain she had found the right girl. But if that was his decision then fine. They talked for a while, then Stephanie decided that she would get a gypsy cab home. It was already in the early hours.

Supreme walked his sister to the cab and returned to his apartment yawning. He looked in on Born before deciding to get some sleep himself. Tomorrow would be father-son day, and they were always exhausting!

Morning was breaking over the Atlantic ocean, Massachusetts, Rhode Island, Connecticut, Westchester and the Bronx. In the next half an hour it would break over Harlem. You could never be too sure, though. There were some days when the sun didn't want to be caught uptown at all.

"Damn!" Supreme said, looking at himself in the mirror. "I'm a ugly mothafucka in the morning!" The transformation his face underwent while he was asleep was incredible. *Damn!* He'd slept in his hat again. He laughed. Everyone wondered what he looked like without a hat. Only Stephanie, Born and Mike knew; everyone else had only vague memories. He took his hat off, took a look, and frowned again. Oh well; the image in the mirror wouldn't improve until he'd taken a shower.

Once he'd showered, he looked in on his son. Born was still asleep.

44

Good. He'd have time to go to the corner store and get the paper. He dressed quickly and hit the streets. It was painfully early and night people were still out trying to get their moves together. A couple of prostitutes up on Lenox, caught on the wrong side of town, trying to pick up a last couple of bucks before daylight. *Who's looking for pussy at this hour except a man with no hands?*, Supreme laughed to himself.

On the opposite side of the road a crackhead and a junkie were arguing over who's high was the best, while each one was secretly trying to steal the other's shoes. A police car cruised by. A young brotha was on the pay phone at the corner—his conversation was clearly audible right across the empty street and growing in both volume and expletives. The bodega proprietor who Supreme bought his newspaper from—a cute young sista who looked like she could have been one of the teenagers that Breeze had been talking about—had been reading a book of poetry when he entered, and seemed efficient. She was probably saving up to go to college. Supreme couldn't help wondering—was the same brotha who was providing her with her future also selling crack to her brother?

Supreme started reading the paper on his way back to the apartment. There was some bullshit article claiming Rhineholt Dunn III didn't give to worthy causes. *That's crazy*, Supreme said to himself. Rhineholt Dunn III owned almost every black business in the metropolitan area, employed almost exclusively black people, sponsored several black scholarship funds of his own, had self-help this, poverty relief that, 'Feed the Homeless', 'Shelter the Hungry'—all kindsa shit. What did these fools consider 'worthy'? He flicked to the sports page. The New York Highrises, the local pro basketball team, had got bumped out of the playoffs. *Damn! The Highrises better hope that when Steve comes out of college, they have a lottery pick*, he thought, chuckling. He read his favourite comic strip, Sergeant Leroy, a cartoon about a black sergeant who was always almost getting kicked out of the army. Nate Allen, one of Mike's customers, was the cartoonist. Leroy had altered his uniform to include red, black and green bell-bottom pants and platform shoes. Supreme laughed all the way to his mailbox. He hadn't checked his mail for two days now and amongst the various junk mail, there was a letter from the Big Money Realty Company addressed to Born.

Supreme climbed the stairs up to his apartment, opening the letter on the way. It was about the seemingly worthless farm in North Carolina that Pop Pop had left Born in his will. Big Money Realty was interested in building a shopping mall and condominiums on the land. Although it covered only about ten acres, it was the ideal location, they explained. Supreme looked over the offer and thought for a minute. It was nearly twice as much as their previous offer, and almost ten times the value of the property as farmland. Supreme decided, on behalf of his son, that

Pop Pop's land was worth more than money.

Born was still asleep. Supreme decided to read the newspaper. He scanned the pages quickly for anything interesting. He paused, reading one of the headlines: 'Mobster gunned down—reprisals feared!' it screamed. Beneath it, was a picture of a body under a bloody white sheet.

'At approximately 12:15 this morning, reputed 'mobster' and drug baron Guido Andolino was shot to death outside his Queens, New York home', the article read. 'No evidence relating to the crime was found on or near the scene, except a half-eaten watermelon rind. Police are unsure whether Andolino himself had been eating the watermelon, or whether it was left there deliberately. No motive has yet been determined.'

Supreme read the story twice. He was sure from the part about the watermelon rind that it was the work of Breeze and the Black Experience! If it was, Breeze had become too dangerous to even think about.

By the time Born woke up, Supreme had fixed breakfast. Single-parenthood had made him a decent cook, and he even managed to keep the house clean. When Born came out of the shower, Supreme passed him the Sergeant Leroy comic. Born laughed until he nearly fell out of his chair.

Father and son ate breakfast together then Born got dressed. Sipping on a glass of orange juice, Supreme nearly choked when he saw the outfit that Born decided to wear. Without speaking, Supreme thrust both hands in the air.

"What?" a confused Born asked.

"You have to be about to rob in that outfit," Supreme said to his big-jeans-sweatshirted-boots-in-the-summer-wearing son. Born looked down at his outfit with a critical eye and then back to his father with the same expression.

"Get in your room and change," Supreme said flatly. His tone left Born in no doubt about what kind of outfit he was expected to put on— but Supreme didn't even notice for a second that he had never bought the one that was about to come off.

Born changed clothes.

Though his Honda was an expensive model, Supreme knew that it would seem like second-best once Slick Shawn's car came out. Supreme laughed out loud. *Damn! Niggas are makin' cars now!* It was long overdue, but African-American craftsmanship was about to go blow-up.

It was time to decide where they were going. Hell, they were in the car, driving at fifty miles an hour. In no time at all, they were at the zoo.

"Why are they kept in cages?" Born wanted to know as they made their way by the big cats' enclosure.

"Wouldcha want that lion walking right next to us?" Supreme asked, prompting him to use his own judgement.

46

Born gave it some thought, then shrugged. "Yeah, why not?" he said.

Supreme had to grin. He didn't have an answer for that one. He changed the subject by buying Born a chocolate ice cream cone, then another when he dropped it. They walked and laughed and laughed and walked, and were father and son.

When Supreme finally looked at his watch it was seven o'clock. Time to see a movie. This was one thing about their father-son days that never changed. They'd see a current movie of Born's choice at the theatre, then rent a movie to take home afterwards. On the way home tonight, they rented *Shaft*—the black classic with Richard Rountree as a black private eye who has to out-muscle and outwit the Mafia, while working for, with and around the black mob and black nationalists in Harlem.

They were on their way upstairs to the apartment when a voice called out: "Supreme!"

He and Born turned around. It was Denise, Born's mother, the 'dead' girl. She looked terrible. Dirty and shabby from head to toe. "You still not speakin'?" she asked.

There was a lump in Supreme's throat as he stood and stared in silence. Born reached for his father's hand. Supreme pulled it away.

"Mama's baby!" Denise said softly, as Born crept behind Supreme's leg. "What's the matter? You're not scared of your own Mama?"

Born started crying and groping wildly for Supreme's hand.

Denise became enraged. "How couldcha turn my child against me?" Her eyes were wild as she yelled at Supreme. "Come to Mama," she pleaded reaching for Born again. "Please baby—"

"Daddy! Daddy!" Born screamed in terror.

"Don't..." Supreme shook his head. "If you love him, don't do this."

She stood up and stared into Supreme's eyes. He returned her gaze for a moment, then turned his back on her to open the front door.

"Don't you have any regrets?" she asked him, pitifully.

Supreme took a good, long look at her. Her hair, once long and shiny, was now a dirty, matted mess; sunken breasts hung in place of the proud, upright ones he used to know, and the drawn, vacant face bore little resemblance to the pretty girlishness he'd once loved.

"One," he said matter-of-factly. "That I wasn't born Supreme." He turned around and walked inside.

CREATIVITY

"Ow!" The toast hit Mike in the face. His apartment housed a wide variety of electronic gadgets and gizmos he'd created in his spare time, and he hadn't adjusted the spring on the toaster. It was seven-thirty on a Monday morning, and he and Riff would be alone at Uptown Heads all day until Supreme arrived in the evening. He knew that if he didn't get moving soon, he'd be late. Uptown Heads opened at nine o'clock on weekdays—not eleven like most barbershops—to capture the morning rush-hour traffic. There were usually a couple of customers waiting outside when he or Riff got there.

Supreme had once said to Mike that anybody who didn't believe in heaven should come to Harlem, and that anybody who didn't believe in hell, should travel a little further down the same block. Only uptown could you find the heights of wealth and depths of poverty sharing the same parking space. Only uptown. And it was only the uptown veteran who knew how to 'stay' in heaven. Who knew how to travel those few 'good' blocks so that they led into other 'good' blocks. Mike was just such a veteran. His walk to work through those 'good' blocks was the favourite part of his day.

There was nothing in the world like Harlem in the morning. Little black children hurried off to school, some with anxiety, some with reluctance. Old women stood on their stoops, or made their way to and from the corner market—"you hafta get there early to get the good tomatoes." Old men in chairs lined the wall of the liquor store. These days, they didn't do half as much drinking as talking.

If a black person from the past were to look at Harlem in the morning, he'd swear that brothas and sistas had finally taken over. The people had so much vitality. Young brothas with their bullshit, shirt-and-tie jobs, who prided themselves only on the fact that they weren't living foul, headed for the downtown subway. Sistas—some glorified secretaries, or entry-level executives, recent business school grads, or with degrees in Economics—stared at the brothas wondering when and if they'd ever get the picture. Yeah, this was Harlem alright. This was Mike's home.

He dropped by Build Your Own Breakfast, his favourite eating spot. It was also his favourite Build Your Own Brunch, Lunch and Dinner spot, since the sign changed with the meals served. After building his low-protein, high-cholesterol breakfast, Mike bought the day's paper. Sergeant Leroy was suggesting that the army trade in their jeeps for long pimpmobiles with eight-track tape players. Mike laughed hard and long. Next time Nate Allen, the cartoonist, came to the shop, he would ask for a copy of the new Sergeant Leroy book. It had only been on the market for

48

two weeks, but was already a bestseller. He turned to the sports page. The Highrises were interested in some eight-foot white guy from East Germany. He frowned. *Whaddaya expect but a scrub team when you got scrubby management!* He read an article suggesting that Rhineholt Dunn III was of Brazilian nobility. He laughed. The subject of Rhineholt Dunn III always made him laugh. Back on the front page was an update on the mob slaying in Queens. He didn't read it. Stuff like that didn't interest him.

He looked at his watch. It was eight-thirty. He was out. He arrived at the shop at exactly nine o'clock to a chorus of shouts of "Yo, Mike!" Riff hadn't got there yet, and already a few customers were standing waiting.

Some of Uptown Heads' more celebrated customers preferred to visit the shop early to duck the heavier crowds that came in the evenings. Graveyard shift people also came early, as soon as they got off work. As soon as he opened up, Mike's old friend Pat Erving, the dominant centre for the Highrises, stepped in. The two friends greeted each other warmly and the other customers gladly offered their place in line out of respect for the popular basketball star. Pat smiled at Mike and sat down in his chair.

"An eight-foot East German?" Mike asked in mock outrage.

"I guess that'll make me a power forward," Erving said with a shrug.

"A forward, but I don't know how *powerful*,"

"We need you out there Mike," Pat said smiling, but only half-joking.

"You do. But I hung up basketball a long time ago. My knees are gone. Besides, what you guys really need is a small forward, not a big guard."

"Man, when I played against you in high school you were a forward," Pat said, daring Mike to find an excuse.

"Yeah, but that was in high school. Pro forwards are a lot bigger than high school forwards."

"Yeah," Pat said, unimpressed.

Riff arrived a half hour later. By that time another six or seven regulars were already there, chatting aimlessly.

"You late, brotha!" Mike called out.

"But I'm good, brotha," Riff replied evenly.

Everyone knew why he was late. They knew why he was suppressing a smile, too. They had all met Stacey. Bumpy, the old-timer in the house, who came early every day for a shave and once a week for a haircut, added some advice:

"Got damn it boy! It only nine o'clock in da mornin'! Ya need ta leave that young girl 'lone till a more respectable hour!"

"Well at least with a wife who's a psychiatrist, you'll know when you're going crazy..." Crazy Injun laughed. *"I had no idea!"*

Dr Andrews jumped to Riff's defence. "Leave the young man alone. Love is a splendid thing."

Bumpy frowned. "Oh there that fool go again with dat 'ole love shit! Ain't no such thing as no got damn love! Just sex and money!"

A few mocking yeahs went up from the regulars; a couple of them sounded sincere.

"Listen to that guy," Crazy Injun laughed, "the man who cried when Elvis died!"

"Ya got damn right I cried!" Bumpy said. "I was sorry I didn't kill dat mothafucka myself! And I'll tell ya anotha thang..."

"No, let me tell you something," Nelson Gibbs interrupted. "I never did care for your choice of language. You demonstrate an utter disregard for decorum and decency. Don't you realise that people's choice of language reflects not only their opinion of the world, but also their opinion of themselves? Now, keeping that in mind, what do you have to say for yourself?"

Bumpy looked thoughtful. "Fuck you! You old three piece suit-wearin', pocket-watch-havin', vocabulary-buildin', Allwhyte University-attendin'—"

The rest of his outburst got buried in the laughter.

"You was kinda askin' for that one, Nellie," Willie T said humbly.

Mike had been following the conversation closely, as he did each time one of these men spoke. Nobody was a better witness to the past than someone who had actually seen it. Those old-timers had lived it, and they wore their battle scars with pride. So what if they exaggerated a little bit? Or just out-and-out lied sometimes? The shit they said they did was more interesting than most of the shit other people dreamed of doing. They weren't pathetic old men wasting the rest of their days rotting in a barbershop. They were warriors taking a well-deserved rest!

It was 9.35 am. Mike was a time fiend. His eyes raced several times back and forth between the head he was cutting and the clock. Time was dragging, the way it had dragged every Monday for the past year and a half. 9.35 seemed to take forever to become 9.36. "What time is it?" he yelled.

"Ain't there a clock on the wall, Brah?"

"Man, you know that thing is either too fast or too slow. I need to know *exactly* what time it is."

"Well, I think it's about...now."

The Uptown Heads crowd, not used to Riff making jokes, enjoyed this rare delight.

"All right, fuck it," Mike said with a hostility that startled everyone. "Will somebody at least tell me when it's twelve?"

"Yeah, man," Bumpy said. "I'll tell ya anything you wanna know.

50

When it's twelve, who *really* killed Kennedy, where to get some bootleg; *anything*."

The laughter that followed and the sarcastic look on Bumpy's face made Mike realise how he must have sounded. He reluctantly joined in the laughter. Somebody still better tell him when it was twelve, though.

By the time twelve o'clock rolled around, Mike had pulled himself together. He waited until exactly 11.59 before he yelled "Lunch!" then eased out the door with the eyes of the whole shop on him. Folks can tell when one of their own is up to something. They can usually tell what it is. And by the way that Mike had strolled way too casually past each of them, it wouldn't' take long before somebody said what everybody was thinking.

"I smell fish," Riff said flatly.

"It ain't on him yet," Bumpy laughed.

'Yeah, but at least he knows where the river is," Riff said with a smirk.

"Tasteless," Nelson Gibbs mumbled to himself, shaking his head. "Simply, utterly, tasteless."

Mike arrived for his weekly pilgrimage at exactly 12.05. He knew that she would already be there—and was hoping that she enjoyed seeing him every week as much as he enjoyed seeing her, and that she would be concerned about missing him if he was late. Their eyes met as he entered. It was exactly the same every week. Mike would feel weak, and almost stumble at the intensity of her glance, but he wouldn't break the eye contact until she did. He knew that if he did, he'd lose an edge that he'd need if he ever did manage to get her alone someplace. He may have been planning to take on Muhammad Ali, but he was loading his pillow case with soda cans

Like any devout pilgrim, Mike studied his temple. He could do so openly, because he knew that she would not look in his direction again. One glance a week, that's all he got. The brotha she was with was so concerned with coming across as smooth, intelligent, classy and sophisticated all at once that he missed what Mike was doing in the next booth. Mike leaned back into the most casual-looking sitting position he could manage. It was a pose, he knew it—anybody looking at him would know it. But he thought it looked cool as hell, and that was what mattered. The temple was in rare form.

There were many beautiful black women in the city, this Mike was sure of. He came to the same conclusion every time he rode the A Train downtown to a club in the Village, or to Fulton Street in Brooklyn, Jamaica Avenue in Queens, Third Avenue in the Bronx, or any of the many neighbourhoods he regularly visited. Even just hanging around Harlem, you were bound to see some of the most beautiful black women in the world. And that was just New York! The thought that there were more throughout the country—and throughout the world—was too much to take. So how could he be so sure that this one sista sitting in the next booth was *the one?* He heard her sigh and felt his heart flutter. The sista was beyond dope. She looked like God's smile. He could stare at her for an hour, and did every Monday. Even though she wasn't looking his way, Mike hoped he was somehow scoring points with her nevertheless. Maybe she could sense him giving her his undivided attention.

When they saw a sista they dug, a lot of brothas would try and play it cool by purposely looking away. Fuck that! Mike looked at her for an hour non-stop. He always ordered lunch, he usually didn't bother to even eat it.

He listened to titbits of their conversation:

"Yes, of course," the brotha was saying, "and then right after I got my MBA, I took a job on Wall Street making six figures. It was my first job after college, you have to understand, hence the low income..."

Bullshit, bullshit, bullshit! Even if it was true it was bullshit! Nobody wanted to hear that garbage. Why didn't he just show her his resume?

Mike's lunch hour was drawing to an end, but he wouldn't leave until she did. He had to see her from behind at least once a week. It was the only way he could make it to the next. As they rose from their booth, the brotha was still talking, and for the life of him, Mike couldn't believe half the things that came out of his mouth. Was he running for office, or trying to get some ass? Then again, was there any difference? He heard the brotha say, "So Andrea, when can I call you about all this?" and near-ly laughed out loud. You never ask a woman like her when you can call her. She was probably looking for the guy to have some balls and instead he'd shown her his had been cut off. *Too bad, Brah, but you're history!*

On his way back to the shop he realised that, after a year-and-a-half, he finally knew her name. Andrea.

"You're always talking about how good you look," Nelson Gibbs was telling Bumpy when Mike got back to the shop. "Look at you, you dress like a bum!"

Bumpy roared. "Handsome ain't somethin' ya put on, mothafucka!"

The barbershop exploded in laughter.

Mike simply shook his head. Why did anybody even try him? Bumpy was the original. Even Supreme didn't try him. Some people just had wit like that, they were just damn funny, and Bumpy was definitely one of them. Still, Bumpy had had his own personal demons to deal with. In Harlem, humour rarely came without a price.

Mike had already called Sharon, his best friend in the world next to Supreme. In some ways she was an even better friend. Whenever a delicate subject arose that Supreme either wouldn't be able to understand, or didn't want to, Mike went to Sharon. She knew about Andrea, Supreme didn't. She knew exactly how broke Mike was; Supreme only had an idea. To Mike, the whole notion of a platonic relationship with a good-looking woman had been ridiculous. "Somebody's gotta wanna fuck somebody," was his rationale. But with Sharon his reasoning had changed. Hell yeah, he'd wanted to sleep with her in the beginning, but she had a boyfriend at the time, so he used the old 'can I still be your friend?' routine, then became and remained her friend. By the time her boyfriend was out of the picture their friendship had progressed to the point where Mike decided it was too valuable to ruin by trying to sleep with her. That was a first. Until then, nothing had ever been more valuable than trying to get some. Now he had an intelligent and dependable female friend he could talk to about anything and everything. Funny, huh?

Mike planned to leave work at nine o'clock that night and meet Sharon for dinner. The shop wouldn't be too busy. It was only Monday. And after all, he was the one losing money when he left early. Money. He had to find a way to make some and quick. He'd talk to Sharon about that too. She knew about money: where to find it and how to keep it. She already had a contract to co-design and help build office buildings for Rhineholt Dunn III—and she was only a senior in college. Rhineholt Dunn III! Mike chuckled. The subject of Rhineholt Dunn III always made him chuckle.

Mike was taking a break, standing by the refrigerator, sipping lemonade when Supreme walked in at exactly 5.30. The whole atmosphere changed with Supreme's arrival. He always evoked the feeling that everything was going to be all right. As it was Monday, Supreme would be more businesslike tonight, but he would still be funny. He would always be funny.

"I'm leaving at nine, man," Mike told him, once he began to cut his first head of the night.

"Hot date with a chick you ain't sleeping with?" Supreme asked with a mischievous grin.

"Yes, I am going out with Sharon," Mike said after a pause.

Supreme shook his head. "Whatta waste!"

Mike understood his attitude. Supreme had never had any platonic female friends, and now that he was damn near celibate, he didn't have any real female friends at all.

"Call Kool Moe," Supreme said, turning his attention back to work.

Kool Moe was the next best barber in New York. He worked at a shop in the Bronx, but whenever one of the barbers at Uptown Heads needed time off, he made any excuse to the owner of the shop he worked at to

53

leave early. He loved to work at Uptown Heads. He was known as the Great Pretender because he was able to flawlessly imitate any of the Uptown Heads barbers' styles. For the longest time, he had been trying to convince Supreme to add a fourth chair at Uptown Heads. Supreme was still 'considering it'.

Supreme's Monday jokes were like preliminaries. They weren't quite as funny as the ones he told on the weekend, but they still raised a laugh. Some jokes were told in installments, so you had to be in Uptown Heads every night to get the conclusion. And you could tell who had missed a night or two—they would be looking around, all confused, trying to figure out what was so funny.

When the door burst open at exactly seven o'clock, no one wondered who it was. Tyrone, Tony and Steve rushed in, sweaty and out of breath.

"Yo, cuts kid, cuts!" Tyrone screamed.

"I just cut your hair two days ago!" Supreme snapped.

"Well just edge us up real quick then. The Black State tournament is tonight and Steve's in it," Tyrone said proudly. "We gotta represent!"

Mike was still shocked by Tyrone's announcement. He could hardly believe it. Although he was all-state in high school and third-team all-American in college, he had never been invited to the Black State tournament. He looked at Steve and smiled. "You better do good work, kid."

"Oh, I intend to," Steve said, confidently.

"Wait a minute," Supreme waved his hands for a time out. Supreme turned to Mike and frowned sourly. " 'Represent'," he said, shaking his head. "I hate that term. Makes niggas sound like either Olympians or dishwasher repair men. If Steve is playing, why do you and Tony need edge-ups?"

"Have you ever seen the *honeys* at Black State?" Tyrone asked.

That was all he needed to say to get Supreme started, and minutes later, using treachery, deceit and even a little blackmail, he, Tony and Steve were able to wangle themselves into the next available chairs. They received quick service and left to help Steve get some last-minute practice.

At 8.45, Kool Moe walked into Uptown Heads, and everyone yelled "Kool Moe!" in chorus. He sauntered casually over to an empty seat, with his usual aura of pleasant cool. Mike smiled. Moe was not only a skilled barber—he was also genuinely funny without even trying. He never told jokes, he just said funny things. Moe was always dressed wrong for the weather—leather in summer, suede in the rain, silk in winter—and was convinced he was misunderstood. He was right!

He hadn't sat comfortably in his seat before it started. Supreme stopped cutting just to survey Moe's faded jean suit.

"Been shopping at the 'Can ya Help a Brotha?' thrift shop again,

Kool?"

"Yo, this is brand new!" Moe said, offended. "Brotha sold it to me yesterday."

"You mighta done better with a lease, Brah," Supreme said.

Customers struggled to stifle their laughter.

Moe looked at them, confused.

Mike decided to let him get started, because idle, he was a sitting duck. He packed up, handed Moe the double adjustable clippers the youngster only got to use at Uptown Heads, then left.

When Mike called Sharon and asked her to meet him at Swahili's in Greenwich Village—one of the most expensive African restaurants in the city—the first bell of her 'women's intuition' alarm went off. When he usually took her out to eat, they went to 'Build Your Own Whatever', never to Swahili's. Something had to be up. When Mike arrived at exactly 9.30 as promised, bells two, three and four went off simultaneously; Mike was never on time for their dates. They hugged. His ear-to-ear grin was infectious. Sharon knew who was on his mind.

"You can't be that happy to see me," she said, as they sat down.

"Yes I is!" Mike said, sounding remarkably like Buckwheat. "Girl, you look better than a plate of biscuits with ribs on the side!"

"And you need to stop hanging around King James," she laughed. "So...you saw your lady today?"

Mike nodded. "And her name's Andrea."

"You spoke to her? About time!"

"Well, no I kinda overheard..."

Sharon was dismayed. For eighteen months she had watched this fool love a woman from a distance, when that same fool could have had any woman in the world. God, she was tired of being every man's mother, but that's what they all seemed to need—mothering.

"Michael, you big, stupid, sexy, black idiot! Be a goddamn man, would you. I mean, damn! God gave y'all the dicks, not us."

Mike looked like a deer caught in the headlights of a truck. "Sharon! I never heard you talk like that before! Cursing...all vulgar and hostile. And you know what...?" he leaned across the table and lowered his voice. "It kinda turns me on."

Sharon laughed. "So what's up with Supreme? Is he gay or something?"

Mike laughed. "I hope not. He's seen me naked."

"Well so have I. And it's definitely something to laugh about." A thick silence followed. "I mean, the way you have almost no body hair."

Mike exhaled. "You need to be a little more specific in future," he said, a little unevenly. "The male ego ain't no plaything."

55

Sharon shook her head. "*Anyway*, what's the matter with your boy?"

"Nothin'," Mike said, a little offended on Supreme's behalf.

"Then why hasn't he tried to get with me?"

Mike's eyes widened. "I suppose he didn't know he was *required* to," he said sarcastically.

"That's not what I mean Mike and you know it."

"Well, what do you mean?"

"I've made it obvious, *painfully* obvious, that I'm interested in him, but he never seems to pick up the signals."

Mike shrugged. "How did you make it obvious? See 'cause that's the thing. Women always expect shit to be obvious to brothas, like brothas are mind-readers or something. Y'all think that if you look at a brotha— just a regular look now, not some ole sultry, seductive shit—he's gonna know when you wanna go out, where you wanna go, what you wanna do, what your favourite food is, your mother's maiden name, all sortsa shit. Y'all are gonna hafta be more than 'painfully obvious'. You're gonna hafta be crystal clear."

"But I thought I was."

"How? By watching the back of his head while he cuts hair?"

For a while they were silent.

Then Sharon broke the silence. "Mike, look at me."

He glanced up at her indifferently.

"No, I mean really look at me."

He sighed, then took a long look at her. Slowly, she began to transform from the trusted friend he had matured enough to appreciate, to the amazingly beautiful woman he'd originally met. He let his eyes roam over her; her rich, smooth skin, her soft, short natural, her innocent eyes, and her mouth...full and beautiful. She was absolute.

Two years earlier, they had gone to Chicago, to watch the Highrisers meet the Chicago Bulls in the playoffs. They decided to share a hotel room because, after all, they were just good friends, so what could happen? It was late when they got back from the game and Mike was all night in the shower, as usual. When he heard the door open, he twisted his upper torso to peer around the shower curtain. Sharon was naked, and heading straight for him. Mike was frozen to the spot. She pulled back the curtain, took a quick inventory of his body, and eased past him to stand under the shower head. Then she grabbed the soap from his hand. "Taking all damn night," she muttered, as she began soaping herself. Mike was still in shock. Was she coming on to him after all this time? Was this a sign? Should he try to make a move? Or was she just taking a shower? He struggled to gather his senses together, but the sight of her body, wet and naked before him, was overwhelming.

She was a series of marvellous curves. There was the curve in from her foot to her ankle. The strong curve of her pronounced calves. The continuous curve of her made-for-miniskirt thighs that led to her gotta-be-a-black-woman hips. The almost ninety-degree curve from her hips to her slim waist. The simple inward curve of her lower back and the round, hanging curves of her breasts. And the innocent curve of her upper back, extending gently to the nape of her neck. As soon as Mike's eyes reached the back of her head, Sharon whirled round to face him and they stood eye to eye. It was at that moment, in that place, at that time, that Mike doubted he'd ever see a more beautiful woman in all his life. He had had to fight to keep down the "I love you" that threatened to jump out of his throat.

Sharon's eyes fell to the area just below his waist. She raised her brows. "*That* looks different."

Mike hid his face with his hands, a second too late to hide his embarrassment. He lowered them again just in time to catch the gentle rise and fall of her buttocks as she walked to the bathroom door.

Mike turned the water to as cold as he could stand, and stayed in there longer than necessary. By the time he went back to the bedroom she was already in bed, sleeping lightly. He eased quietly in beside her and didn't sleep a wink all night.

"Am I the type of woman a man would be attracted to?" Sharon was asking him now.

"Any man who already has a dick and doesn't want another one," he joked.

Sharon frowned. "You can be so tasteless sometimes."

"Yeah, but I'm always honest."

"That you are," she agreed. "Anyway, forget Supreme. What's up with this money situation of yours?"

"Can't be a money situation if there ain't no money."

"Is it that bad?"

"Worse."

"Are you desperate?"

Her tone made him slightly suspicious. "Kinda. Why? What did you have in mind?"

"Nothing," she said, innocently, "apart from doing what you do best."

He looked confused.

"Cut hair!" Sharon screamed, not even bothering to imagine what he might have been thinking. You have a beautician's license, don't you?"

"If it's hair, I'm licensed to cut it."

"And you know all the real money's in women's hair, right? Well, I happen to know that Ensembles is hiring..."

"Ensembles?" Mike interrupted. "The *fag* spot?"

"You said you were desperate."

"Yeah, but not insane! Listen, I can't work with a bunch of gay moth-afuckas. I wouldn't feel comfortable."

"Why not? I bet a lot of gay people hang out at Uptown Heads."

"Yeah, but they know enough to keep that shit in the closet."

"So what's the difference?"

"The difference is, if you're gay, that's your business. As long as you keep that shit at home, or save it for other people into that shit. Don't come fuckin' with me! Don't run up into my shit, trying to convert me or make me sympathetic to your cause."

"What's your point?" Sharon asked, doubting there was one.

"The point is, Ensembles is their spot. I'd be an intruder. At any moment, I might just tell 'em about their faggotty asses, and that would-n't be right. They're supposed to feel comfortable in their own spot."

"Your problem is, you're homophobic."

Mike didn't try to deny it. "No question! Girl, I'm scared of the *dark* so you know those homos scare the shit out of me!"

Sharon laughed. "I guess you can't be *that* desperate then."

Mike had never been so broke in his life and the thought hit him that very moment. The mortgage payment on his mother's house was due. His sister had just had another baby. His brother was in jail again. And his own rent was overdue.

There was a long, flat silence. Finally, he asked, "You know how to sew?"

Sharon frowned. "A little. Why?"

"I may need you to sew my butt-cheeks together."

Vic Juliano was a rebel; or maybe maverick was a better word. It was-n't that he'd ever really rebelled, he had just blazed his own path. He was the only son of a prominent Italian dry cleaner, who had himself rebelled against the ethnic traps that befell immigrants in America. He didn't open a pizza parlour, he didn't join the Mafia, and he didn't do anything else that Italians were expected to do. He did his own thing. And he raised his son to do the same.

As a boy, Vic loved the music of legendary soul crooner Marvin Gaye, while Frank Sinatra bored the hell out of him. His religious interests ranged from Judaism and Hinduism, to the Black Muslims. Catholicism, to Vic, was illogical. Why should he confess his sins to a guy who was just as prone to screw up as himself? As an adult, he dated girls from every country, culture, race and colour on the planet. Of course, he still dated the occasional Italian girl,

"But why limit yourself to only one flavour when the world is Baskin

Robbins?" he reasoned.

Now, at age thirty-five, Vic was the man. He had opened a beauty shop called Ensembles in his basement twelve years earlier, after visiting a black beauty shop with a girlfriend. Seeing the profitability of the establishment immediately, he got a loan and opened up his own shop. He hired only one beautician, rumoured to be the best in the city, but Vic saw much better work every day. So why, he wondered, did this guy do so much business and have such a rep? He soon found out. He was a prolific gossip, and was also openly homosexual. Women would come from far and wide to hear the latest, and knew that he always knew it.

Vic's plan was to draw all the best beauticians from all over the city by letting them keep seventy-five per cent of what they made—it was a better deal than any other shop could offer. Meanwhile he operated at a loss for a few months, but worked nights as a school janitor to subsidise the shop. His plan worked. Soon he had leased the entire bottom floor of a trendy midtown office building and was now thinking about leasing the whole building.

Midtown was a different vibe. White people. Loads of 'em. And in such a big fuckin' hurry to get where? Work? If a job in midtown meant having to hustle like that every morning, Mike didn't want one. But he had to admit, some of the suits were incredible. Mike knew a tailor-made when he saw one. He could sometimes even name the tailor. Suits were supposed to be personal. They were supposed to fit like the tailor made it around you. Like you just walked off the stand with it on five minutes ago. No sags, no bulges. No high-water pants, tight-across-the-backs, or short sleeves. If you lose or put on weight, get a new suit. If you grow; new suit. Get it soiled; new suit. Mike could tell who lived by the code, and who was faking it.

The buildings in midtown seemed to be alive. Nothing but a living thing could be of any use to so many people. People in constant motion. Nobody just chillin'. Everything seemed so imperative, so life or death, that Mike wondered if anything down here was really important at all. Traffic was a mess. Fifty cabs to every car. Trucks making deliveries. Messengers by the posse. Insanity, given jurisdiction.

Mike loved looking at the black people in midtown. A lot of them were his shirt and tie brothas and glorified secretaries from uptown. He also dug looking at the brothas and sistas who he knew instinctively to be from other boroughs. Brothas from Brooklyn just looked rough; like at any moment, they might just start killing people or something. Sistas from Brooklyn had a raw defiance that radiated in everything they did; from walking to talking, to just sitting down, looking evil. Both brothas and sistas from Queens were always clean. The dopest fashions, the newest styles, every hair in place, Queens brothas and sistas always had the look of a black fashion magazine. You could tell that they were from a borough where there were actual houses to live in. Most of them were probably from two-parent homes too.

The Bronx flavour was so similar to the Harlem flavour that occasionally Mike mistook them. Bronx brothas and sistas, like Harlemites, had the most imitated style on earth; freedom. They didn't have it where the Harlemites had it, though. Bronx brothas and sistas had it in the dress, hair, walk and talk—but they didn't have it in the eyes. Harlemites had it in the eyes.

Mike seldom wasted time with the 'spin-offs', as he called the brothas and sistas from Upstate, Long Island, Connecticut, and New Jersey. Their flavours were imitations of the brothas and sistas from the boroughs. To Mike, the world began and ended with Manhattan Island, Harlem being the Garden of Eden.

He was relaxed when he walked into Ensembles that Thursday morning. It helped that Sharon actually knew Juliano, so he didn't have to go through all the application forms and interview bullshit. To Mike all the beauticians were gay, or at least looked gay. He gulped. He figured the white guy in the office at the back of the shop was Vic, and walked straight through. He had expected some fat, razor-stubbled, pony-tailed Italian in a Hawaiian shirt to greet him. But Juliano was slim, with hair cut neat, and dressed in slacks. Mike was surprised at how young he seemed.

Juliano welcomed Mike into his office. "You're Mike Edwards from Uptown Heads, right? I'm Vic Juliano. Call me Vic."

Absolutely. Mike had never met a white man in his life he'd even consider calling mister.

"I heard about your work. I hear it's fantastic," Juliano said.

Mike breathed a silent laugh. "Sharon, right?"

"Hey, she should know," Vic said. "She used to be one of my best customers before she cut all her hair off and went natural."

"That's what's in," Mike told him simply.

"I just saw her recently. Do you do her hair now?"

Mike nodded.

"Fantastic," Vic said genuinely. "Fantastic."

Against his will, Mike was beginning to like the guy. He had never met a white man who wasn't a cop, teacher, or some other authority figure, so like most inner-city kids, he had developed a deep distrust of all white people. But somehow, standing here now, with this hip, Italian, Black beauty salon owner, he decided that here was a white boy he'd hesitate to kill in a race riot.

"We got one little problem though, Mike," Vic said after a moment.

"What's that?"

"You're not gay, are you?"

Mike burst out laughing. "That's a problem?"

"Yeah, it is. For me."

Mike felt a little angry at himself. White people. They were all the same. What the hell was he thinking a minute ago?

"Mike," Vic began again, "I would love to have you for Ensembles..."

"But..." Mike interrupted.

"But I have this policy about only hiring gay beauticians."

"It's a power thing, huh? What? You got a thing for black faggots? What d'you do...fuck 'em in the ass when business gets slow?"

Juliano looked like a man about to throw a punch. Mike noticed, and welcomed it. He hadn't had a fight in almost a year, and breaking a white man's jaw would be the talk of Uptown Heads for weeks.

"You have every right to be hostile," Vic conceded, having regained his composure.

"You wanna tell me my rights now?"

"No, no, you got it wrong—" Vic tried to explain. "I didn't mean to come off as a cop."

His change of attitude made Mike cool down a little. "Well what you trying to say?"

Vic took a deep breath. "Ensembles isn't the best place in the city for black women to get their hair done. To be honest with you, most of my beauticians are garbage. Ensembles is, however, the top-rated gossip house on the east coast. Women come from everywhere just to swim in bullshit. And when the subject of black men comes up..." Vic waved his hand for emphasis, "...forget it! The women and the beauticians get along great because they are all after the same thing; black men. They get to compare notes, give sexual tips, all kindsa sick shit."

"So you think I would disturb the groove?"

Vic nodded. "Hey, I'm not gay, but even I can tell that you're a good-looking guy. Sure, you might get customers because of your talent, but you'd fuck up the real juicy bullshit throws."

Mike nodded. "How much do chicks pay to get their hair done here, anyway?" he asked out of curiosity.

"Two to five hundred dollars," Vic said matter-of-factly. It took every bit of Harlem cool Mike had to keep calm.

"What kinda cut do you take?"

"Twenty-five per cent," Juliano said.

"Damn! That's a good piece of change for the beautician."

"I try," Vic said.

"Well look," Mike said, his mind now on leaving, "I can dig where you're coming from. I don't agree with it, but I understand. I'm gonna leave my number with you in case you change your mind or have any

61

other ideas. Two to five hundred a head is good dough, I damn sure wouldn't mind having a piece of that."

Vic nodded.

"I'd probably raise the quality of the work in this place, too."

Vic nodded again, this time more vigorously.

"Give it till Sunday." Mike told him. "If you can't think of anything by then, forget it."

Two hours later Vic was in his office with the door closed, watching his favourite show in the world, *The Little Rascals*. It was the episode where all the fellas join the 'He-man Woman Hater's Club', but Alfalfa goes over to Darla's house and has to dress up like a girl to keep the fellas from kicking his ass. Vic was howling. Alfalfa looked cute as a little girl and Spanky, Buckwheat, Porky and the other fellas were all trying to get into her pants. Vic realised then, that he didn't have to wait until Sunday. He already had an idea.

If you catch a train uptown from midtown in the daytime it's the regular New York melting-pot scene. *Hell, white people even have the nerve to be in Harlem in the daytime!* Mike figured it was their equivalent to a jungle safari, they were doing something brave and dangerous. Young white boys would come uptown with their girlfriends, as if to say *look baby, I'm a real man 'cause I've got the balls to walk around where all the niggers live.* Older white men were in Harlem looking for new property to buy and new slums to create. And if it was late enough, you might catch a white man uptown trying to pick up some black tail.

Mike never usually caught the train uptown in the daytime, since that was where he lived and worked. If he was coming from somewhere like a club, it was usually very early morning. The inhabitants of uptown-bound trains at that time were only two colours, black and brown; the pot had already melted and the other colours would by then be safe in their suburbs and condos. Even the young white boys were smart enough to stay away from uptown at night and they damn sure kept their girlfriends away. No big, black stud was gonna come and 'Jungle Fever' their woman.

Riding an uptown train during the day felt weird. Like being a tourist or something. After being in midtown all afternoon, Mike desperately needed to get back to a place where people moved slower and thought faster. He observed the stops on the train as they passed. Fifty Ninth Street, Seventy Second, Eighty First...oh God, why didn't he take the express? He got off a stop early and walked up to One Hundred and Twenty Fifth, happy to see real people again. *How could any self-respecting brotha live anywhere else in Manhattan but uptown?*

Kool Moe had been filling in for Mike at the shop all day. Mike had wanted to get back before 5.30 so that when Supreme got there he wouldn't have to do any explaining. He couldn't tell Supreme he had applied for a job at Ensembles. Not Supreme. Never Supreme.

Mike reached the door of Uptown Heads at exactly 5.25. Supreme would be hot on his tail. Kool Moe was in the middle of cutting a customer's hair when Mike walked in. Without explanation, he ushered Moe out the back door quickly and finished the cut he was working on. Supreme walked in at exactly 5.30. Mike let out a sigh of relief.

"So whatcha sayin' Tim?" Born asked.

"We got dough, but it ain't no Rockerfeller money," Tim said a bit dejectedly. It was Saturday morning, all the reports were in, the kids had made a little bit of money, but not as much as they'd hoped. Some of the kids were making more money than their fathers. The notion was incredible.

Supreme flung open the door suddenly. The kids were playing innocently. Too innocently. He closed the door.

"I know Born's up to something crooked back there," he whispered to Mike.

"With a father like you, whaddaya expect him to be doing? Playing bingo?"

Customers were already beginning to pile up outside.

"Where the hell is Riff?" Supreme asked, more worried than angry. Mike shot him a 'think about it' look.

A moment later the street doors nearly swung off their hinges as Riff came through them. "Let's get ready to rumble!" he yelled.

"Time, time for some, time for some action!" Mike sang, picking up the cue.

"Ok, Redmen," Supreme said, calming them both down. "If you look outside, you'll see we got more work to do than a little bit."

It was an especially busy Saturday. As always, many of the customers didn't leave after they got their hair cut, but hung around to wait for the main feature: Saturday night at Uptown Heads. It was destined to be a vintage one. Most of the regulars were in attendance. Fat Freddie and Supreme were going at it as usual.

Nate Allen walked in and everyone yelled "Nate!" It had been a while since they had seen him. He had been in Hollywood negotiating a deal for *Sergeant Leroy, The Movie*. Jungle Jim was to produce and direct it, King James would star, Hot Rod would provide the soundtrack, Freddie would rap and Natalie would sing on a couple of songs, and Angie would choreograph the few dance numbers. Black joy was at an all-time high.

"Yo, Nate!" Mike called. "Gimme that copy of the Sergeant Leroy book I know you got in your pocket, arrogant bastard."

Nate pulled out a copy and tossed it to him.

"He probably got a whole trunk full of them shits," Supreme laughed. "Don't even have room for a spare. If the nigga gets a flat or something, all he can do is wave a copy of his book in the air and offer to to autograph it for anybody who'll give his ass a ride!"

The rest of the shop joined Supreme in laughing.

Tyrone, Tony and Steve burst through the door. They were, of course, sweaty and out of breath, but just in time for their regular seven o'clock appointments.

"What? Do y'all just finish fuckin' each other every time you come in here?" Supreme asked.

Tyrone just looked at him deadpan. "No, but if you find you got a little brotha in nine months don't expect him to look like your father."

The "Ooohs!" came out in full force.

"See that's what I do for these young people. You hear that wit? How clever he is? He was nothing when he came to me, now look at him. I swear to God I should start my own school."

Supreme was able to rally a few more laughs from Mike and the rest of the shop, but on balance he knew he had lost that round.

With all the pride of the victor, Tyrone pulled a magazine from his back pocket.

"Check this out...Steve got his picture in *Sports Illustrated*."

"Lemme see that," Supreme demanded. He fumbled through the magazine before he asked, "What page?"

"Seven," Steve replied, ready to step into the spotlight.

Supreme turned to the page, then sucked his teeth.

"Aw man, this is just 'Faces in the Crowd'. Anybody can get their picture in this shit. Look, right above Steve is the hundred-year-old lady who ran the Boston Marathon in seven hours."

"Why you so jealous of everybody?" Tyrone asked.

"I'm not jealous. You just can't impress me with no bullshit."

"How many points didcha score in the Black State tournament, yo?" Mike asked Steve.

"Thirty-two."

Mike raised both eyebrows. "I'm impressed"

"Man, he probably shot the ball sixty-four times!" Supreme teased. Steve just sat there, soaking it all in, happy to be the centre of attention.

"There's no way you'll give the brotha props 'til he's in the NBA is there?" Tyrone asked.

"Naah, there's a way I could give him props tonight." Supreme told him.

"How's that?"

"If he beats Mike."

Tyrone literally screamed with laughter. Mike was a bit surprised to hear his own name mentioned and hoped the conversation wasn't going where he thought it was.

"Wait a minute, wait a minute!" Tyrone said, catching his breath after his laughing fit. "You saying you think pretty boy Mike could deal with Steve on the court?"

"Now that ain't what I'm saying," Supreme told him.

"Well at least you ain't crazy."

"Naah, I'm saying I think Mike could *bust* his *ass*."

The "Ooohs!" were back.

Tyrone stared off into the distance, stroking the side of his face with his thumb. "Well there's only one thing to do, then," he said after a pause.

Supreme smiled. "Like my grandfather used to say, 'You ain't said nothin' but a word'."

Mike closed his eyes tight. God, he didn't wanna go through with this.

"Uptown clearance!" Supreme screamed.

An official Uptown clearance. Everyone would leave the shop and go to a predetermined area, in this case the basketball court. Supreme was the only person authorised to issue an Uptown clearance. They were issued for various occasions—like spontaneous stick-ball games, grudge slap-boxing, major events on the street and occasionally, like tonight, for a challenge issued in the shop that could only be settled outside.

Mike looked over at Steve who was pimping hard beside his boys. Damn, the youngster looked smug! Then again, why wouldn't he? He was sixteen, about to sign to Black State University, projected to be a definite starter by his sophomore year and he wasn't even a senior in high school yet. And now he was being challenged by a barber in a smock, jeans and work boots! He had good reason to smile.

Mike hadn't played ball in a while and he knew you lose shit when you don't play. Your game is off. You give your body orders and your body's like, *What? If you really expect me to do that shit, you shoulda stayed in shape!*

He would go out there and make a fool of himself. Why did he agree to this? Oh yeah, he didn't agree to anything.

"Knees," he remembered telling Pat Erving. It was his knees. The sense of helplessness he felt after the knee surgery in his sophomore season in college, then throughout the whole rehab process, had made him see sports in a whole new light. Questioning his body; would he ever be able to play again? If so, would he be his old self? Or would the strain of a game make his knee pop and leave him in pain. The fear was all in his mind, he knew—the doctors had told him that a million times—but didn't they realise that the worst place for fear was in a person's mind? If your body was afraid, your mind could rationalise. But who rationalised when your mind was afraid? And what if the doctors were wrong? What if the injury wasn't just a routine arteriole cruciate strain? What if every time he went up for a dunk or blocked a shot, or lunged to make a steal, or pulled up for a jumper, he jeopardised his chances of walking again? Was basketball worth it? Hell, was any sport worth it? Mike had decided it wasn't. He finished his last two years of college eligibility as half the ball player he had used to be, but still twice as good as most. Now he only played in pick-up games which he was sure wouldn't get too strenuous.

"All right, all right, we're here," Tyrone stated the obvious once they reached the basketball court. "What's the game to?"

"Seven," Supreme said. "Winner take out?"

"Of course."

Steve and Mike didn't mind having no say in the terms of the game they were about to play.

"You wanna take it out?" Steve asked.

Mike shrugged. "Whatever..." he said, lost in his thoughts.

Supreme was concerned. He had an idea what Mike was going through, but he also knew that nothing would cure it faster than his first basket. That first one would mean everything.

Steve passed Mike the ball. He caressed it like a newborn, feeling the rippled texture and creases. He bounced it and judged the weight. He seemed to be in another world.

"Hey, Kareem!" Tyrone called out from the sideline. "We got a game to play. Save that 'memory lane' shit for later."

Mike quickly came back to reality. He checked the ball with Steve, then rocketed past him as if shot from a cannon for an easy basket. *You never lose it*, he thought as he watched the ball flow through the net.

"He's still pretty quick," one of the Uptown Heads crowd said matter-of-factly.

A slow smile crossed Supreme's face. "Hey Steve!" he yelled. "You musta been too young to read the papers back when Mike was playing. Then you might know who you was fuckin' with."

"One-zip!" Mike said to Steve as if reading a box score.

Steve nodded. He and Tyrone looked at each other. Mike walked back to the foul line and checked the ball with Steve again. He noticed the space Steve gave him, guarding against him blowing past him again. Mike pulled up for a jump shot from where he stood. Nothing but net.

"Damn, I'm hittin' my jumpers!" Mike said to himself, but loud enough for Steve to hear.

Steve's face looked as if he was trying to swallow a lemon.

"Hey Steve," Supreme yelled from the sidelines. "You got to guard him out there, you just can't give him the open jumper."

"Shut up, Supreme," Tyrone said.

"Two-zip."

Mike checked the ball once more. After a couple of cross-over dribbles, Mike breezed past Steve again, but Steve caught him and pinned his shot attempt against the backboard. The Uptown Heads crowd, which had been silent until that point, erupted. Steve smiled as he cleared the ball. He dribbled to the middle of the lane, head faked Mike who left his feet for the block and sent a pretty overhand left-handed lay-up kissing off the backboard and in. Steve was clearly more of the crowd-pleaser.

As they both walked back to the foul line, Mike asked, "You left-handed?"

"Nope."

"Then nice move."

"Yo, Mike, you shoulda took your vitamins before this one!" Tyrone screamed from the sidelines.

Mike nodded in agreement, never one to be easily heckled.

"Two-one!" Steve said as he checked the ball. Realising he had the crowd's support, he went into a dribbling and head faking routine that would have put the Globetrotters to shame. Mike merely waited for his opportunity, reached in, stole the ball, raced to the basket and dunked backwards.

"Here comes the brand new flavour for your ear!" Supreme sang.

"I believe that was in his face. Yo!" Riff said.

"Time for the brand new flavour for your ear."

The uptown crowd began chanting. "I'm kicking new flavour for your ear."

Supreme concluded with, "Mike put the brand new flavour in Steve's ear."

The crowd was hysterical.

"Maybe on his head?" Tony asked.

"Maybe on his ass!" Bumpy called.

"Personally," Tyrone interrupted, "I didn't think it was all that."

"Three-one."

"I know, man. I know." Steve said back.

Mike checked the ball. After a couple of quick cross-over dribbles he made another explosive move towards the basket and felt an equally explosive pain in his knee. A pain so severe that he couldn't even cry out. He fell down in a heap. Supreme heard the 'pop' from the sidelines. He raced out to his best friend's side. Steve wondered if Mike was just faking to get out of finishing the game.

Mike was in true agony.

"Where the hell is Gary?!" Supreme called.

The short, light-skinned youth was already emerging from the crowd. Thank goodness there was a medical student in attendance.

"Yo, check this guy out, man," Supreme demanded roughly, concern on his face.

"Sounded like it just popped out of place," Gary said, bending over to feel Mike's knee.

"Did anyone ask what it sounded like, mothafucka?"

The crowd's tension exploded into a roar of laughter.

Gary kneeled down and felt the uneven curvature of Mike's knee. Outta place, like he thought. He could provide temporary relief, but Mike would still need follow-up medical attention.

Gary looked off into the crowd with sudden interest. "Damn, look at that!" he exclaimed.

All eyes, including Mike's, followed his field of vision.

Snap!

"Oooooowwwww!" Mike screamed as his knee popped back in place. Once he was able to speak again, he added, "That was fucked up, man!"

"You still need to get yourself some x-rays," Gary said, helping him to his feet. "And you'll probably need some crutches or a brace."

Supreme patted Gary on the shoulder. "Glad to see my tax dollar's going to work."

"Glad enough to give a brotha a free cut?" Gary asked.

"Man, I'm never that glad."

Mike limped his way back to Uptown Heads followed by the slow-moving crowd. The first thing he noticed was that the lights were on. That was strange, because he remembered Supreme turning them off. Then he noticed that the door wasn't locked. He paused. Robbers? And if so, who, when half of Harlem was right behind him? By this time Supreme and Riff had reached and figured something was going down. Supreme slowly pushed open the door...

To his relief, Stephanie and Born were sitting in the barber's chairs playing a spelling game. Stephanie was the only other person with keys to the shop, but she hardly ever used them because there was usually someone there.

Stephanie looked at everyone piled in the doorway and frowned.

"Let me guess," she said tiredly, "an Uptown clearance?"

Supreme nodded. He and the gang walked in and took up their posts. "What are y'all doin' here?" he asked.

Stephanie looked him straight in the eye but didn't answer.

"Say it," Supreme demanded.

She remained silent, only now she looked uncomfortable too. "There ain't nothing wrong with needing money, girl. We're family, one should-n't be in need if the other one got some."

A thick silence followed.

Mike, using his chair like a brace, was the first to speak. "What kinda down-south wisdom was that, Reverend DoRight?" Supreme sighed. "I'm just saying Stephanie's all on this 'Modern Black Woman' shit..."

"And Supreme's all on this 'SuperNigga' shit," Stephanie interrupted.

"So whatcha sayin' is you both are on some shit," Riff interrupted.

"Look Sis, don't ever be embarrassed to ask me for money; any amount, no matter how much or how little."

"Well then, give me five hundred." Stephanie was only joking, but she didn't hand the money back when Supreme counted it out from his wallet and handed it to her.

The Uptown Heads crowd were stunned.

"Hey Supreme, did I ever tell you my mother looks just like you?" Tyrone called.

"And I got an uncle that could pass for your brother, man," Fat Freddie chipped in.

"Yeah, yeah, yeah!" Supreme said wearily. "Ain't nobody in this shop related to me but Stephanie and Born."

"Don't be too sure, man," Tyrone cut in. "I got a cousin—"

"Yeah, but do you have a father?" Supreme interrupted.

The "Ooohs!" had their longest chorus of the night.

"That was foul, man," Riff said quietly to Supreme.

"Yeah, that was a little low, yo," Mike added.

Supreme shrugged. He'd go easy on him for the rest of the night.

"Stephanie!" Slick had called out evenly. Everyone turned to face him. Nobody but Supreme, Mike, and Riff had ever said Stephanie's name out loud in the barbershop. The word out was that brothas were scared to. "Would you come here for a sec?" Slick continued. Stephanie turned to face him. The corner he was standing in immediately cleared. What did he want, she wondered.

All the brothas in Uptown Heads were of one mind as they watched that big ass of Stephanie's carry her across the floor. Stephanie was a thing of desire for most of them, just as much and just as distant as that big money new job, that fly new apartment, and that dope new ride. The problem was most of them couldn't even see themselves approaching a woman like her until after they'd gotten all three of the above. But what was she supposed to do in the meantime—wait? And what the hell was Slick doing now anyway?

Stephanie approached Slick slowly like an assassin deciding which verbal weapon to use to kill him with. Slick stood there casually, almost stupidly, like a man waiting for a bus or something. Stephanie walked up to within inches of him. When she was right on top of him, he merely raised both eyebrows.

"Well?" she asked flatly. Slick smiled a wide, ridiculous smile. He looked happy, genuinely happy—not at all intimidated, as most of the brothas in the shop felt they themselves would be in a similar situation.

"I was just thinking..." Slick began.

"Oh, you do that?" Stephanie interrupted. "Think, I mean."

"From time to time," Slick said without missing a beat, and, believe it or not, smiling even wider. "But really, I was just wondering..."

"Get it straight now," Stephanie said, interrupting again. "Were you thinking or were you wondering?"

Slick paused, then frowned, mocking intense concentration.

"Actually I was thinking about wondering whether I should take you to dinner or a play for our first date." There were all kinds of grumbles coming from the brothas in Uptown Heads—half of them sounding impressed, the other half shocked.

"Didcha hear that?" Tyrone asked Steve and Tony. "That shit was dope. I gotta use that line on a honey."

"How?" Steve snapped back. "Every girl you know is here right now."

Stephanie was smiling and nodding her head.

"That was cute," she said, impressed by the good-looking Slick.

"Do you wanna know which one I've decided on?" Slick asked.

"Oh, you've already decided?"

"Yeah. It don't take me too long to make up my mind about anything." Stephanie smiled again. This guy was saying all the right things—this could be interesting.

"Which one?" she asked.

"Neither," Slick said flatly. Stephanie frowned, confused. "I just remembered that Stevie Wonder's coming to town—and if you don't like Stevie, then I don't wanna be with you anyway."

Tyrone was bouncing up and down in his seat now, and the grumbles from the brothas sounded like shock.

"Did you hear that?" Tyrone asked Tony and Steve in a loud whisper. "Get me that brotha's autograph!"

"I like Stevie," Stephanie said simply. It was just that easy. The brothas in the shop—who for two years had been trying to figure out a way to do what Slick had just done—were heartbroken. Supreme turned to Mike.

"Did you just see what I saw?"

"I think so," Mike said. Supreme shook his head.

"Did you know I used to change that girl's diapers?"

"I know I heard you say you did."

"Well don't you think that after being that close to somebody and after being around them all their life, I should be able to say that I knew them by now?"

"I would think so," Mike said. Supreme just shrugged, and returned to cutting hair. Mike laughed at the image of Supreme changing diapers.

"You know who's got a mad crush on you?" Mike asked. Not now, Supreme was thinking. It was almost midnight, still humid outside, he had at least a ten-block walk home ahead of him, and Lenox Avenue could be less than beautiful at that time of night. It was no time for guessing games, especially games involving random girls and stupid crushes.

"Agnes," Supreme said tiredly, referring to Mike's mother, and hoping that Mike would get the point that he didn't wanna be bothered.

"You like playing with your life, huh?" Mike asked flatly.

"I forgot you was a cold blooded killer! That limp just adds to the persona."

"That's right," Mike said, not biting at Supreme's sarcasm about his leg. "I'll hurtcha if I gotta."

"Yeah I remember back in third grade when you hit me with that mud-pie, that was some fucked-up shit. I mean people have done some foul shit to brothas throughout history; slavery, lynching, castration, and all that, but hittin' a nigga with a mud-pie has to be among the worst." The only thing that made Mike angrier than Supreme's speech was the fact that he had been serious; he really felt that way about getting hit with a mud-pie.

"Man, are you ever gonna forget that I hit you with a mud-pie in the third grade?" Mike asked.

"Hell no!" Supreme shouted. "That shit was a turning point in my life!" Mike shook his head and decided not to comment.

"A mud-pie," Supreme continued. "In the face! Do you know how mentally fucked-up I was after that? I almost needed therapy!"

Mike sighed and let the conversation pause.

"Look man, do you wanna know who digs you or not?" he asked after a three-block silence.

"Who?" Supreme asked hotly. Apparently he was still angry from discussing the mud-pie incident.

"Sharon." Mike said just as angrily. He should have known this would happen. A conversation about dust could degenerate into a slug fight with Supreme, and now his knee was starting to really bother him.

Supreme's eyes lit up.

"Sharon's dope," he said thoughtfully. Mike just nodded. There was

71

another silence. Supreme looked over at Mike, whose limping had grown more obvious. "You sure you don't wanna just catch a cab or something?"

"We shoulda just hopped on the train."

"And pay a subway fare for ten blocks?" Supreme asked incredulously. Mike shook his head again.

Supreme would willingly pay for a cab, but was too cheap to ride the subway—where did get his logic? And what about Sharon? He hadn't said anything else about her. Damn, the people you love the most always made the least sense. There was another silence. Mike was almost dragging his leg now.

"You look horrible, yo!" Supreme said, sympathetically. He stopped walking. "Here," he said, cradling his arms as if preparing to pick up a baby.

"Get the fuck outta here!" Mike laughed and dragged on.

"Naah, I'm serious man. I can't bear to watch you walk any more. You only live two more blocks from here."

"So whatcha gonna do? Pick me up like I'm your girl or something?" Mike asked, becoming half-serious.

"You are a little sweet-ass," Supreme joked. "Come on," he said, motioning with his head for Mike to let him pick him up. Mike considered Supreme and his offer. Here they were, at the corner of One Hundred and Thirtieth Street and Lenox Avenue, inches emotionally from hating each other—at least for the rest of the night—and now the brotha was gonna go and do something like this? Mike decided that he was gonna look up the word 'friend' in the dictionary when he got home that night. If Supreme's picture wasn't next to it, he was gonna throw the book out.

"See now, I'ma letcha get away with the 'sweet ass' shit cause I'm injured," Mike said, climbing into Supreme's arms.

"Yeah, yeah. By the way, nice game."

"Thanks."

The room was pitch dark. Mike was holding the soft flesh of her naked hips, his body moving in a rhythm. Her breathing was a little quicker than his, although his was fast as hell. He was dripping with sweat, and he laughed because it was so dark he couldn't see where the sweat was landing. He imagined that it was landing right in the middle of her forehead; payback for when she had been on top and had sweated on him. He had wanted to come for the past half hour and the only thing holding him back had been pride; pride and basketball memories. If he had even dared to think about how heavenly her ass felt in his hands, he would've been history.

You never get back the first time, he reminded himself. He altered a stroke; the result was a sound from her that contained so much pleasure that his image of himself at the free throw line disappeared—and the reality of where he was and what he was doing rolled over him like an ocean wave. "Oh Andrea!" he moaned, as the first and largest of the rushes flowed from him. She stopped moving instantly. So did he. *Shit, why did that name come out of his mouth?* He now needed a lie.

"What did you say?" the woman asked, breaking a silence so loud that Mike could almost hear the morning coming. He was happy that it was too dark in the room for her to see his expression.

"I said 'oh, I'm there'. 'I'm there', as in: 'I'm coming'." Mike could only imagine what her face looked like then. However it looked, though, he was happy that he didn't have to see it. There was a long pause. Mike weighed up all the possibilities of escape, even though they were in his apartment. His knee had begun to hurt like hell again.

"And I'm saying 'I'm out'!" she said finally. "'I'm out' as in 'I'm leaving'." Secretly, Mike had been hoping she would leave. He had been hoping that she would simply get dressed, leave, and forget about the whole ugly incident. There was no way to apologise. Now he was hoping that she would just go. And if she was going, she could do anything she wanted. Anything. She could hit him, spit on him, kick him, curse him, anything; except turn on the light.

Mike listened as she fumbled around on the floor, searching for her clothes. He wanted badly to help her, but was afraid to touch her. When he heard something that sounded like a sob, his heart dropped. What was he becoming?

"I'm sorry," he said finally, his voice breaking and uneven. "I am sorry." But his words seemed to hurt her more. Her sobs grew louder. "Listen..." Mike said, reaching out and grabbing for a motion in the dark that turned out to be her arm.

"No, please," she said weakly, pulling away. "Don't touch me. And please, don't say anything. Just let me go." Mike buried his face in his hands and started waiting. Waiting for the only thing that could free him from this fucked-up night. Waiting for the sound that would allow him to start trying to forgive himself and forget the whole thing. Waiting for the sound of the door opening, and then closing...

Supreme's voice screaming down a pay phone was not how anybody wanted to be wakened from a bad dream on a Sunday morning—and Mike was no exception. Supreme and Born were in Washington DC for their 'father and son day'. Supreme was ranting and raving about how dirty the real city was and how the government only cleaned up the areas that they knew the tourists were gonna see. Mike asked to speak to Born.

When Born asked him how come no black people had any monuments, Mike told him it was because no black people had been president yet. When Born asked him how come that was, Mike told him to have his father call him when they got back to New York if he didn't get thrown in jail first.

Mike tried to go back to sleep, but Sharon phoned up too. She had just had 'date from hell' number two thousand, four hundred and seventy-five, and wanted to know where all the good black men in New York were. Mike said that he didn't have one single address for any of them. Very funny, she said, and asked him what he was doing for the rest of the day. Committing suicide around one, he said, then probably going out and getting something to eat later on in the afternoon. Call her after he was dead, she said.

He couldn't go back to sleep now, so Mike decided to get up and try to do something with his day. No ideas for new gadgets or gizmos hit him, so he decided to work on the video game that he had been trying to design. He had come up with the idea because there were no video games that were black-oriented. Black kids just had to play what the white kids played, whether the games related to them or not. His game would be one that every little nappy-headed kid in Harlem would be dying to play!

He had already designed the lead character: It was a black man with an afro, black leather jacket, jeans, and black boots. The character would roam through a generic city taking on thugs, hoodlums, and—of course—the cops, all the while losing energy and needing to stop and feed himself at various soul food restaurants. He would also have to avoid winos by the liquor store, who tried to detain him by begging for money—thereby making him lose energy—and drug addicts who tried to jab him with a heroin needle—thereby making him lose control and wander in and out of a high.

Mike figured that that part of the game would be the most difficult to design, but also the most rewarding. He was hoping that kids who played the game would get the message that drugs made you lose control. It was a lot to hope for, but worth a try.

When Mike's phone rang again, he already had it in his mind that he was going to tell Supreme that there was no way in hell that he was coming down to DC to bail him out. Vic Juliano's voice startled him.

As Juliano rumbled through an awkward series of prolonged pleasantries, Mike wondered what that man was coming to. Juliano had struck him as the type of individual who liked to get right down to business. But now he was using up Mike's time talking about The Little Rascals and some other bullshit. Just get to it, Mike was thinking; whatever it is just get to it. Then Juliano got to it. Mike just sat there, struck dumb, holding the receiver as Juliano began to ramble again; this time about great opportunities, and how much he could use a hairdresser/beautician with Mike's talent.

Then came the laughter. Tons and tons of unstoppable laughter. Mike knew that it was rude to laugh in the man's face and all, but hell, could he expect a brotha to be serious with the ridiculous shit that he had just proposed? "Yeah, yeah, I'll take your number. Yeah, yeah, I'll think about it," Mike said after he had calmed down—knowing that he would do one but not the other. Mike jotted the number down, and allowed his thoughts to return to the video game. Supreme and Juliano should hang out, he mused. They could get into some crazy shit!

His brother Ronnie was the last person Mike expected to hear from on that particular Sunday. Then again, with the way the day had gone, he shoulda been expecting anything. Ronnie had had the nerve to call him and tell Mike that he was in jail. Mike already knew that. No, no, you don't understand, Ronnie was saying, he had been out—for a week. He had just got thrown back in the night before. Out for a week and you didn't even call, Mike was thinking. Anyway, this was some bullshit, Ronnie was saying. Of course, Mike was thinking. He could get out on bail in the meantime, Ronnie was saying. He figured that, Mike was thinking. That's why he had called—because he needed a couple of bucks, Ronnie was saying. I knew it wasn't because you loved me, Mike was thinking. So what was up, could he have the money, Ronnie was asking, Mike was silent.

"C'mon, Mike, you know what Pop always said about having a family member in jail that you could get out," Ronnie was saying. C'mon Ronnie, not that 'Pop' shit, anything but that 'Pop' shit, Mike was thinking.

So what's it gonna be, brother, Ronnie was asking. A job at Ensembles for Ron Sr.'s youngest, Mike was thinking

"It's your fault," Mike said next morning to the faded old photo of his father that he carried in his wallet. "If you've got any objections to this, tough!" Ron Sr. didn't seem to have any.

He had spent the better part of the night in Harlem Hospital's emergency room, getting a brace that fitted his naked knee so awkwardly that he walked like a peg-legged Frankenstein. Mike had left Harlem so early the next morning that only the old ladies with their tomatoes had seen him—and boy, did they look at him funny.

So did the brothas on the train—some of whom he recognised. I *knew* he went that way, a lot of them were thinking, having figured Mike to be just a little too damn pretty. He was never so relieved to reach midtown in all his life.

The first thing Mike spotted as he wobbled upstairs from the subway station was a suit crossing the street in his direction—a suit so stylish, so well tailored, so chic that it could only be worn by one man; Rhineholt Dunn III. Dunn saw Mike and stopped dead in his tracks.

Dunn must have had a business meeting or something in midtown; Mike knew for certain that he worked in the Wall Street district. Mike hurried off as best he could; Dunn nearly got run over by a delivery truck.

Slipping into the door of Ensembles, Mike limped straight to the back office to, see Vic Juliano.

"You gotta have some place I can change in here because I am never coming downtown on a train dressed like this again as long as I live."

Juliano nodded unevenly. "Just bring a big bag full of clothes tomorrow and you can leave it under my desk."

Mike decided to get straight to work. No introductions were necessary, he'd meet the faggots at lunch, he figured. In the middle of putting his combs, brushes, sprays, greases, shampoos, conditioners, mousses, gels, clippers, and scissors in order, Mike had a thought. No, he wouldn't meet the faggots at lunch today. By lunch he was gonna hafta find a place to buy some decent clothes, catch the train back uptown and head to Build Your Own Lunch because it was Monday, and after all...

Before he could complete his thought, Mike looked towards the door, and saw Andrea walking right towards him!

That fine ass brotha from Build Your Own Breakfast is gay?, Andrea was asking herself. No wonder he had never approached her! After all the times she'd seen him up there and thought that he was staring at her. He had probably been staring at the brothas she was with. He was probably mad at her for taking all those men away from him. Well, he could have them. She didn't have a use for them. Damn, this brotha had looked like he could've been the one, too. Oh well, she might as well have some fun. Andrea walked over and sat down in Mike's chair, as Mike seemed to be choking on something.

"Can you see the bob style my hair is cut in now?"

Water. I've got to get some water, Mike was thinking. His throat was dryer than King James' old jokes.

"Yeah," Mike said in a voice covered with sand. "I see it."

"Good. Change it."

"Waddaya want?" he asked. His voice was now covered with asphalt.

"Be creative. That's what I'm paying you for."

Mike laughed in one loud, awkward gasp. He raised his hand like a diner summoning a waiter in a restaurant. Juliano spotted him.

"Uh, Vic, can I get a glass of water over here?"

Andrea thought it was odd for a beautician to ask the owner to get him a glass of water, and even odder that the owner went and got it. Mike took a gulp. As he started to do her hair, she found the sensation of his hands on the back of her head and neck startlingly relaxing. Damn, this brotha had some smooth hands!

"Aren't you the guy who always goes to Build Your Own Lunch at twelve o'clock every Monday?" she asked mischievously.

Mike wanted to say no; hell no. He knew the guy she was talking about. Good looking guy that worked at the Uptown Heads barbershop named Mike Edwards. He couldn't see how she could mistake him for Mike Edwards. He was just a faggot without a name.

"Well, uh... um...", Mike stammered.

"Yeah it was you," she interrupted. "Do you come all the way from down here to go up there for lunch?" she asked.

"No I useta work at the Uptown Heads barbershop during the day," Mike managed to answer. "I still work there now, it's just that I work there at nights. A guy from the Bronx fills in for me during the day."

"You really didn't seem gay when I useta see you up there. What, are you in the closet or something?" Mike was silent. "Come on, you can tell me," Andrea said in the tone of a confidant. "Were you in the closet?"

"Naah... you could say that I was more like... in the basement," Mike said, not trying to be funny, but having to laugh himself when Andrea started to. This was going better than she had expected.

"Do you have a boyfriend or something?" she asked, always up for a bit of salacious gossip. For some reason, the picture of Supreme sitting on his sofa, watching TV and scratching his balls flashed through Mike's mind. He figured he'd better say he did, or else she might try to introduce him to some real homo.

"I guess you can call him that," Mike said frowning.

"What's he like?" Andrea said, sounding truly interested. The picture of Supreme came up in Mike's mind again, although this time with him picking his nose and burping.

"Well, he's tall, good looking, a killer in the sack..."

He paused, allowing for both of their laughter.

"I don't know how else to describe him, he's just mine."

"Awww," Andrea said, turning around in the chair to face him. "That's so sweeeet. I wanna meet him."

"You can't," Mike said, almost ferociously.

"Why not?"

"He doesn't like people."

"That's ridiculous," Andrea said quickly, turning her back to him again. "He likes you, doesn't he? And you're 'people'. Tell you what, me and my girlfriend... oh, I'm sorry, I shouldn't have put it that way. Me and a close female friend—with whom I'm not sexually involved with in any way—are going to Zimbabwe's this Friday for her birthday. Meet me there with your boyfriend so I can check him out."

"We can't," Mike said disappointedly. "It's our first anniversary and we're having dinner at home alone." The picture of him and Supreme eating by candlelight flashed through his head; Mike was happy that he hadn't eaten breakfast—if he had he would have most likely tossed it!

Andrea turned to face him again.

"You'd better. Or I might just make a little visit to that barbershop, and bring that basement of yours up above sea level." The picture he got this time—of him and Supreme being accused of being gay, and then being laughed out of Harlem—was too much for Mike to deal with.

"What time should we meet you?"

"Twelve."

He finished the cut in silence. When it was over, Andrea simply paid for it and left. She didn't even bother to scrutinise it. That was particularly painful for Mike; Mike, who never even judged his own work when it came to haircuts, but was sure—absolutely sure—that this particular cut had been his best ever.

"Yeah, but do you have a father?" Supreme had asked him. It was only supposed to be a joke but that shit wasn't funny. No, he didn't have a father.

Tyrone was not only a member of Harlem's majority that didn't have fathers, but also one of that group's minority who had never known their fathers. Had never even seen him. Most people who complained about not having a father were complaining because he wasn't living in the same house as them; he wasn't a part of their day to day lives. Most of them had at least seen the man. A lot of them even knew where they could find him if they wanted to—even if it was just down at the liquor store, or on a given corner shootin' up.

Tyrone wondered if any of them understood what it was like to have no idea about your own father. No idea at all. No idea what he looked like, where he was from, what he liked or disliked, and no idea in the world where he was. How was a person supposed to know anything about themselves if half of who they were was missing?

Some people he knew in a similar situation tried to turn it to their

78

advantage. They would argue that—not knowing anything about their father—they could imagine that he was whoever they wanted him to be. A pro athlete, a great entertainer, an African prince; anything but what Tyrone believed his father must've been: a bum.

How could he be anything but a bum, having fathered a son and abandoned him? 'But what if he didn't know?' was the question that some used to defend their absent fathers. They knew, Tyrone would argue. They knew.

The hurt of being fatherless didn't hit Tyrone until he realised that he was supposed to have one. So few of his friends had fathers at home that he had always kinda considered them "extra" people in a family.

I mean, to a little black boy in Harlem what role did they serve? There was you; a mother to work, pay the bills, and cook; maybe a brother or sister or two to get on your nerves, and that was it. But Steve had a father, and his father seemed to do things. Things that nobody else in the house did. First of all he worked too, and he fixed shit, and he always wanted a beer, and he complained a lot, and he grabbed Steve in headlocks and said, "You is my main Negro," and he was always hungry, and always eating, and he wore funny old clothes, and he pinched Steve's mother's butt, and he made people laugh. Suddenly, it had seemed to Tyrone that that type of person should be in his house too. And Tyrone wondered why he wasn't.

When Tyrone was younger, he had looked for his father. Looked for him in the eyes of any brotha old enough who he passed on the street. But he was older now. And older people don't believe in Santa Claus, or in fathers who are just as imaginary.

It was with this in mind that Tyrone approached Vince that day in the street. Vince had always liked him, even though Tyrone had sided with Supreme in the rift between them. Tyrone had trouble expressing himself to Vince, but made his intentions clear. Vince listened, and wanted to know what had brought about this turn of events. A conversation, Tyrone told him, that he had just had with his girlfriend. Vince nodded, and left it at that. Tyrone was happy that he didn't probe any further.

Tyrone had known two pains all his life; the pain of being fatherless, and the pain of being poor. Either pain can destroy a man, but each one can also make him stronger. After talking with Sylvia earlier that day, he had made a decision. No child that he brought into the world would ever know either of those pains.

Sharon couldn't be called in on this one. Mike needed 'the Man' himself. Especially since what Mike planned to put down directly involved him.

A train ride seems shorter when your mind is going faster than the subway. Mike could usually count the number of stops it took to get back to Harlem from anywhere else in Manhattan, without listening to the conductor's voice or looking up to see where he was. Today he missed his stop and damn near ended up in the Bronx. He switched platforms, and headed back in the right direction. Exactly how was he gonna put this down? And how in the world was he gonna get Supreme to agree to it? These and a myriad of other thoughts were swimming around Mike's head as he dragged himself and his leg out of the subway station two blocks from Uptown Heads.

Mike noticed Vince and Tyrone standing together, five feet away, talking. He and they exchanged confused glances.

"Whas happenin', fellas?" Mike asked—knowing why he was looking at them funny, but only now realising why they were looking at him funny; he had on one of Sharon's blouses, butt-tight jeans, rouge, and eye-liner.

"Yo, Mike," Vince offered weakly, staring.

"Hey, man," Tyrone mumbled.

"What are you two brothas doing out here?"

"Just talkin' business," Vince said casually.

"Oh," Mike said with feigned indifference. He shook both of their hands, turned and hobbled away. Oh well, he thought. This was just another fucked-up thing on a long list that he had to tell Supreme about.

JUST THE THREE OF US

Supreme stood in front of the Apollo theatre at five the next morning dressed in a sweatshirt, baggy jeans, a hat—of course—and boots. He was blowing hot air into his hands as if it were cold. It wasn't; it was just early. He was certain of two things: one—for the life of him, he couldn't remember the last time he had been up so early, and two—yes, his best friend Mike was clearly certifiably insane. When Supreme noticed Mike peg-legging towards him down One Hundred and Twenty Fifth street from the direction of St Nicholas Avenue it didn't surprise him, even though he knew Mike lived in the other direction. He was still wondering what the hell he was doing out in front of the Apollo at five in the morning, wearing a sweatshirt, baggy jeans, a hat—of course—and boots and blowing into his hands.

"I got some bad news and some horrible news," Mike said when he reached Supreme. Supreme eyed Mike with concern, and ran his left thumbnail back and forth between his front teeth. Mike stood there waiting. Supreme sighed.

"Whatchu mean is that you got some news worse than me standing outside the Apollo Theatre at five in the morning dressed like a rap star."

Mike nodded.

"Where would you have me meet you for good news—Africa?"

Mike shut his eyes tight.

"Not now, Supreme," he said in a low even tone, his eyes closed. This is serious."

"I hope so," Supreme said with a sigh. "I gotta get home and change soon. What's the bad news?"

"I think Tyrone's selling now." Mike said, opening his eyes and fixing them dead on Supreme's. A shadow crossed Supreme's face.

"Damn," he said, as if cursing some mistake of his own. "How'd you find out?"

"Him and Vince were standing around talking together about a block away from the shop. Said they was talking business."

"Damn," Supreme said again. The next look Mike saw cross his face—the look of confusion and pain, was a familiar one. It was funny how life worked, Mike was thinking. First Vince, then Tyrone; same look.

People always harp on about how times change. In Harlem a lot of things stay the same.

Cars, clothes, and appliances change. Heroin has been replaced by crack as the new 'get high'. All the kids want to be rappers when they grow up now instead of soul crooners, and there has even been a new black mayor for a second time. But none of these things are actually changes.

The people still get high, the kids haven't learned to grow up wanting to *own* record companies, and the new black mayor is still working in the same old government. But you'll hear people say it. People in Harlem will say 'times have changed!'

Well, some things change. It changes from the 1980s to the 1990s, from spring to summer, from Monday to Tuesday, from five a.m. to six; the decades change, the seasons, the days of the week and even the hours. But have times really changed?

At eight years old Supreme had walked across a muddy school yard at lunch-time on his first day there. He had just moved to Harlem from Co-op City in the Bronx and it seemed to him, even at that age, that the new apartment was a bit of a dump.

It was a little further down on his father's continuing downward spiral; but Supreme was too young to be concerned with that thought. He just hadn't wanted to leave the Bronx. All his friends were there, it wasn't too far from where his grandfather lived in New Rochelle, and when his father wasn't drunk—which wasn't often—he had talked about buying a house in nearby Mount Vernon. Now all of that seemed like a dream. Here he was in Harlem; a place where kids would cut you open and watch you die if your sneakers were untied—or so he had heard. He didn't really believe that, but his Pro Keds were in a double-knot just in case.

Mike and Vince had known each other all their lives and had been best friends from birth. They had lived right next door to each other on One Hundred and Forty Second and Broadway until they were five—when Mike's father, Ron Sr., bought the family a house and they moved to the more affluent Striver's Row.

Vince was one of those kids without a father. His had died, but Ron Sr.—being the man he was, and realising the relationship that existed between Vince and Mike—would pick up the fatherless boy and take him along on family outings so that he and Mike could remain close. Two years later, when Mike was seven, Ron Sr. died.

It takes a lot for a seven-year-old who worships his father like a hero to accept his death. Mike blamed Ron Sr. for leaving him, and then resented him, and ultimately just missed him. Missed him terribly. So terribly that he was given to fits of anger and uncontrollable crying which would alternate on and off, day to day, for the next two years.

It was only a year later when Supreme walked across Mike and Vince's school yard. Desperate to make a friend, Supreme stopped in front of the first two kids he came to.

"Hey," he said to both of them.

"Hey," they both greeted him back. Then it started.

"I just moved here from the Bronx. Co-op City. This is my first day in school and everything. This school is kinda funny looking. The teacher's all old and ugly. Are all the schools in Harlem like this? My mother says that I don't have to go to high school in Harlem. She says that I can apply to go to high school anywhere in the city, even Brooklyn or Queens, but I'm probably gonna go back to the Bronx. What's there to do in Harlem? I mean in the Bronx, we played kickball or dodge ball, or basketball, sometimes we even jumped rope with the girls. They say some funny things when they're jumping if you listen to them. Do y'all play kickball, or dodge ball, or basketball here in Harlem? How about skully? Y'all gotta play skully... everybody plays skully. Do you know what I'm talking about? The game when you get the bottle caps and you draw up some boxes on the ground with chalk, and you shoot one bottle cap into another. You know what I'm talking about? Y'all have bottle caps out here, right?"

Whap!

Supreme dug the mud-pie out of the creases of his face and looked at Mike in amazement. His first instinct was to fight. He'd been the best fighter his age at his old school. But this was Harlem. And there was no telling what kinda weapons these crazy-ass eight-year-olds had here. He felt completely helpless.

"Why'd you do that?" Vince asked Mike, feeling a little sorry for the new kid with mud on his face.

"He wouldn't shut up."

Supreme looked at Vince and tears swelled in his eyes. "He hit me in the face with a mud-pie, man!"

Vince looked truly apologetic.

"He didn't mean it. His father died not too long ago."

"So! I didn't kill him!" Tears streamed down Supreme's face and mixed with the mud.

"I know," Vince said, then walked over to Supreme and put his arm around him.

Mud-slingers and sissies, Supreme thought. *Is everyone in Harlem this crazy?*

"What's your name, kid?" Vince asked him.

"It," Supreme answered between sobs.

"Is that your real name?" It was bad, but he'd heard worse.

"No. When I was born, my father said 'I'm only having one kid and that's it.' So that's what my mother started calling me."

Vince bit his lip to stop himself laughing. Mike was not so kind.

"My Pops was wrong anyway," Supreme said. "I got a little sister."

It didn't take Supreme long to realise he needed Vince as a friend, even if he was a sissy. Vince could protect him from Mike, who Supreme was sure must have already killed a few kids. As time went by Supreme realised that Vince wasn't a sissy at all, he just wasn't the biggest soul brotha in the world. Soon Supreme and Mike started edging towards a friendship themselves. By high school, the three were inseparable.

The Islamic religion of Five Percent hit Harlem hard, and had young brothas calling themselves 'Gods', and the sistas 'Earths'. Vince, Mike and 'It' became 'Justice', 'Reality' and 'Supreme'. They formed 'ciphers' with other brothas and 'knowledged' each other on the science and mathematics of their new religion. If eighty five percent of the population were deaf, dumb and blind, and ten percent were the purest of devils, that only left five percent. The five percent who were the poor, righteous teachers. The religion had this one simple premise at its heart, but infinite ways of expressing it, so it caught on quickly with a young Harlem crowd tired of Christianity. 'Justice'—or rather Vince—having been raised a devout Catholic by a mother who 'didn't play that', lasted the shortest time with his new moniker. 'Reality' went back to Mike when everyone refused to use his new name. But Supreme endured. And even though he lost the religion before his eighteenth birthday, he refused to answer to any other name.

Supreme, Mike, and Vince found that they needed each other more and more as their own personal problems developed and intensified. Both Supreme's and Mike's home lives were deteriorating fast, although for different reasons. Even though Ron Sr.'s death was now years behind them, Mike's mother, older brother, and older sister still continued to live as they had when he was alive; as if however bad they messed up, Ron Sr. could come behind them and fix it. Mike often found that he was the one trying to play Ron Sr. and fix things. Supreme and his father had reached an impasse. Supreme had too much mouth, was too damn cocky. One day, his father warned, he'd get knocked off that high horse, and back down to the low ground. Supreme didn't have a problem with that, he argued. But why was his own father trying to be the one to knock him off?

Vince didn't really have any problems with his home life. He and his mother were as tight as a drum. Every now and then, he would try to complain like Supreme and Mike; she makes me eat this, she won't let me buy that, she gets on my nerves, but his complaints either sounded insincere or childish. He would just have to face the fact that he loved his mother, she loved him too, and they got along. So you can imagine how he felt when he met his 'dead' father?

A pair of clippers? Supreme was thinking as he left Pop Pop's house. For his seventeenth birthday. The old man had definitely gone senile.

"Use 'em," Pop Pop had told him. "Use 'em on your own head. They'll save you some money."

"How much did they save you when you coulda bought me a real gift?" Supreme had joked.

Whap!

The old man was still quick, Supreme was thinking as he rubbed the back of the head. And still as mean as a snake, but not the type of mean his father was. Supreme was sorry that he didn't get to see Pop Pop like he used to. Well hell, he lived in Harlem now, and New Rochelle wasn't the hop, skip, and jump it used to be when he lived in Co-op City. He was gonna come up every weekend from now on, Supreme decided as he waited for the bus. Pop Pop was too much of a character not to see on a weekly basis. Besides, the old man always gave him wisdom. Wisdom on how to make it. It was through Pop Pop that Supreme first learned that there were two sides to himself.

"All us men folk in the family have 'em," Pop Pop had explained to a frightened eight-year-old about to move to Harlem. "We got a side for fuckin' up, and a side for takin' care of business."

"So what's wrong with Daddy? I only see his fu—," Supreme corrected himself: "—messin' up side."

"That's cause that's the only side he chooses to use," Pop Pop said simply. You just couldn't beat wisdom like that.

"A-C-P-You! A-C-P-You! A-C-P-You!" Each section of the huge gymnasium pointed to the other as they chanted "You!" loudly. A seventeen-year-old Mike sat with the recruiter in the press box. *Damn, this shit is big time!*

"So, Mike, with your talent, you could be starting by your sophomore year, maybe by the end of your freshman."

Mike continued nodding. He hadn't heard a word the man had said for the past twenty minutes as he was too busy being impressed by the enthusiasm of Adam Clayton Powell University. The campus was dope. The students were just the kind of upwardly mobile young brothas and sistas he wanted to surround himself with. And the basketball program was on the verge of becoming a national power. The only thing stopping Mike from signing his letter of intent and committing to ACPU was Black State. They had made it to the final four in the NCAA tournament the previous year, and stood a good chance of winning it all this year.

A lot of that chance, some believed, rested on where the 6'4" forward Mike Edwards, out of Father Divine High School in Harlem, decided to study. Mike, who used to struggle in pick up games with Supreme and Vince, had become one of New York's top prep stars and now had universities falling over themselves to offer him a scholarship and other incentives. He desperately wanted to go to Black State, for two reasons.

First, he wanted to go to a real powerhouse team, the kind of squad where a pro career was a foregone conclusion and if the team won a National Championship, even its bench players would get drafted into the NBA. Second, he was desperate to get away from his family, and give them a chance to mature. Black State was in Atlanta—which was fourteen hours away from uptown and his boys Supreme and Vince—but he would do it given the opportunity. Problem was, Black State wasn't exactly banging down his door with enthusiasm. That's why he had decided to give nearby Adam Clayton Powell University in Patterson, New Jersey the visit they had practically begged him to make. At least they showed the kind of appreciation a skilled basketball player like himself deserved.

"Ladies and Gentlemen," the announcer said at half-time, "we have a young man here tonight who we hope this university will see a whole lot more of in the future!

"Please join me in welcoming New York State player of the year—runner-up MVP of the New York Inner-City Round-Robin Classic—and three times first-team All-New York State forward, Mike Edw-a-a-rds!"

Damn! Mike was thinking, impressed. They knew his bio.

When the crowd rose to their feet, chanting "Mike! Mike! Mike! Mike!" it was all over for Black State.

People always talked about how bad it was being a latch-key kid, but for Vince it was part of everyday life. He'd been coming home to an empty apartment since he was seven, when his mother had decided he had sense enough not to kill himself by accident or do anything stupid. He proved her right. She took it as a personal compliment each time somebody commented on her son's good sense. Vince was better than a good kid. He was damn near perfect. And in Harlem, that was no small accomplishment.

Vince shied away naturally from the things that other mothers worked hard to protect their kids from. At seventeen, he had an academic scholarship to Garvey X University; didn't smoke—cigarettes or marijuana—didn't use cocaine or crack; would never even consider heroin and on the one or two occasions when he let a sista 'seduce' him, he insisted on wearing *two* condoms. His only surrender to peer pressure was to drink a little beer on the weekends. To Vince, he was only doing what came naturally. He had never seen his mother smoke, drink, use drugs, or have any 'uncles' stay over?

"If Mom don't do it, it ain't worth doing," he would say—a sentiment that would get him laughed off many an uptown block. But Vince didn't care. He had his two partners, Mike and Supreme, and they were all the friends he needed.

One day Vince had been on his way home—wondering what Supreme had wanted to tell him that had to wait until Mike got back from his ACP University visit. Supreme could be 'iffy' like that sometimes.

To his surprise a stranger was sitting in the apartment when he got home. In cheap, awkwardly fitting clothes and with a nervous expression, the man looked lost rather than dangerous. But Vince wasn't in the mood for company, and didn't like the fact that this particular company had invited himself.

"The homeless shelter's that way, Brah." He pointed out the window to the street.

"I'm no bum," the man said simply.

"Well you ain't no land baron either, so what are you?"

The man sighed, took a deep breath then looked upwards as if searching for the answer.

"I'm just a brotha tryin' to catch up with his life."

"Well catch it down the block. It's called the A train," Vince said hotly. But the man just sat there shaking his head.

Vince decided it was time for some action.

"Yo, Supreme," he spoke into the phone a minute later. "I got some nut who broke into my crib over here. Hurry up and come over. And bring a baseball bat or something."

Supreme ran the several blocks to Vince's place, turning down brothas offering to help beat down whoever he was on his way to beat down. That's the way uptown was. If somebody warranted a beat-down, he probably warranted a bad one. But Supreme knew better than to invite a whole crew to Vince's mom's apartment. So he ran by himself, bat in hand, across One Hundred and Twelfth Street, up St Nicholas, right on One Hundred and Twenty Fifth then back up Frederick Douglas.

Ten minutes later he arrived at Vince's door breathless, his adrenaline pumping. Vince opened with a surprised expression on his face—looking dazed, and almost offended, that Supreme had come. Supreme was ready to commence the beat-down, but Vince held him back at the door.

"My mistake, yo," he said calmly.

"Whassup?"

"It's not all that. The guy's cool."

87

What?! All this running for nothing? Somebody was about to get their ass kicked!

"Well let me at least come in and check him out or something" he insisted. But Vince held surprisingly firm.

"I said, he's cool. We're talking right now. Come back later. I'll give you a call." With that, Vince slammed the door on his homie's face.

Come back later? Mothafucka, I shoulda kicked your ass for making me come now!

Pop Pop looked at his grandfather clock and kept stuffing his pipe, as if he hadn't heard the bombshell that Supreme had just dropped. Supreme was growing anxious. Pop Pop was the first person in the world he had told. Neither his parents, nor Mike and Vince, knew yet. The old man's reaction was critical to him.

"He gets the land," Pop Pop said eventually, as if he'd been thinking about something else.

Supreme nodded. He had long known that the old man had a farm in North Carolina, which he'd decided to leave to his first great-grandchild. But it was his opinion, just his opinion, that Supreme needed right now.

"Well," the old man began after a long silence, "at least you know what to name him if it's a boy."

"Oh, *hell* no, Pop Pop."

Whap!

As always, the slap found its mark. Supreme rubbed the back of his head. "Look, I know it's family tradition and all, but it's an ugly, stupid name."

"You calling my name ugly, boy?"

"And stupid!"

Whap!

Supreme rubbed the back of his head.

"Look, Pop Pop. I can't give that name to my son. I don't know how you and my father had the nerve to give it to anybody. It should have stopped with you, and it should leave the earth with you."

"Funny you mention leaving the earth—"

The old man was cut short by a horrible hacking cough. "You know, I ain't got too much time left..."

Supreme smirked. "Pop Pop, you ain't had too much time left since I was born."

"Naah, I'm getting up there. I ain't nowhere near as spry as I useta be."

"Yeah, but the left you keep hitting me with is just as quick," Supreme joked. "Anyone would think you useta be a boxer, not a barber."

"Did a little of both," the old man said with a wink. "Useta barber at the shop in the daytime and box with your grandmother at night."

Supreme laughed. But then Pop Pop grew suddenly sad, as he did whenever he thought of his wife who had died twelve years earlier.

"Well that's all I got to say on the matter," the old man said after a while. "Your mother raised you fair enough. You're decent compared to a lot of 'em. You'll make a good father."

"Thanks, Pop Pop," Supreme said, more flattered than he'd ever been.

"No way I can get you to reconsider the name?" the old man asked slyly. "I ain't got too many days left, y'know."

"Pop Pop, I wouldn't reconsider if you died tomorrow," Supreme joked.

Had everybody gone crazy? Mike wondered. Vince had been acting especially shady lately. Supreme had gone up to New Rochelle to visit his grandfather, but a conversation they'd had while Mike was at the university left him wondering if Supreme had finally crossed the border into Belleville's psycho ward express line.

"We need to talk about our futures," Supreme had said. "Me, you, Vince—all of us."

Supreme thinking past tomorrow? This is a first!

"Well, I'm going to ACP," Mike told him. "I just decided. And Vince is going to Garvey X—that's as much a fact as you is black. That leaves you, Brah. *You* need to talk about *your* future. Or go out and find one." He didn't mean to sound as hard as he had, but Supreme's lackadaisical attitude to life had bothered him for some time now. Supreme didn't have to be good at ball like him, or as smart as Vince—but he had to do *something*. Mike didn't want Supreme to be the homeboy he visited in jail when he was home on vacation from school.

"Point taken," Supreme had said evenly.

Taking an insult without even attempting a comeback? Another first. He must be really about to lose it.

Mike decided to find out what was on Supreme's mind.

"So when do you wanna talk about all this?"

"Sunday. I'm going up to check the old man on Saturday. I'll meet you and Vince at the Apollo at two."

At the Apollo? Who does he think he is, James Brown?

The Sunday after he returned from Adam Clayton Powell University, Mike stood in front of the Apollo and waited; and waited. In the two hours he was outside, it seemed like half of Harlem came up to congratulate him, having read that he had committed to ACP. Finally he went to a pay phone. Supreme picked up almost immediately.

"So what happened? Couldn't find your way outta the apartment?"

"Oh, shit! Mike. Man, I'm sorry."

"Damn right you are!"

Mike could hear the sound of women crying.

"What's going on over there?"

"Man, the old man just died," Supreme said gravely. "My moms went up to bring some soup for his cough and found him dead on the sofa."

"I'll be right over."

Mike left the handset hanging as he dashed towards Supreme's. Much, much later, he began to wonder where the hell Vince had been.

The kid was smart, there was no denying that. Reggie Regg had seen plenty of street corner and jailhouse intellectuals, but *this* kid had the book learning to back it up. Maybe he *could* be of some use...

Life was too much of a gamble. What was the sense of going to college, wasting four years of your life getting a degree, when after you graduated, you weren't guaranteed anything? Especially when you could've been making money from the beginning. It didn't make any sense now that Vince thought about it. He wondered how it ever had.

Black kids in colleges were suckers. There they were, supposedly the smartest young black people around, yet they couldn't see the obvious; niggas didn't have shit! Didn't have shit, didn't own shit, didn't create shit. So when those same kids came outta those colleges, they'd have to take their black faces—with the white education they just received, wearing some white suit—up into some white man's face so he could play God and decide whether they could work or not. What kinda sense did that make? It had always been that way and it would always be.

Things would be different if niggas owned something. It's not as humbling to ask your own for a job, and not as humiliating being turned down either. But niggas didn't own shit and the ones that tried got no support from their own people. What kinda people were they, anyway? Did they wanna keep being backwards—the kinda people who would step over something valuable with a Black man's name on it, just to get to the shit with the white man's name on it? Was there any hope for a people like that?

Vince had once envisioned himself as the hope of his nation. He saw himself leading masses of black people to a promised land of abundance and opportunity. black folk weren't backwards, he had reasoned then. They had just been manipulated since being brought to this country and had never known what they were capable of. His mother had been the sole source of many of his beliefs, and this was her theory on her race. But now he knew that she had lied to him about the most important man in his life—his father. She had looked in his face and said:

"Your father is dead."

Now, everything he'd ever learned from her was brought into question. He began to see things a little more clearly. He could see that niggas had had the greatest collection of leaders ever. Malcolm X, Marcus Garvey, Martin Luther King, Harriet Tubman, Sojourner Truth, Kwame Nkrumah, Nelson Mandela, Nat Turner, Haile Selassie, Jesus Christ—everybody! And if none of them could turn niggas around, how in the world could he? Naah, niggas weren't worth it. It wasn't worth trying to save a people that don't wanna be saved. Better to just give them what they want. And if he happened to make a little money from the deal, that was fine by him. All it was gonna take was an OK from Reggie Regg and a block on which to set up shop.

Two sides to his personality, Pop Pop had said. If that was true, Supreme thought, it was time for the 'taking care of business' side to show up. All he'd known up to then was the 'fuckin' up' side. The old man had died too soon. There was so much more to learn. Supreme wondered how he'd make it without Pop Pop.

"Denise?" Mike asked, as if Supreme could be mistaken about who the mother of his child was. "Aw man!" was all he said when it was confirmed.

Supreme hadn't seen or heard from Vince since he'd called to arrange the meeting at the Apollo. The brotha just hadn't been acting right since his crib got broken into. Supreme felt comforted by Mike's presence. Although he valued both friends equally, he and Mike had never been as close as he and Vince or, for that matter, Mike and Vince. Of his two best friends, Mike was the one who never let him get away with anything. But now, watching Mike comforting Stephanie and his mother on the sofa, Supreme realised that Mike would be his friend for life. The thought lightened his grieving slightly.

Supreme motioned to Mike to join him in the bathroom.

"So what are we gonna do now, take a shower together?" Mike asked, only half-joking, hoping that his friend was finished with *all* of his major revelations for the day.

"Naah." Supreme pushed him to sit down on the toilet seat. "We're gonna cut each other's hair." He pulled out the clippers his grandfather had given him, plugged them in and turned them on.

"Have you ever done this before?"

Supreme laughed. "That's the same thing Denise asked the first time we did it."

"Yeah, but she shoulda stopped you like I'm about to," Mike said, getting off the toilet.

Supreme pushed him back down. "Chill man, just let me do this. I'm about to become a father and my grandfather just died."

"That's why I should let you fuck up my head?"

"Tell you what; if I fuck it up, I'll letcha cut mine any way you want to."

"I wanna get to cut yours regardless!"

The haircuts weren't that bad—though neither friend told the other that he kinda liked his cut. Instead each raved about his own skill, and how much the other had benefited from it. Harlem saw it differently.

On the train, a young brotha complimented Supreme. "That cut is dope, yo!"

"You go to a shop around here, man?" an older brotha asked Mike after a game.

Encountering such comments everywhere they went, Supreme and Mike came to the same conclusion. *That other nigga must be able to cut some hair!* And so, after a brief argument about which one was really the better barber, they were in business.

There's a line in the movie *Mahogany* where Billy Dee Williams tells Diana Ross: "Success means nothing without someone you love to share it with." It wasn't that Supreme and Mike weren't looking for Vince to share their new found success; Vince was just nowhere to be found.

During those first few days they spent as travelling barbers—visiting different brownstones, apartments and housing projects to cut hair—neither Supreme nor Mike had time to notice the absence of the third musketeer. Making some money of their own became so absorbing that everything else, including life-long friendships, was overlooked. They figured Vince was simply taking some time out; they all got sick of each other sometimes, as even close friends do.

But rumour had it that Vince was making a little money of his own.

Mike's brother Ronnie had broken the news to Mike and Stephanie had told Supreme. Supreme and Mike laughed like brothas at a Richard Pryor gig. Vince, a drug dealer—how ridiculous! Vince's mother wouldn't even let him take Aspirin, and now here he was selling crack? But for real, they could go up and see for themselves, he was right up there on One Hundred and Thirty Fifth and Amsterdam. Nobody went over by One Hundred and Thirty Fifth and Amsterdam except people buying or selling crack, or people that lived there; and nobody 'lived' there.

Supreme and Mike met up the same night they had both heard the rumours, and set off to One Hundred and Thirty Fifth. On the way the conversation changed—from jokes about Vince getting sick off cigarette smoke, and standing out on the block reading a verse from the Bible, to questions like *Where has he been for the past couple of weeks? And what if he is selling crack?*

One Hundred and Thirty Fifth and Amsterdam had not changed since the beginning of time. It was one of those places just damned to be a get high spot. Crack was—of course—the current drug of choice. Coke had been big twenty years before. Marijuana was always popular. Heroin had had its day at the top. It was even said that that particular corner was where the Indians of Manhattan Island used to come to get fucked up off of their peace-pipes.

Now it was Harlem—every inch of land on One Hundred and Thirty Fifth and Amsterdam was paved, and there were hideous tenements as far as the eye could see. The Hudson River ran at the bottom of the hill— an escape route for anyone who just couldn't take it anymore. It was against this backdrop that Vince stood. He had known that his two best friends would seek him out, so he wasn't surprised when he saw them.

"Man, what the fuck?" Supreme had demanded. But Vince's manner was cool. Remember that day?" he asked Supreme. Remember that day when he had called 'cause some dude had broke in? Supreme remembered. Well it was his father!

"Oh shit!" said Supreme and Mike in unison. Yep, his father. The dude had just gotten outta jail. He had been in for sixteen years on a series of breaking and enterings. That's why he found it so easy to get into the apartment. Supreme nodded slowly; Mike just stood there dazed. So what did that hafta do with anything, Supreme had wanted to know. It had something to do with everything, Vince had told him, and proceeded to explain his new outlook on life to the two of them.

Mike looked at Supreme, unimpressed. Supreme just shook his head and looked off towards the river. The brotha had gone nuts! So having a father makes people sell crack, Supreme had laughed. He had always thought it was the other way around. Supreme didn't understand, Vince had argued. No, he didn't, Supreme had argued back. Mike just stood there, waiting his turn. An opportunity for him to say something would come, but it wouldn't be while Supreme was saying all these things.

Did Vince know how many niggas would kill to be in his shoes? Supreme was asking. Would kill to have an academic scholarship to Garvey X University waiting on them? Man, most niggas wasn't out on the block pumping drugs because they wanted to be! Most niggas was out there 'cause they had no alternative. Vince wasn't in that category. And the fact that his mother had lied to him was no reason for him to throw away a future. Mike would understand, Vince thought.

"Mike, you understand why this is what I gotta do?"

"Naah," Mike laughed. "As a matter of fact, this is the first time in my life that I ever remember agreeing with Supreme."

"Man, I'm ain't fuckin' with you while you're out here, Yo," Supreme said, preparing to leave.

"Then you're not fuckin' with me at all," Vince said flatly.

"Oh, it's like that?" Supreme asked incredulously. Vince nodded.

"Man I'm leaving, Yo," Mike said after a silence.

Mike would come around, Vince reasoned. Supreme was a different matter. Mike and Vince shook hands in parting as Supreme continued looking at the river. As Mike turned to leave, Supreme turned to follow.

"Ain't you at least gonna say peace to Vince, man?" Mike asked him.

It was funny that Supreme had been thinking about both Denise and Vince. It was funny that the next time he'd see either of them they'd be together—her completely naked, head down on her knees, him completely naked behind her, inside her. It was funny if Vince didn't know that Denise was two months pregnant by him, even funnier if he did. It was funny that on his way from her house he had planned to go and find Vince and apologise for calling him dead. They were supposed to be each other's boys; and boys helped each other through each other's problems—they didn't abandon each other. It was funny why he had been on his way over to Denise's apartment in the first place.

Looking at the ring now, he figured that he'd give it to Stephanie, never telling her why he had bought it, nor the fact that he had had to cut half of Harlem's hair to pay for it. It was funny that Supreme's mother had warned him about Denise.

"Got that wild look in her eye," she had said.

"But Ma, she's a church girl."

"Those is the worst kind," his mother had said, without missing a beat. Oh yeah, it was funny. So funny it was damn near hysterical. So Supreme did what he did whenever something was funny. He laughed. He laughed all the way back down Denise's fire escape. He laughed all the way back down the block. He laughed all the way back to his building. He laughed all the way up in the elevator to his apartment. He laughed all the way from the front door of his apartment to his room, so hard there were tears in his eyes. He laughed for the rest of the day, pausing only to wipe away the tears. Life was funny like that.

For the next year, Mike would watch what seemed like two Supremes battling it out for supremacy. There was, of course, the old Supreme— telling jokes, bullshitting, talking too long and too much. But a new Supreme was developing, and he seemed almost serious. Supreme, who had been unreliable, late, truant or just plain absent, was now everywhere he said he'd be—and when he said he'd be there.

He never missed a haircut appointment, and rumor had it that he was also getting good grades. When Mike had asked him about it, Supreme had said some insanity about the old man and a 'side for taking care of business and a side for fuckin' up'. Mike asked where the other side had been for so long. But there had been a change.

And when Supreme asked Mike if he thought that there was any way Mike could use his influence to get him into ACP, Mike's heart almost stopped. College? Supreme wanted to go to *college*? Mike said that he'd try but that Supreme had *better* not embarrass him. When Supreme came back with "Have I ever?" Mike was kind enough not to answer him.

Mike's first Godchild had two names, which had made enough sense to Mike since the child's father had two personalities. Mike had learned that Denise, like Vince, was 'dead'—although Supreme would never say why. Mike had joked about the wonders of medical science—taking a live baby out of a woman who had been dead for seven months. But times were about to get hard.

Supreme's father, who had been laid off from work six months earlier, had begun to resent the son who he used to point to and say wasn't gonna be shit. Supreme was now making all the money in the house— his mother didn't have a job and the only other person living with them was Stephanie.

Denise and Vince were a couple now, and so even Mike could figure out how she had 'died'. The shit was poised to hit the fan, and when it did, surprisingly, it didn't splatter. Supreme had his son, no place to live, and all the money that Mike had saved cutting hair. Why hadn't Mike worried about all this at the time? He had. But the next day, he had his first real talk with Supreme's 'taking care of business' side.

"Are you gonna say something, man, or what?" Mike asked him. Supreme frowned bitterly.

"It's not like you left me a whole lot of room to say too much of nothin'," he said finally. Mike looked taken aback.

"You mean *you* can't think of anything to say?"

"Well as a matter of fact, I can think of one thing," Supreme said.

"What?"

"What's the *horrible* news?"

THE GOOD NEWS

"I'm *gay*, man?" Supreme asked incredulously as he and Mike trudged through the rain on their way to the *Zimbabwe's*. He thought it funny that Mike had picked now to tell him the 'horrible' news. Mike, still walking like a penguin.

"You weren't listening," Mike said shaking his head. "Not only are you gay, *I 'm* gay too."

"Well you *are* gay, man," Supreme laughed.

"Fuck you," Mike said.

"Apparently you do," Supreme laughed again. Mike just shook his head. They walked a couple more blocks in silence. Supreme was thinking of joke after joke and letting them pass because Mike had been acting strange all week. There was more to this bullshit date than he was letting on. All Mike had told him was that he had met a chick whilst he was working at *Ensembles*, who he had to lie to and so he had said he was gay. Mike hadn't said *why* he had had to lie to the chick, *why* he had to go out on this date, or even for that matter, why he was working at *Ensembles* - something Supreme had had to find out from another source!

"I get to play myself," Supreme said out of nowhere. Mike whirled around to face him.

"What the hell are you talking about *now*?" he asked, frowning.

"I get to play the 'guy' fag," Supreme said. "You're the 'chick'."

"Look," Mike said tiredly. "We're a *modern* gay couple, there's no 'guy' fag, there's no 'chick'. We're just two men, neither of us flaming, who happen to be a part of the gay lifestyle." Supreme stopped dead in his tracks.

"Yo," he began deadpan, "you are taking this shit just too *serious*."

"C'mon," Mike said evenly, demanding that Supreme pick up the pace, thereby having to watch the faster version of Mike's grotesque walking.

Step-crank-thud-step, step-crank-thud-step, step-crank-thud-step.

Supreme couldn't take it any more.

"You sure you don't wanna just catch a cab or something?" he asked innocently.

"Supreme, I swear to God, if you start that shit right now I'll kill you.," Mike said. Supreme shrugged.

They were around the corner from *Zimbabwe's* when they noticed the line. It was incredible. There was a sea of about two hundred faces. Nowhere near that many would be getting in.

"Damn," Mike said frowning, "I feel sorry for anybody who gotta wait on this."

"I know," Supreme laughed. "In the rain too!" They walked to the front and under the rain shelter, shook a few hands and waited. They were early. Supreme was deep in conversation with somebody about something when Mike noticed Andrea and her friend in the distance, approaching the club. *Damn*, even her friends look good, Mike thought. Mike elbowed Supreme, who elbowed him back, not wanting to be interrupted. Mike elbowed him again, and Supreme whirled around as if about to punch Mike. "What, man?" he demanded. Mike motioned with his head to the approaching Andrea and her friend. Supreme looked.

"Daaaaaaaaaaaaaaamn!" Supreme said slowly, in awe, but the brotha he had been talking to suddenly made a good point, and not to be outdone, Supreme whirled back around and rejoined the conversation.

Seeing Mike again, Andrea was suddenly sorry she had pressed him into this. The last thing in the world she needed was to be bothered with another half-assed man. I mean, everybody had problems, but why did the brothas she dealt with have so many? And the thing was, she didn't even consider herself choosy! Just be *about* something, she always said to herself, whenever brothas approached her. Just have all your teeth, most of your hair, love your mother, *not* have killed your last wife, and be *about* something. Was that to much to ask for? A man with not only a goal, but a *purpose* in life? But brothas she encountered never had both. They could either tell you what they expected to be doing in five years, but had no idea how in the world they would get there, or they could tell you what they were doing right this minute, but not what they would be doing tomorrow. And now here she was with one of the finest brothas she had ever seen in her life; a brotha who she could just look at and tell that he had both a goal and a purpose, and he was a *faggot*. Well, she had asked for it.

"You know something? I don't even know your name," Mike said, lying his ass off, after Andrea and her friend had come close enough. He remembered that they had never exchanged names at *Ensembles*, and didn't want to give away the fact that he knew it.

"It's Andrea," Andrea said in a low, almost sad voice, "and you know something? You should always dress and act like you are right now. I like you better like this." Her words sounded sincere.

"This is my girl..., uh, I mean, my friend Vanessa," Andrea said introducing her awkwardly.

"Hi, I'm Mike," he said. Great, Andrea was thinking, now I know his name too.

"Hi," Vanessa said.

"So, uh... Where's your boyfriend?" Andrea asked, looking around.

"...Well look, *all I know is*...," Supreme's loud voice boomed to whoever he was talking to about whatever, when Mike grabbed him by the

97

shoulder and twisted him around. Mike knew that he had better grab Supreme quick because when Supreme began a phrase with *"all I know is,"* he told you all he knew; about *everything*. Supreme stood, a little dizzy from being twisted, and frowning, as he peered back and forth between the two women in front of him.

"Ladies, this is Supreme," Mike said evenly. Supreme held up a weak hand in greeting, but didn't say anything. Great, he was thinking. Mike introduces me as a faggot to the woman of my dreams.

Rhineholt Dunn III had been a Wall Street sensation for the past two years. He had apparently come out of nowhere, with no known history. There was tons of information on his career but almost no information on his personal life in the newspapers And he also always managed to avoid having his photo taken. All that was known about him was that he was young, black and handsome, and that he had a business mind such as New York had never seen. Everything else was rumoured. Most of the rumours claimed that he was of old African ancestry and moneyed. Others said he was of Brazilian nobility. There was even one that claimed he was from Harlem! All that was known for sure about him, was that nothing was known for sure about him. Vanessa had decided upon hearing about him, that he *had* to be her man, much as Mike had decided that Andrea *had* to be his woman. Dunn seemed so charismatic, so mysterious, that Vanessa couldn't settle for a lesser man. And now some dopey faggot with his hat turned backwards stood gaping at her. The guy wasn't even one of those smooth or classy faggots. He was one of the ones that tried to seem like they were 'street'. What was he trying to prove by looking at her that way? What, did he go both ways? And if so, couldn't he tell that she was taken?

The four headed straight for the door. With Supreme and Mike's clout throughout the city, there was never a need to wait on lines. On the way through, Supreme was bumped roughly from behind by a large man in a leather jacket. Like a cat, Supreme spun, had both hands up and ready, and was looking for a spot on the man's face to attack. The man was smiling. Supreme paused, frowned, then began to smile himself. It was Rock Killer, the menacing heavyweight champion with the even more menacing looks, and he was also one of Supreme's best customers. The men hugged and shook hands like fraternity brothers. Vanessa wondered about Rock Killer, who she also had a little crush on. Did this mean that *he* was gay too?

The music was blaring as Supreme led the way into *Zimbabwe's*. Vanessa watched him; the way he moved, his style. She concluded that he was the type of fag who acted 'street'. Maybe he was bisexual. Or not even gay at all? She was amazed by how many people he knew. Celebrities came over to shake his hand. The deejay gave him and Mike a 'shout out'. And people seemed so happy to see them. She sneaked a look at Andrea who seemed to be in another world. She'd been that way ever since she'd arranged this date. Vanessa would have to find out what was wrong with her girl.

They took seats at a table near the bar.

"So Supreme," Vanessa began as they sat, "are you a beautician like Mike?" She was becoming more and more curious about this homo-hoodlum,

"Nah, I'm a barber."

"So, how did you two meet?"

"In a school yard when we were eight," Mike said.

"Yeah, that's when you hit me in the face with that mud-pie."

Mike sighed. "*Again* with the mud-pie? Are you ever gonna forget about that damn mud-pie?"

"Hell no. That shit coulda been fatal."

Vanessa and Andrea just looked at each other.

"What's it gonna take for you to never mention it again?"

"An apology might help?"

"Okay, Here, now; I'm sorry."

"You hear *that*?" Supreme asked Andrea and Vanessa incredulously. "He's apologizing now. He hit me with a mud-pie fifteen years ago and today he's apologizing."

Mike stood up. "I can't stand any more of this. Andrea, do you wanna dance?"

"Yeah!" Supreme cut in. "Please do. That should be funny as hell, Peg-leg!"

Andrea looked confused, but stood and walked to the dance floor with the hobbling Mike. Any doubts Vanessa had had about Supreme not being gay had been quelled. *Nobody* fought like that but lovers!

Supreme was sorry that he had chased Mike off. Vanessa made him uncomfortable as hell. A woman had never done that to him. Why outside, he'd damn near made a fool of himself, the way he was staring at her and all. He hoped she hadn't noticed. There was something about this chick. It wasn't just her looks, it was her look. He could tell she looked good when she was approaching, but when he looked in her eyes, something fucked up his equilibrium. He had started hearing love songs and poetry and shit. Something had to be wrong when a nigga started hearing poetry! But he'd be cool from this point on, though. Cool just like he'd always been. She was still just a woman. Even if he did all of a sudden remember all the words to some Nikki Giovanni shit he had read back in high school.

"Do you mind if I ask you a personal question?"

"Shoot," Supreme said, with just a little too much cool.

"How long have you known you were gay?"

Supreme looked confused. He'd completely forgotten he was gay. "Actually, I found out on the way over here," he said blankly.

Vanessa laughed, either because what he had just said had sounded so ridiculous, or so honest. "So you cut hair."

"So I cut hair," he said back. That was cool, sounded almost natural too.

"Do you cut any famous people's hair?"

He nodded slowly.

"Well, who's hair do you cut?"

"Well...," Supreme said, then paused frowning. He had a list ready to shoot to her off the top of his head, but he didn't want to seem like a celebrity name dropper. "Rock Killer, Jungle Jim, Fat Freddie, 'Slick' Shawn Sanders, a whole bunch of people."

"Where do you work?"

"Uptown Heads in Harlem."

"So you probably know my girlfriend's brother. He works there too."

"Who's your girlfriend?" Supreme asked.

"No, her name's Stephanie...damn, what's her last name again?"

"Tall, brown skin, medium length hair...?"

"Yeah."

Supreme smiled. "I happen to know her brother pretty well."

"Oh, you're *that* Supreme," she said. "Stephanie said you were cute." *Sis!* Supreme was thinking. Always looking out for big bro! "She didn't say that you were gay though," Vanessa added with a frown.

"That's probably cause she doesn't know," Supreme said with a shrug.

"Your own sister doesn't even know you're gay?" Vanessa asked incredulously.

"Naah," Supreme said.

"You mean you never told her?" Vanessa asked.

"I never knew myself," Supreme said evenly.

"So Mike was your first?" Vanessa asked.

"First what?" Supreme asked, genuinely confused.

"First gay lover?" Supreme waved his hands and shook his head an amount of times that was just within the permissible boundaries of being cool.

"Wait a minute, wait a minute," Supreme began, "Mike has been a lot of things to me: best friend, confidant, homey, partner, damn near brother, but I ain't never touched his booty, not even in a basketball game."

100

Vanessa was nodding like she understood.

"So what you guys have is a purely oral relationship?" she asked. Supreme felt a rush of bile in his throat that tasted just like the Chinese food he had had for lunch. Vanessa couldn't understand why he was grabbing his throat and changing colour.

"Oral?" Supreme managed to get out, in more of a cough than a word.

"Yes," Vanessa said, a little put off by Supreme's clowning. "We're both adults."

"I'm sorry," Supreme laughed, having successfully fought back down the General Tso's Chicken, "But if being mature means giving another brotha head, I ain't never gonna grow up!" Against her will, Vanessa laughed. That one, Supreme had been hoping on. It was time to change the subject, Supreme figured. Let's go back to Uptown Heads. He always felt comfortable talking about Uptown Heads.

"So if you know my sister, how come you never came to Uptown Heads?"

"I wanted to go a few times, but she said it was a waste. Just a bunch of brothas playing Superfly."

"And The Mack," he added. "Don't forget The Mack."

Vanessa laughed.

Supreme felt a little more at ease.

"Who actually owns Uptown Heads?" Vanessa suddenly asked.

"Rhineholt Dunn III."

So it was true. Vanessa could barely control her enthusiasm. She grabbed his arm. "Do you know him?"

"Yeah," Supreme said, watching her fingers sink into his flesh. "I grew up with the brotha."

Vanessa's eyes widened. "You did? I am in *love* with him! Tell me all about him."

What the hell had come over her. "Tell you what?"

"Well, for one, what does he look like?"

"Hold up!" Supreme laughed. "You saying you love a guy and you've never even seen him before?"

"Well, uh...technically...No."

"Then how are you in love with him?"

"I've just always had this thing for men of power, and hoodlums too. Like Rock Killer—I've always had this crush on him because I thought he was both."

Supreme glanced over at Rock Killer, who was by the bar looking his ugliest.

"If he gives you a crush, then I must pulverise you!" He burst out laughing at his own joke.

Vanessa remained serious. "It's not about looks."

"It couldn't be!" Supreme laughed. "So what is it, money?"

"Yeah."

Her honesty surprised Supreme. He thought she'd talk around that question, like most girls would.

"But I don't want a man for his money," she continued. "I want him because of it."

If there was a difference, he would have liked to have known what it was. "Yeah, that makes a whole lotta sense to me."

"It does when you think about it. A man who has money has pride in himself."

Supreme frowned. "Yeah? And I know poor folks with pride too."

"Just not as much as rich folks," she said conclusively.

Supreme studied her a while in silence. He had come to a conclusion, but he wanted to make sure he had all his shit together before he spoke. "You went to a white school for undergrads didn't you?" he asked finally.

"What does that have to do with anything?"

"Your thought process is entirely Republican."

"I don't understand what you're talking about," Vanessa said, sounding a little offended.

"I mean, no matter what's on the surface, you're just looking for a kitchen to be barefoot and pregnant in."

That did it! Vanessa shot her feet. "Who the hell do you think you are? You little bitch-ass faggot! And you've got the nerve to be questioning me?" She started waving her index finger in his face. "You better pray God forgives your little Sodom and Gomorrah ass, then try and find a sista who'll forget your past!"

Supreme couldn't help but laugh. "Oh, so there is some sista in you."

Vanessa's anger subsided into an easy laugh. She sat back down.

People in the club who had witnessed Vanessa's outburst were still peering at them. "Go on, there's nothing to see here. Go on 'bout your business now!" Supreme called out to them, raising a laugh.

Vanessa looked embarrassed. "I didn't mean to get all black like that."

"You didn't get all black," Supreme told her. "Sista, you just got ignorant."

"Well, I didn't mean to get ignorant then."

"No, I'm glad you did, 'cause if you'da kept taking shit from me, I'da kept dishing it out."

"Wait a minute," Vanessa said, raising her hand. "I'm the one who's supposed to be picking your brain."

"You gotta get through my naps before you can start picking my brain."

"Nappy hair, huh? Is that why you wear that hat?"

"That and the fact that I don't wanna be recognised."

"By who?"

"People mistaking me for Rhineholt Dunn III."

"Honey," Vanessa said, shaking her head, "I don't think you have to worry about that."

They shared a laugh, then something tingled in Vanessa. "So, you cut hair?" she asked again, a little surprised by the undeniable attraction she was beginning to feel for this backwards-hat-wearing fag. "So are you any good?"

"Look around," he said casually.

"You cut everybody's hair in here?"

"Most, not all."

"So can I recognise your style?"

"If you can recognize style itself," Supreme quipped with all the smoothness of a Barry White intro, Vanessa formed an 'o' with her lips as if impressed, and began to look around from head to head.

Supreme grinned. This should be fun, he thought. "Ok, well, you know I cut Fat Freddie over there. And Rock Killer and Jim and Slick. And Mike cuts Nate Adams, King James, Hot Rod and Pat Erving."

Vanessa studied the brothas he pointed out with deep concentration. Now she was going to try and select who else was a customer.

"Okay," she said finally, and pointing out heads in the crowd, "you cut him...him...and him..."

She was right.

"And Mike cuts him..."

Right again.

"You cut him..."

And again.

"And Mike cuts him."

Right again. Supreme was amazed.

"And..." she paused for a moment, to look at someone who's haircut fit the pattern of a Supreme cut, but somehow just didn't seem right. "I think you may have cut him."

"Almost," Supreme smiled. "That was a Kool Moe cut. Also known as 'The Great Pretender'. He imitated my style."

Vanessa came across another tough call.

"I can't tell who cut that guy! Looks like you both did it."

"Right again. That's Mack the Nut. Mike starts and I finish. You did pretty good!"

"I'm an art minor at Midtown Tech," she said, smiling. "I can always tell a man by his work."

"Well then you need to come by my studio in Harlem one Saturday night. I'll show you how art is born," Supreme said with a smirk.

Mike opened his eyes and squinted. He looked at the clock, then the phone, then back at the clock just to make sure. It could only be Supreme. What did he want now? Calling him at 5.30 on a Saturday morning. He answered the phone with a groggy "Hello."

"You looked like an idiot tonight," a drunk sounding female voice laughed down the line. "Dancing around on one leg with people chanting, 'Go Peg-leg! Go Peg-leg!' " The voice exploded into high pitched, howls of laughter.

It was Sharon! The female Supreme. Mike had forgotten that he'd seen her at the club. What did you want at this time of morning?

"Just to make fun of you."

She could have done that anytime, he reminded her.

"Not as good as I can right now," she laughed.

Was she drunk, Mike asked.

"No, just happy," she said. Happy she'd been drinking.

There had to be more to it than that, Mike guessed. Sharon wouldn't have called at this time unless she had something to tell him. "What is it?" he demanded, after a pause.

"What's what?"

Mike began a silent mental countdown; *three, two, one...*

"I met a man!" Sharon screamed.

Progress. "Yeah? When, last night?"

"Yep!" she said, then gave Mike a run down of their entire meeting. "You know who you are," he had said to her, as she walked past him in Zimbabwe's. Sharon asked him to repeat himself. He did. She asked him to explain. He said he could tell that she knew who she was. From her hair, and the style of her clothes, to the way she carried herself, her walk and attitude; she radiated. Despite the depth of the trance she was in, she came to her senses quickly. Then she wanted to laugh. First, because the line the brotha had used was the most rehearsed line a brotha had ever used on her. And second, because for a moment, just one fleeting moment, it almost worked. It was the eyes that actually did it.

Mike was sceptical. Yeah, the brotha had said some dope shit; he might even use that line himself one day. But who was this brotha? The name definitely didn't ring a bell and he knew damn near everybody in the club that night.

"What does he do for a living?" he asked.

She said he was a part of a group. Their name didn't ring a bell either. Mike racked his brain, but couldn't come up with anything. He'd have to ask Supreme.

Sharon said she just wanted to tell him the good news and that she was tired and should try and sleep now. With that she hung up. *Damn!* He didn't get to tell her who *he* was dancing with.

It was Saturday morning and the shop had not yet opened. Supreme flung open the back room faster than he ever had before. Born and the other kids were sitting down, studying him, curious. Supreme had caught them, he was sure. He just didn't know what he'd caught them doing. Where was the incriminating evidence? He'd have to be even quicker next time. He closed the door slowly, then opened it quickly again. Nothing. They were hip to that one.

"Now," Born said, a little annoyed by his father's ridiculousness, "back to business."

"You're father's a nut, you know that dontcha?" Tim said.

Born shrugged and handed each of the kids a quantity of money, then started to talk about productive ways to spend it. Ice cream sounded good.

Back in the shop, the three barbers were getting everything ready for the Saturday morning rush.

"Riff did you know that your boss is a homosexual?" Supreme stared at him deadpan.

"Nah," Riff said, with only mild interest.

"Well, neither did I. But I am," Supreme continued.

Riff shrugged and continued tidying up his workstation. He was in no mood to indulge Supreme. Mike just stood, shaking his head.

"See, I met this girl last night," Supreme began again. "Dope. Bad body, dark-skinned honey, long thick legs, and lips...? Man, you shoulda seen them lips. And her eyes; man they were like stars—I swear to God."

Riff nodded, but didn't look towards Supreme.

"But, I'm gay so none of that matters," Supreme said quickly. Mike sighed.

"Man, that's fucked up!" Riff said matter-of-factly.

"Tell me about it!" Supreme said, shaking his head.

Mike began to wonder how much time he'd get for shooting a barber.

"I wanna get with this sista, Riff," Supreme announced.

"So why dontcha?"

"Because she knows I'm gay."

Riff looked up from his workstation, opened his mouth to speak, paused, then closed it again. *I'ma take a chance,* he thought, *that the next thing outta this mothafucka's mouth ain't as crazy as everything else he's been saying.* "Well if you're gay," he said slowly, as if speaking to a child, "why do you wanna get with her?"

Supreme shrugged. "I dunno. Ask Mike."

Mike was sitting in his chair, rubbing his closed eyes with his fingertips. He could feel both pairs of eyes on him.

"Look Supreme," he said, without opening his eyes. "I appreciate what you did for me last night. Most brothas wouldn't have said they were gay, no matter how much you paid 'em. But you did it because you're a friend. I realise I put you in a fucked-up position and probably fucked up an opportunity with a beautiful sista that coulda meant something to you, and I deeply regret that. Now...is there anything else you need to hear?"

"Yeah," Supreme said in a tone a little too serious. "Does this mean that I'm not gay?"

Even Riff had to shake his head.

It was early evening and the Saturday Night crowd began to roll in; Freddie, Natalie, Nate, Keisha, Gary, Sharon, Jungle Jim, April, Hot Rod, Angie, King James and Cee Jay. When Slick and Stephanie entered arm in arm, the whole shop fell silent, and stared. Stephanie looked happy, and happy made her breathtaking. And Slick just looked happy to be Slick. Supreme watched Stephanie revel in all the attention she was getting. The woman who had argued that men didn't even exist, was now happily dangling off the arm of a six-foot two, something, apparently without classification. It looked like a man to Supreme, from where he was standing. But then again, real men don't exist, according to Stephanie. But Slick Shawn apparently did and was making her eat her words.

She caught her brother's eye and knew exactly what he was thinking.

"How does that taste, Sis?"

Smack, Smack, Smack!

"You ain't funny Supreme," she said, fighting back a smile.

The night kicked off with it's usual excitement. Fat Freddie and King James were in a hilarious argument. Jim and Rod were talking about movies and music. April and Cee Jay were talking about marketing hair care products. Sharon was in and out, saying she had to be somewhere, with somebody.

"Who?" Mike asked. "Everybody's here already."

She just laughed, and was gone seconds later.

Everyone was so immersed in themselves that they forgot something that they had all just recently heard, and wondered how they were going to deal with. Something of definite importance that they were sure would be of relevance this Saturday night, and for Saturday nights to come. When seven o'clock rolled around, Mike was the first to remember. *How is this gonna go down?* he wondered nervously.

Tyrone wasn't trying to fool himself. He knew that everybody at Uptown Heads knew he was selling by now; they all probably knew why too. Selling drugs in Harlem was no big deal. Selling drugs in New York was no big deal. Hell, selling drugs anywhere was no big deal these days. The idea was to not be broke. And he wasn't; not anymore. In only four days, he had already made more money than he had made the entire summer working at the Bronx Zoo. And was he supposed to be sorry because of it? The only thing that he was sorry about was that he was getting further away from his original intentions. He had only gotten into this because he had a child coming, but since the money had started rolling in he kept finding more and more things that he needed. A new leather for winter. Those boots he'd seen in the Village. A colour TV with a remote for his own room. And hey, didn't Supreme have that new twenty-four disk compact disc changer?

Tyrone was comforted by the certainty that the money would keep coming. He felt confident he could provide for his child. This lifestyle had possibilities he'd never imagined before. He could actually have anything he wanted. That thought alone was incredible. He had convinced himself that the downside was minimal. He'd already had his first arrest, which was bullshit. He was both too young and too unimportant for the cops to do anything to. They tried though, with their typical uptown 'white cop, black cop'—good cop, bad cop—bullshit duo. No imagination. But they hadn't found anything on him. And they wouldn't have either, unless they had looked in those little balloons he had swallowed when he saw them coming. He'd end up in a pine box, the black cop warned him.

"So will you, eventually," he'd replied.

"So will we all," the white cop said, with an air of finality that no one dared to challenge.

Tyrone slipped into his new leather and his new boots, then met up with Steve and Tony before heading off to Uptown Heads to find out his fate.

Nothing had changed about their entrance, except for the fact that none of the three were sweaty or out of breath. They all arrived at seven, and they entered, as always, Tyrone first, then Steve, then Tony. The barbershop fell deathly silent as all eyes turned to Supreme. He continued working.

A few low whispers broke the silence intermittently as Supreme finished the cut, with more care and attention than usual. He brushed the customer off, turned around and looked Tyrone deep in the eye for what seemed like an eternity.

"Next!" he said, looking straight at Tyrone.

There were at least a dozen people ahead of Tyrone, but they knew now was not their turn. Tyrone got up slowly and looked around the shop. All eyes were on him as he approached the barber's chair. He sat down uneasily. Supreme noticed the new jacket and boots. Tyrone obviously couldn't wait until the winter to model them. He began to clean his clippers and scissors. "You know what I hate, Riff?" he asked loudly.

"What's that?"

"I hate young niggas with futures," Supreme told him. He began to cut Tyrone's hair.

"Futures?" Riff asked, with sudden interest.

"Yeah, 'cause you know, us older brothas, we all got pasts. Most of of us ain't done half the shit we said we was gonna do when we was young."

There were nods of agreement around the shop.

"But these young niggas today man, they got a chance to actually do what they say. They can have pro ball careers, or be doctors, lawyers, even engineers and builders and shit."

Riff nodded his head, but remained silent.

"But you know who I hate even more, Riff?"

"Nah, who?" Riff asked evenly.

"Young niggas who go on and do what they said they was gonna do. You wanna know why I hate them?"

Riff nodded. "Sure, Brah."

"Because they make me feel like I ain't shit, 'cause I didn't live up to my own expectations."

"So what about the young niggas that fuck up their futures?" Mike asked from across the shop.

Supreme looked up, and Mike saw anger in his eyes. *Don't do it, Brah*, he thought. *Remember how sorry you were about Vince.*

Supreme looked away. "Oh, I love those niggas that fuck up their futures," he said, in a slow even tone. " 'Cause then I say, 'Hey, I might only be a barber, but at least I'm not out there selling crack'."

Mumbles of disapproval hummed throughout the shop.

Supreme leaned forward. "Who's paying for this haircut, brotha?" he whispered in Tyrone's ear.

"I got money." Tyrone said, pulling a twenty from his pocket.

"Uh-uh, that money's got blood on it."

Tyrone studied the bill momentarily, before he caught Supreme's drift.

"Get out of my shop!" Supreme whispered hoarsely. "And don't come back 'til you got clean money to pay with."

Tyrone hopped up out of the barber's chair with his half-finished cut, and disappeared quickly through the door. Steve and Tony ran out behind him.

"I don't think Supreme is gay," Vanessa told Andrea, crooking the phone between her shoulder and ear. She had phoned to tell Andrea her plans for Saturday night. She had decided to visit Uptown Heads with her girlfriend Stephanie.

Andrea was silent for a while. "So why would he lie?"

"I don't know, but he said some strange things for a homo, like he ain't never touching Mike's booty. Unless it's just Mike he doesn't like..."

This conversation was not helping Andrea. She needed to believe that Supreme was gay, that way she could accept that Mike was gay and life would start making sense again. "Maybe he's in denial," she offered weakly.

"If he was in denial, he would have come straight out and denied it. Played straight from the beginning."

Logic, Andrea thought. She didn't need god-damned logic right now. She needed Supreme and Mike to be lovers. It was that simple. "Why would a man pretend to be gay if he's not?" she said quietly.

Vanessa noticed Andrea's tone. She heard it every time Andrea talked about Mike. She guessed that Mike was having more of an effect on her friend than Andrea was willing to admit.

Vanessa tried to think of something that would lighten the mood a little. "Maybe some chick's sweating him, and he's trying to get her off his back!" she laughed.

Then she heard the dial tone.

109

A DUNN DEAL

"Where to today, kid?" Supreme called to his son.

"Let's go over to the Polo Grounds and watch the Rutger's Tournament," Born called back from the next room.

Supreme was surprised by his son's choice. "You wanna watch basketball today?"

"Yeah, Steve's playing, so Tim's gonna be there."

"Wait a minute. This is father and son day and you wanna hang out with your friends?"

"No-o-o-o-h," Born said, coming into the room. Supreme knew he was about to get conned. "I wanna hang out with my dad," Born said with a smile that would have melted the devil's heart.

"So let's go somewhere else then."

"Okay," his son said, with a shrug. Supreme was satisfied until Born added, "Can Tim come too?"

Supreme sighed.

"I'm going to the store to get the paper." Born was missing the point of these father and son days.

It was still early on a Sunday morning so Harlem wasn't awake as Supreme stepped out of the bodega where he bought his Sunday paper. Across the street a large woman was yelling abuse from a fifth-storey window at a brotha leaning on the wall outside, who was paying no attention.

As she shouted, pointing her fingers and waving her arms, her heavy breasts and the flesh under her arms swung furiously back and forth. Supreme watched for a while with interest. *The brotha better answer her,* he thought, *because she's the kinda sista that would hit a nigga with a rolling pin or something.* Another brotha approached and the two exchanged greetings. The woman in the window kept yelling. *Oh, Brah please don't try to impress your boy!* But sure enough, the brotha went into a show.

"Bitch, shut the fuck up!" echoed up the wall of the building. When the woman disappeared from the window, Supreme took a deep breath. The brotha's friend was smart enough to leave, but he continued leaning against the wall casually. Suddenly the fat lady sprung out the front door of the building. The brotha had a second to make his move. He was two seconds too late. He went to make a dash, but she was on him before he took his first step. Supreme watched as she raised an iron skillet and brought it crashing down on the brotha's head. He collapsed like a dead man.

"Get up, chump!" she roared, kicking the brotha in the ribs. *Stay down, Brah, stay down,* Supreme prayed as he watched from a safe distance. The brotha showed no signs of life. The woman, apparently tired from all her activity, started back towards the building, cursing and muttering and blowing. She'd only gone a few steps when the brotha was up and sprinting down the block.

Supreme looked around him. Of all the people passing on both sides of the road, he alone had bothered to observe the drama. Back in the days, a crowd would have gathered for the entertainment value. Was he the only one that still enjoyed living in uptown, he wondered.

A little boy toddled by holding his mother's hand on the way to church. He was wearing a suit that was entirely too cute. Suddenly Supreme felt down. Born didn't even own a suit. He had never gone to church. And he was terrified of his own mother. Supreme began to wonder whether he was a good father. Sure, Born was one of the few kids in Harlem who always knew where his father was—but what else did he know? Supreme wandered back around the corner with one thought in mind; he just wanted to hug his son. Hug him and apologise. Apologise because shit was not perfect yet. That's all he had ever wanted for his son; for things to be perfect. If he had his way, they would be. Real soon.

How could I have missed a headline like this? Supreme wondered when he finally did look at the paper. 'Ace Challenges Dunn For Wisconsin Deal' it read. How could he have failed to see that coming?

Donald Ace had been the white Rhineholt Dunn III twenty years before. Unlike Dunn though, Ace wasn't an enigma—everybody knew everything about him. His father had been a shoelace manufacturer. Ace had gone to Yale where he had double-majored in Accounting and Political Science. He had graduated with honours. He became a CPA first, then a licensed, practising lawyer. He left his law practice to become a broker on Wall Street, a move which many considered bone-headed. On Wall Street, though, he dominated. Years before the insider trading scandals had broken out, Donald Ace became known as the man who 'always kept a hundred in your pocket'. If you saw anything and you told him, you got paid. If you heard anything and you told him, you got paid. If you had even thought you had seen or heard anything and you told him, you got paid.

"You don't win by playing fair," Ace had written in his autobiography, long after he had made too much money for it to matter anymore. By that point, he was rumoured to be like an old elephant—looking for a place to die.

Ace had grown old and bitter. His hair had gone grey, he had begun to put on weight and he looked beaten. He was beaten; but not by defeat, by victory. He had married a model right out of a magazine. He had bought the house that people said would never go on sale. He had even bought himself a term as Mayor of New York City, then resigned when he saw what the pay was like. Winning all the time, he had come to find, could be dull.

When the city contract for the maintenance of the Port Authority had come up for bidding two years before—and Ace's contracting company had been a day late with the paperwork—he found that the city had already hired a contractor. That was ridiculous, he had argued. For fifteen years he had been providing maintenance for the Port Authority. No one would have been foolish enough to bid on the job. But someone had. A young black man, he was told. Rhineholt Dunn III.

A nigger? Of course they weren't all niggers. Some of them were people, he had reminded himself. He had been a liberal in college, had listed the United Negro College Fund as one of his main charities, and had even dated a black woman during his rebellious years.

Six months later, when the same thing happened with the contract on the George Washington Bridge bus terminal, the old Donald Ace returned with a vengeance. He dyed his hair back to jet black, shed the extra weight, and the look in his eye—which had begun to dim—was back to killer intensity. There was going to be a war. He would go on to buck and challenge Rhineholt Dunn III at every opportunity, regardless of the stakes. Ace had left Dunn frustrated by seeming to always beat him to the punch. With this Wisconsin deal Dunn was sure that he had something even Ace could not ruin. But of course, Ace—who by his own admission never played fair—had spies everywhere; spies who made it their business to follow Dunn's activities closely.

So when the *Homer Today*, a small Wisconsin newspaper, published an article on the poor farming couple who had discovered oil on their property and intended to sell their farm to Rhineholt Dunn III, it was only hours before the story was headlines everywhere. Dunn had given the already agreeable couple three months to think things over back in early June and now, with September approaching, the deal would have seemed certain to anyone but Dunn and Ace.

Dunn planned to fly to Wisconsin with the preliminary paperwork in about a week's time. But the newspaper article reported that Ace had just returned from Wisconsin, and had offered the couple significantly more than Dunn. The poor couple agreed that Ace's offer was more lucrative, but Ace had been gruff with them, trying to press them into making the deal right away.

They said they would agree to Ace's offer, but only if Dunn couldn't match it by the time the three months was up. The couple couldn't understand why Ace had laughed when they told him this. He seemed like he wanted it that way.

Ace pitched his offer just out of Dunn's reach. His people calculated just how much resources and capital Dunn could liquidate, and bid just over that amount. Both men knew there was no way that Dunn could come up with that kind of money in the time that remained—less than one month.

But Dunn also knew Ace was playing a very dangerous game, because although he did have more resources than Dunn, he didn't have much more.

Supreme continued skimming through the paper. The only other article that caught his eye was the one that said that the authorities were beginning to connect the Guido Andolino murder and thirty or so domestic and international drug-related assassinations that had taken place since. A watermelon rind was found at each crime scene; even 'New York's finest' couldn't miss that connection.

He folded the paper and put it down. It was father and son day and he had his own concerns. Born had missed a loop in his pants with his belt and mis-buttoned his shirt, and they still hadn't decided what they were going to do that day. Supreme needed to deal with the matters at hand—without wondering how long it would take Breeze to get caught, and without worrying about some rich brotha and some place called Wisconsin.

It was a more soberly dressed Mike that Andrea saw as she walked into Ensembles the next Monday morning. He still had a questionable shirt, but he had given up the butt-tight jeans. *Damn, he looks like a man*, she thought. He held his head like a man. He moved his hands like a man, held his shoulders like a man and kept his back straight like a man—a *straight* man. Andrea wondered if she really wanted to go through with this.

It had been her intention to have him do her hair since she'd last seen him at Zimbabwe's, so that he could caress her. But now, as she watched him, she was losing her nerve—or rather her control. He had to be gay. Had to be. If he was, then there was nothing a woman could offer him. If he wasn't, then there were a lot of things a woman could offer him; though obviously not her.

Mike noticed Andrea standing uneasily by the door. When he smiled that big, black All-American-Boy smile, Andrea wanted to slap him for making her feel this way. This was crazy. She didn't even know him and here she was, all uptight over his sexual preference. *I don't even want him*, she told herself. *Yeah right*, herself told her back. She wanted him all right. She had wanted him at Build Your Own Lunch back in Harlem. He was the reason she always took her clients there for lunch. All he ever had to do was say *Hi!* She could have taken it from there. But he never did. He just looked at her. And his look never said anything concrete. It didn't say *I want you*. It didn't say *I dig you*. It didn't say *I'm interested in you*. It didn't even say *I wanna fuck you*—most guys managed at least that much. Those damn brothas from Harlem. You could never read them. She tried to face the very real possibility that, for the first time in her life, she wanted a brotha who didn't want her. *Naah*, she told herself immediately. *He's gay. He has to be.*

"You look almost normal," she mocked, sitting down in his chair with her back to him.

"I'm feeling more like myself too," he laughed. *Like himself*, she wondered. Did that mean that he wasn't himself the first time they had met?

"A trip to the beauty shop the first day of every week, huh?"

Andrea nodded.

"Today's the day I meet with prospective clients," she said.

"Prospective clients?"

"Yes, for my Yellow Pages—or rather, black pages. That's what I do. I set up advertisements for black-owned businesses in a special phone book the company I work for publishes."

Mike nodded. A progressive sista.

"So what, do you take 'em out to lunch or something?"

Mike had yet to make the connection between what she'd told him and the way he had spent his last year-and-a-half of Monday lunches.

"Yes. I take them up to Build Your Own Lunch. But I always get my hair done here first."

"So that's why you always looked so good when I used to see you there."

The connection had slammed straight through his head and come out of his mouth. The silence that followed was nearly fatal. *What the hell did I just say?* he wondered. He had admitted that he had seen her too? Oh, God! Whatta fuck-up. It had been cool when she had asked him if it was him that she had seen there. But now he was admitting that he had seen her too! That he had always seen her. Any slim chance that he might have had to convince her that he wasn't gay was definitely gone now.

How would he be able to explain seeing her for over a year-and-a-half without even trying to start a conversation? Prospective clients; those were the brothas she had been with. So they stared and gaped at her. Who wouldn't? She was fine, and now, she would never be his. If he had only just approached her or said something. Winked, smiled, whatever: That damn Harlem cool!

Sometimes it was better to just take the chance of getting your feelings hurt.

'...You always looked so good...'

The words echoed through Andrea's head like it was empty. Would a

114

gay man have noticed how good she looked? Would a straight man have noticed and not acted on it? Maybe, if he had had a girl or a wife—but most married men still went out of their way to flirt with her, and brothas with girlfriends; *please*.

A black man with a girlfriend was like a kid with a bad tooth; they didn't think about her unless she was bothering them at the time. So then what was wrong with this brotha? You see, because there had to be something wrong with him. He had to be gay, or married, or one of those brothas she had only heard about; one that had a girlfriend he treated with respect, or something.

There couldn't be any other possibilities. Except the one possibility that she refused even to acknowledge; that he just might not have been interested in her.

They were both silent as Mike finished up the styling. He surprised himself by making her hair look even better than it had done the last time.

"Looks great," she said emptily, without even looking at her hair; paid the cashier and left. No *see you next week*? No nothing, Mike was thinking. Well, at least this time she had *said* she liked the hairdo.

Andrea stepped out of Ensembles with nothing but time on her hands. It was only nine thirty; two hours before she needed to meet with the client at Build Your Own Lunch. She decided to start heading uptown anyway.

Monday was 'new business' day for her, and Andrea really didn't have to drop by her office at all. But she liked to go by to pick up her mail and messages. There was no mail this morning, and only one phone message: "Bitch!" an angry-sounding female voice said, then hung up. Andrea laughed. She'd have to call Vanessa and apologise for hanging up on her Saturday night.

You had to go through at least four socio-economic scales heading uptown on Amsterdam Avenue from Andrea's office on Seventy Second Street. The journey began in Whiteville. Rich Whiteville. They had Manhattan town houses, don't-call-'em-brownstones-but-they're-brownstones, and duplexes. Restaurants and cafes lined the streets, imitating Parisian and Italian flair, but with 'Joey from Brooklyn' as the maitre-dee. They had fancy office buildings, much hipper than those slobs in midtown, but safe from those savages uptown.

Next, you passed through Beigeville. Puerto Ricans, Dominicans, South Americans, Latinos; Andrea was never sure what those people were, she was just sure where they were. Their spot on Amsterdam started at about Eighty Eighth Street. 'Beigies' went out of their way to make it known that they were whatever they were. Now they all tried to act like niggas. Especially the kids. The way they walked, talked, dressed and acted, you would have thought they belonged further uptown. *It must have something to do with hip hop.* Being black was in vogue again because of rap, but Andrea wondered if the 'beigies' and other 'new niggas'—as Vanessa called them—understood the lyrics. If not, they'd revert to being Puerto Ricans, Dominicans, South Americans and Latinos as soon as niggas went back out of style.

Next came Junior Whiteville, as you passed through the campus of Columbia University. Junior Whiteville wasn't as affluent as the senior one forty blocks south, but it allowed its inhabitants to indulge in the delusion that they were living independently; they only went to their parents' places to eat dinner, do laundry and get money for food and rent. They also got to believe that they were living in Harlem. It would be a cool story to tell at dinner parties a few years down the line.

"Yeah, I useta live in Harlem, Bob. Ha, ha, ha!"

"Really Rick? Weren't ya scared?"

"No, you see I know how to communicate with those people. I speak the lingo."

Never mind the fact that, 'speaking the lingo' amounted to screaming *please don't hurt me!* every time a black man got in the elevator with them.

Finally, you reached Harlem. Although Andrea had been born and raised in Jamaica, Queens, she thought of Harlem as her second home. You could tell so much about a place just from the brothas on the corner. From the way they stood, the clothes they wore, their movements, and their eyes—if you could read them. Was it just an 'everything is everything' gathering? Did they have a beef with the brothas on the next block? Were they getting their plans together to make a record demo? Play some ball? Write a movie script? Go by that girl's house party? Or just get some forties, smoke that blunt and cool out for the night?

You could also tell who didn't belong, or didn't belong any more. The visitor from out of town, another part of the city, or another block. The brotha who was home on vacation from college or the military. The brotha who had made it—in any of the ways that 'making it' manifested itself—and was now just reminiscing with his homeboys, who hadn't.

When Andrea finally got to Build Your Own, the lunch itself was exciting for a change. The prospective client was an older brotha who designed and sold shoes, sneakers and boots. He seemed delighted with the notion of a black Yellow Pages, but even more delighted with Andrea herself. They were less than half an hour into their conversation when he offered her a job as Regional Supervisor at the office he planned to open in Atlanta.

Andrea was flattered, and declined graciously. But the brotha insisted that she at least give the offer some thought, and maybe even consider a visit to the proposed site. *Atlanta?* She had been there before, but thought it had absolutely no culture or happening social life. If she decided to take a job there, what would she do to keep from going crazy after work every day?

Tyrone spotted Breeze in the distance that Friday. He had seen him around and had always wanted to get to know him better. Breeze seemed to have his own thing going. Even though Breeze and Vince were supposed to be down, they were very different. Even the brothas that worked for Breeze were different. Breeze was standing near the door of a shiny new black car, speaking to a small group of brothas about what looked like it could have been anything from politics to rap music. He wore light, earth-toned, summer apparel; a thin, cream-coloured cotton blazer, a tan T-shirt and mauve, had-to-be-linen pants. This guy was too smooth. Tyrone noticed he used small, but very expressive, gestures when he talked, and was never more than a decibel or two above a whisper. And he seemed to listen carefully and respectfully when other brothas talked, but there was no mistaking the authority he had over them.

If Tyrone was going to pattern himself after a drug dealer, he decided, this was definitely the one. Tyrone approached, and one of the brothas standing with Breeze indicated his presence. Breeze stopped talking to look him up and down.

"Yeah?" he asked.

Suddenly Tyrone felt unsure of himself.

"Whassup?" he asked, smiling nervously.

"Gas prices," Breeze replied, before returning to his conversation. Tyrone knew he was supposed to take the hint and leave, but he didn't. The brotha indicated to Breeze that he was still there.

Breeze turned to look at him again.

"Whatcha want, man?"

"I just came over to...you know...rap a little and what not."

"What's 'what not'?" Breeze asked, deadpan.

"Rap about, you know...hanging out with you brothas on occasion," Tyrone said, with as much fake cool as he could muster.

Breeze studied him closely, then chuckled. "Ain't you Mr. Garvey X?"

Tyrone had no time to wonder how Breeze knew that. He simply answered, "Maybe. In the future."

Breeze shook his head. "Not if you try to get with my program."

"Why? What's your program about?"

"What's *yours* about?"

Tyrone shrugged. He figured he'd need to say something cool.

"Makin' money, livin' well, gettin' bitches, you know."

117

Breeze shook his head at Tyrone's foolishness.

"So what's your program about?" Tyrone asked him.

"Dying painlessly," Breeze said evenly. A slow smile spread across his face; a smile so sinister, it made Tyrone turn on his heels and walk away—fast.

If you didn't really know Supreme, you wouldn't know how hard he was working. He seemed normal enough; funny as ever. You would have thought that it was just another typical Saturday night at Uptown Heads. Almost everyone was present and accounted for. For many of them, tonight was destined to be the first good time they'd had all week. Supreme indulged them, but it was a strain tonight because he was so tired.

Mike noticed that Supreme wasn't up to it, but tonight the regulars needed cheering up. Gary was about to start his final year of medical school. Jungle Jim's current movie project was dangerously near going over budget. Fat Freddie was being taken to court over allegations that he had illegally sampled music from some toothless old rock star. Hot Rod, owner of Rough, Rugged & Raw Records, was having a terrible time finding new talent for his label. King James had just lost a part in a movie. Angie, the choreographer had sprained her knee, so she was now peg-legging it like Mike. Natalie, the singer, had just had her tonsils taken out. Kookin' Keisha, chef extraordinaire, had missed an opportunity to set up restaurants on highway rest stops. Naturals and dreads were in with the sistas, so Cee Jay's perm products weren't selling like they used to. April's advertising agency hadn't had a large, national contract since their *Bad pipes make me plumb loco!* ad for Wild West Plumbing. The Uptown Heads crowd was a pretty sad group tonight, but you would have never been able to tell from the laughter.

At almost exactly seven o'clock Supreme started working at a fevered pace. His humour was vicious, ripping strips off everybody. The only thing that saved most people from being genuinely insulted was the fact that he was still funny, funnier than ever by some accounts. Mike wondered if anyone beside himself had noticed the connection between the time of day, the day of the week and the beginning of Supreme's onslaught. If they had, they would have realised that it was on this day, and at this time, that Supreme usually got his favourite victim—one of three young brothas who'd burst in the door sweaty and out of breath.

At seven thirty the crowd seemed to emit a gasp of hope as the doors were flung open. Mike knew for sure who it wouldn't be. Tyrone was as stubborn as Supreme if not more so. When Stephanie and Slick entered, Supreme smiled.

Smack, Smack Sm...

Then Vanessa walked in. Mike whipped a look at Supreme, who instantly looked away from the door and back to the head he was cutting. Supreme, who had been in mid-Smack when Stephanie and Slick walked in, went dead silent. Mike had to bite his bottom lip to keep from laughing.

"Looks like a cat's got somebody's tongue," Riff said. He had also noticed the change in Supreme.

Supreme greeted his sister and took it upon himself to introduce Vanessa to Uptown Heads as, "the marvellous young woman I had the pleasure of making the acquaintance of."

Next, he began the personal introductions. There was Riff, "a fine, fine barber and all in all, an excellent human being." Gary, "the future of medical science as we know it"; Jungle Jim, "the maker of powerful, explosive films that awaken our consciousness"; Fat Freddie "who brings class and elegance to a musical form overrun by thugs and hooligans." *Hooligans?* Hot Rod who, "knows the dimensions of sound and its variables perhaps better than anyone"; King James, "the man for whom comedy becomes genius"; Angie, "the woman for whom the term 'poetry in motion' was coined"; Natalie, who "sings with a voice so rich in intensity that it makes the angels jealous"; Kookin' Keisha, who "makes food the pleasurable experience it was intended to be"; Cee Jay, who "made your hair as much her business as her own"; and April, who "could coin a phrase that would make hell sound inviting".

All the Uptown Heads regulars just sat there; waiting for a nuclear bomb to drop, the sky to open up, or some other sign of the apocalypse. A serious Supreme? A gracious Supreme? Just five minutes earlier he'd told them they were bum-ass this and that's, and low-lifed-assed that and the others. Now they had class, elegance, and intensity, were the futures of this and made powerful and explosive that!

If anybody had been impressed by this beautiful stranger, they were in awe of her now. She had done something more impressive than making a pig fly. She had made Supreme a gentleman.

When the phone rang and Supreme asked:

"Get that, would you my dear sister?" Stephanie was convinced that there was something really wrong with her brother. Unlike the rest of the Uptown Heads crowd she hadn't been impressed by her brother's earlier show of graces. Stephanie had seen Supreme resort to more than a little show of class to impress a woman in his day. But for him to address her courteously, her—his insult practice pin-cushion—there had to be something wrong.

What it was, she didn't know. But she'd be damned if she didn't find out.

It was Stephanie and Supreme's mother on the phone. Born had thrown up. He wasn't too sick, but she had wanted to call to tell him. As soon as he hung up the phone, Supreme was in motion.

"Great heavens! My lad is ill," he muttered to himself, then rushed out of the barbershop. This didn't surprise anyone. Supreme was the king of over-protective fathers.

"That was ugly," Mike said with a mocking smile.

"No, your fuckin' walk is ugly," Supreme corrected him. *Nine more blocks of this?* He wondered if he could stand it.

Mike looked up into the night sky. "It's a pretty night, man."

"Yep. Won't be too many of these left. Summer's almost over."

"So whatcha wanna do?" Supreme asked hotly. "Go someplace and neck?"

"Naah, you blew your chance to do that earlier," Mike laughed.

Supreme shot him a look so cold, Mike felt a chill.

"Easy, baby!" Mike said, smiling. "Wasn't me who turned into Nat King Cole back there in the shop."

"Nat King Cole?"

"Yeah, that shit you tried to pull was 'unforgettable'."

Mike laughed.

"See, that's why some people shouldn't even be allowed to make jokes," Supreme said. "You should have to check with a referee, your shit be so foul."

"Like that was funny."

"I wasn't trying to be."

"So what were you trying to be back in the shop, Rhineholt Dunn III or something?"

Supreme stopped walking dead in his tracks. "You didn't have to say that," he said evenly.

"I'm sorry."

They started walking again.

"So what was wrong with you back there, man?" Mike asked.

"I dunno," Supreme shrugged. "I guess when Vanessa came to Uptown Heads, she was up in my spot. She was there. Seeing me for who I really am. I mean, before—at Zimbabwe's—we were on neutral ground. I coulda acted any way I wanted and she would've never known who I really am. But up in Uptown Heads, that's me. I mean, that's where I work, that's what I do, that's where my friends are, that's how I act, that's me. I just felt kinda...I dunno...naked out there, with all that 'me' showin'."

Mike laughed, but not a mocking laugh; he understood. He hobbled over to Supreme and put his arm around his neck. "C'mon, let's find some place to go and neck," he said smiling.

Supreme gave him a wry look. "You think I don't know you're serious? Ensembles got you all twisted like that. You ain't my type any way. I like a brotha with some hair on his chin. That clean-shaven shit is too bitchy."

Mike laughed. Then he thought of Sharon. She had missed her first Saturday night at Uptown Heads in a long time.

"By the way, Yo, you ever heard of a rap group called The Black Experience?"

Sharon and her new man sat across from each other, waiting for their dinner to arrive. They gazed only into each other's eyes—the effect that he had hoped the restaurant would have on her lost. It was located near Chinatown, almost exactly under the Manhattan Bridge. Brooklyn could be seen across the water. It was almost nine, and in the light of the full moon even something as ugly as the East River looked romantic. Things had happened so fast. It had only been a week since they had met. They had spent every night together since. *At last,* she thought, when they had first met. *A brotha whose hand I don't have to hold. A brotha who doesn't need a mother.* She could tell that much about him from the very beginning. The rest of it—her emotions—weren't so clear.

Sharon had never been one to rush head-first into a relationship. Brothas had always been so reluctant to admit how they really felt, even to themselves. Sharon liked to wait until she was able to tell how long, and what kind of games, a brotha would be playing, before she decided whether or not it was worth getting involved. Her new man was different. He had put his cards on the table at the beginning.

She remembered the first night that they had slept together, the Saturday after they met, he told her exactly who he was and exactly what he did. He ended by saying:

"So if you're gonna hurt me, get it over with."

She hurt him for the rest of the night.

Now she sat in the restaurant beneath the Manhattan Bridge, waiting for Ethiopian food, and thinking life was too short for moral differences to get in the way. Her new man was real—that was all that mattered. She wouldn't have to change him or even try.

This was too much. Andrea had kept her eyes closed during the entire styling because she couldn't bear to look at him again. There he was, right behind her, strong hands massaging her scalp, chest occasionally brushing against her back, and scent so masculine she wanted to leave scratches on his back. *He's not gay* kept echoing through her head.

But he wasn't. Not today at least. Not dressed in those loose-fitting jeans, cotton blended T-shirt and low-cut work boots. Not without any make-up. Not without a trace of the faggoty attitude he had shown on her first two visits. He wasn't gay today. It was that simple. Andrea didn't worry about the rationality of it all; of a person actually being able to switch back and forth between being gay and straight. She just knew that on this occasion he wasn't gay.

So if she was planning any move at all, she'd better make it now.

"Write down your phone number and address," she said, after her hair was finished. Mike frowned and looked at her oddly.

"Why?" he asked sceptically.

"Because I told you to," she said flatly. He complied, and waited for her next order.

On her last two trips to Uptown Heads, Supreme had seemed more like the guy Vanessa thought she had met at Zimbabwe's that night. Her first night there had been a nightmare. Everybody she knew who had been there before except Stephanie had always ranted and raved about how good a time she would have if she went.

They had told her Supreme would keep her in stitches. When she went for the first time, she'd feel like she'd been there all her life. But that first night, she had thought she might never want to go again. Supreme hadn't been funny at all. And when she walked in, there had been an awkward silence followed by insane laughter after the barber introduced to her as 'Riff' had said what must have been some kinda inside joke about cats and tongues.

This was what everybody was going so crazy over? she wondered about the shop. Then Supreme made those asinine introductions. *"Yes, I'm the person who makes dynamic this and that about that and the other—who are you?"* Vanessa read in the faces of everyone Supreme introduced her to. Who was she? Just a college student who occasionally worked for her father. And here she was meeting the inventor of this and that, and the creator of x, y, and z. It wasn't that she had minded meeting these people. A few of them she had recognised from newspapers and magazines, and some she had wanted to meet. But why did Supreme have to introduce her to them all at once? Why couldn't she have just gotten to know them in passing, like everyone else in the shop seemed to have done.

She felt like the outsider she had desperately *not* wanted to feel like on her first time there. And about that 'marvelous young woman' crap; did Supreme honestly expect her to be flattered by that nonsense? The last person she had referred to as marvelous was Marvin Hagler, and if Supreme had been comparing *him* to her, he might have found a right hook waiting for him the next time they met—which might have been never.

But Stephanie had been persistent in asking her to return. Her winning argument was that whatever ridiculous thing Supreme did the following week, he *couldn't* introduce her to everybody again. So she returned. And it was in returning that Vanessa again saw in Supreme what had so captivated her in the first place.

A strict father and a private school upbringing can be hell on any young sista, but it's a blistering hell in New York. The distance that's imposed between you and the rest of your race seems uncrossable. But you're expected to maintain. *You're* the one who's supposed to make something out of yourself, *you're* the one who's special, *you're* the one who's going somewhere in life, *they're* not. So how come *they* always seem to be laughing at *you*? Laughing at you and calling you a 'little white girl' when nothing could be further from the truth. You were black. Very black; and pretty, if what your parents told you was true. You were supposed to be better than them. So how come they seemed so much smarter? Not book smart, but street smart. You tried to console yourself by telling yourself that book smart was more important; that anybody could have street smart. But if anybody could have it, why didn't you? And how come their girls seemed so much more pretty? You were naturally beautiful, you were told—but as your hair was pressed and your naked face scrubbed and presented to the world, you longed for the braids and lipstick that would turn your beauty pretty like theirs. And how come their boys were so much cooler? Sure, there were black boys in private school, but they didn't seem like *real* black boys. Real black boys were supposed to curse. Real black boys were supposed to steal. Real black boys were supposed to smoke marijuana and drink vodka without a chaser and say nasty things to girls and get in trouble all the time. Except for the occasional rebel, or the child of parents with new money, all the black boys at Vanessa's private schools acted whiter than the white boys.

Vanessa had eventually grown out of her warped perception of her own people, but not its effects. The beginning of her undergraduate college career was a period where she made up for what was, to her, lost time. She wore her hair exclusively in braids, owned between thirty and fifty different shades of lipstick, and developed a 'street' personality so convincing you would have thought she'd grown up in the toughest section of Brooklyn, rather than one of the better sections of Long Island. The only thing that Vanessa hadn't tried in college was the boys. She dated the same whiter-than-white black boys in college that she'd seen all her life in private school.

Vanessa had always wanted to try a 'ruffneck', but had always been scared of them; probably for the same reason that she had always been attracted to them. She had watched them, on the trains, leaning easily

123

against the railing, clothes too big even for someone twenty pounds heavier, nodding their heads to Walkman beats, reading rap music magazines or rapping to their partners. She had seen them on the streets; walking to a cadence that only they heard, strutting like they had either too much change in their pockets, or too much air in the soles of their sneakers, looking at her sideways or full in the face, challenging her with their gaze. She had heard them, speech flowing endlessly, until you wondered whether the listener actually heard the words, or just deciphered the rhythms. She had wanted them; all of them, or at least one of them...to try. But they were too dangerous. Their lives seemed too unpredictable, too transient, as though at any moment they would be shot, killed or arrested. She still wanted one, though. One with the same cadences and rhythms, just less danger.

So when Supreme came along with his thugish, street arrogance, backwards hat, bad grammar, rugged good looks, and bastard son, he was just the brotha Vanessa had been looking for.

'The Black Experience Found Out', the headline read. In an almost perverse way, Supreme was happy. He was concerned for the safety of the brothas in the Black Experience—particularly Breeze—but he was happy that, for the first time in the last three weeks, the headline was not another article about Rhineholt Dunn III or Donald Ace. The article went on to say how a police informant named Vincent Carr had called the paper with a story that explained the recent assassinations of reputed drug dealers that were taking place all over the world. In the article, Vince admitted that he himself was a drug dealer, but under the control of some black, criminal mastermind named 'Breeze'. Vince went on to say that the 'Black Experience' was an all-black group of drug dealers who planned to take over the entire drug trade by force.

Supreme could only shake his head as he thought of Breeze now. Breeze was dead. Someone in the Black Experience had turned Judas and sold him out to Vince, who had in turn sold him out to the newspapers and the law. To the average person, it was supposed to look like either the police, or some vengeance-seeking international drug cartel, had taken care of Breeze's hit. But Supreme could see further than that. Vince's fingerprints were all over this murder.

He would have had Breeze killed before the newspaper story broke and the body stashed, just to make sure that the hit was taken care of. He would then leak the story to the newspapers to scare the members of the Black Experience by blowing their cover. He would probably go into hiding himself for a while, just to be on the safe side. He would then have Breeze's dead body resurface to make it seem like the hit had taken place after the newspaper story had broken, and that it had been carried out by people seeking revenge. Knowing Vince, he would then probably hire some foreign-looking dudes to walk around Harlem looking suspicious, as if they were looking for other members of the Black Experience to kill. Vince would cover all the angles.

'Two Days Left', said the article on about Dunn and Ace on the inside page of the paper. It was too much to hope that there wouldn't be one at all. The article referred to the days remaining for Rhineholt Dunn III to match Donald Ace's offer on the Wisconsin deal. Supreme looked at the article half-interested. He had never worried about what the newspapers wrote about the 'incredible' Rhineholt Dunn III before, and he didn't intend to start now.

Vanessa was ready to get down to business. She would have thought that a brotha like Supreme would have been in a rush to get the booty. But on the contrary, he seemed almost tentative. And now Vanessa was tired of it. She was a little unsure herself as to whether or not she really wanted to sleep with him. But then she had got to know him better. She had sat in on his sessions at the shop, watched him interact with the uptown crowd, laughed at his jokes, met his son and saw how it was only his son that could bring out a side of Supreme that was just outright goofy. He had turned out to be such a beautiful young brotha that now she really didn't have the heart to hurt him, the way she knew she eventually would. But then Supreme was a man. And men can handle things like that—much easier than women, at least. Could anyone honestly admit to knowing a man who claimed to be hurt because he had been used for sex? Supreme was a big boy and if she did hurt him, he'd get over it. It was important to get this 'bad boy' craving out of her system before she met Rhineholt Dunn III—rather than have that desire surface after they were engaged or married.

Vanessa marched from the cab up to Supreme's apartment building, loaded down with more procreative items than a pharmacy. She arrived uninvited—having already arranged for Born to be 'kidnapped' and taken to the circus by Stephanie and Slick—but she didn't feel she'd be intruding. If there was another sista there, she'd leave. If not, Supreme was getting screwed, whether he wanted to or not. But he would want to. She'd make sure of that.

Vanessa deliberately buzzed the wrong apartment and lied about free pizza to the man who answered the intercom. He buzzed her in immediately. Then she crept through the hallways of the building until she arrived at Supreme's door. She put her ear to the door to hear if he had company, but all she heard was mellow jazz at a low volume.

Supreme was lounging on his sofa, in boxer shorts and a holey T-shirt, listening to John Coltrane and reading an article in *Essence*, when he heard the knock. He ignored it. Probably the crazy kids from next door playing 'hall football' again. Another mid-season rug-burn for one of the running backs, no doubt. When he heard the knock again he got up, went to the bathroom and came out with a packet of Band-Aids. When he opened the door, holding the Band-Aid can, a look of shock crossed his face.

There she was, looking better than ever, at his doorstep, with her fine, uninvited ass, carrying a big bag that might have contained a campsite or something.

There he was, no longer the dominant force behind New York City's most popular barbershop, no longer looking street 'chic', in his jeans, button-down shirt and boots, but instead wearing his boxer shorts and T-shirt—looking quite ordinary for the first time she had seen him; looking quite hatless, and because of the fact that he was hatless, looking quite beautiful. He slammed the door in Vanessa's face.

She put her ear against it and heard a series of sounds. Heavy footsteps moving frantically, then stumbling, then falling, glass breaking, a stereo being turned off and a TV being turned on, then both sounds again in reverse. Finally, Supreme opened the door again—this time wearing a bathrobe, slippers and a hat.

"Mike cuts your hair, huh?"

She could tell for sure by the style.

He leaned against the door.

"When I wanna look pretty. When I wanna look mean, I do it myself." He stood back to invite her in.

Vanessa breathed a sigh of relief.

"I'd have thought you'd be wearing a tuxedo, the amount of time it took you to come back to the door."

She stepped into the apartment.

"Maybe I would've if you'd called in advance. But if you're just gonna drop by on a brotha unexpected, don't expect nothing special."

"So what took you so long?"

"I was alone, I'd gotten comfortable...couldn't let you think I keep a sloppy place, with a son to take care of and all."

It was then that Vanessa noticed his apartment for the first time.

Some brothas spent all their money on their cars. Others on their wardrobes. Supreme's car was nice enough—not flashy, no spoiler kits or any of that nonsense—and his wardrobe was street, but always fashionable, and bought for the way the clothes looked on him, not for the name on the tag. So his apartment was his money pit. It had to be. There was no other way that a barber could live this way and be spending big money in other places. It was surprising that a barber could live this way at all!

Oak, marble and lacquer furniture blended to produce different effects. The man's sense of taste was fine. Very fine. The living room was huge and the furniture was arranged to reflect that fact. He had used the far corners to accentuate less important furniture, while making the central area cosy with the TV, stereo and sofa.

"You wanna put your life down, bag lady?" Supreme asked.

Vanessa whirled to face him. He was back on the sofa, with his magazine, scratching himself on the upper thigh. She put her bag down. Supreme didn't look at her, nor did he seem compelled to act the gracious host. She took this as a cue to look around his apartment some more.

Born's bedroom was adorable. The bed was neatly covered with a cartoon bedspread. He had the cutest toys and games. A huge poster of Huey Newton hung alongside one of Tommie Smith and John Carlos giving the black power sign at the '68 Olympics. Vanessa wondered if Supreme was trying to make him into a junior Black Panther, since those posters couldn't have been requested by a five-year old.

Next was Supreme's bedroom. From the layout and decor, you would have thought he was trying to impress somebody. The huge bed. The satin sheets. The cream coloured wall-to-wall carpets. Mirrored doors on the closets. She mentally disregarded what looked like packed suitcases on the floor. Instead she wondered how many women had been seduced by the room itself, without having to be seduced by Supreme. One closet door was open, so she wandered over to it. It contained more jeans, button-downs, and an occasional sweat or T-shirt. Nothing. But there was another closet right next to it. Vanessa tried to open it, but it was stuck. This heightened her interest. Closets revealed a lot about a person. Where else would you hide your skeletons? She tugged harder.

"It's locked."

Vanessa started, turned to see Supreme standing in the doorway. He was hatless again as if he knew the effect his bare head had on her.

"It's rude to be going through people's closets anyway," he said evenly.

The two of them just stood, thinking the exact same thing, but each waiting for the other one to do something about it. They came together in a collision.

Vanessa just sort of noticed that she was naked. Naked, sitting on Supreme's chest. Her becoming naked wasn't anything that she could trace. All she knew was that she and Supreme had been attacking each other like wild animals, and her clothes must have been torn to shreds as a result. She paused from the menacing tonguing she was giving Supreme to look down at him. He was naked too. It was then that she realised that they had not had sex yet.

127

For some reason that she couldn't understand, Supreme had seemed a little reluctant to initiate the act. She knew why she had been. The apartment. Not that it was stylish and neat. But the fact that it seemed so personal, and Supreme seemed so comfortable in it. Most brothas who had nice apartments, had them for the sake of the people they planned to invite over. They could have lived like slobs otherwise and it wouldn't have mattered to them. The fact that Supreme could be so comfortable in the sort of elegance he surrounded himself in, made a statement about him that Vanessa did not want to hear. That he was not somebody for her to just play with. It was time for her to come to a decision. Could she really have something with a brotha who was just a barber?

Supreme reached his hand behind her head and began to caress the back of her neck. She looked back down at him, into his eyes, and at his beautiful, hatless face. She nodded evenly, and he began to pull her upwards, backwards for what seemed like an eternity, then he let her slide slowly, carefully, down.

Andrea decided to go through with it. It wasn't while she was in her apartment, it wasn't on the train ride uptown, and it wasn't on the cab ride to follow. It was on One Hundred and Twenty Fifth Street that she had decided. On One Hundred and Twenty Fifth Street; passing the Apollo Theatre.

If Supreme wasn't gay, then that probably meant that Mike wasn't gay either, and judging by what Vanessa had told her about what had happened the night before, then Supreme definitely wasn't gay! So Mike hadn't wanted her. It was that simple. The only thing a logical person could do would be to accept it. But Andrea wasn't being logical right then. Didn't want to be. So she decided to go through with it in front of the Apollo Theatre. The Apollo, a place that had seen people with no talent decide that they could sing, dance, tell jokes, rap, and other illogical shit. So another illogical decision made there wouldn't make too big a difference. Besides, this would probably be her last ever visit to Harlem—and what was it they said about 'going out with a bang'?

Mike hated to feel good because that meant that something bad was gonna happen.

Besides, he had enough things to feel bad about already. Andrea hadn't been in the shop that Monday. She hadn't called and she hadn't come by. His money situation had only improved to the point where he could now almost eat and pay bills. And his brother Ronnie was back in jail again—for a record three times in one summer. But Mike still couldn't help but feel good.

He had laughed when he dropped off an exhausted Supreme and

Born, having picked them up from the airport. They looked so much alike when they were happy or tired. His mother had finally paid off the mortgage for the brownstone on Striver's, so that was one less bill to worry about. He had finally gotten his knee brace off so there'd be no more peg-legging. And he was being completely himself at Ensembles. He was getting more customers by being the straight brotha who created the best hairstyles and gave better advice than the gays. Vic Juliano couldn't have been happier.

But Mike still knew that something bad was gonna happen. Without a doubt. So he shouldn't have been surprised when he opened the door to his apartment and saw Andrea standing naked in his living room.

He shouldn't have been, but he still was...

Not a whole lot, just maybe like ten or fifteen. Twenty would be dope, but just maybe like ten or fifteen. That's all he'd need. A coupla lay-ups, maybe two jumpers, a nice post-up move, and a dunk. He'd definitely need a fat dunk. If he could get two dunks though, that would be so dope! Or maybe like, a variety. One one-handed, through the lane, in traffic, and one on a fast break where he could get creative. Yeah, 'The Lawyer' would have to give him his props on those! He'd definitely get some respect outta the man. But how was he gonna stop the Lawyer though? Hopefully, his team would play a zone, and there'd be no need to worry about any individual match-ups. But what if they went man? What if they played a man-to-man defence, and he found himself matched up one-on-one against the greatest player to ever put on a pair of sneakers? He'd get embarrassed, that would be for sure. The Lawyer would probably dunk on him, or worse yet, come through the lane puttin' up one of those pretty finger rolls, which when Steve reached out to block it, would vanish, only to reappear in the net seconds later. Steve had seen that move make fools of some of basketball's best for years. He had worked on, and nearly perfected his own version of the Lawyer's finger roll, as he had nearly every move in the Lawyer's arsenal. Damn, Steve thought, shaking his head, him and the Lawyer on the same court!

Jerrod Lane was nicknamed the Lawyer because of the way he ruled the courts. It was the ultimate compliment when Steve heard his game compared to Lane's.

"Look at that move. Man, that's a straight-up Lawyer move!" or "Man, the last dude I seen do some shit like that was the Lawyer," Steve would hear as he back-pedaled up the court to get on defence, fighting the urge to smile. Tomorrow, Steve would be facing the real thing. It didn't really matter if the Lawyer didn't praise his game. All he wanted was to be acknowledged by the man. To be acknowledged as a young brotha who could play. To be acknowledged, and have just maybe like ten or fifteen points, a coupla layups, maybe two jumpers, a nice post-up move, and a dunk. Definitely a fat dunk.

"Where'd you get that diamond ring from?" he had finally brought himself to ask her that night. She had been wearing it since the first time he had seen her.

"It's an engagement ring," she said simply.

"Who'd you get it from?" he asked, frowning. She laughed.

"From my brother," she said, smiling.

"Supreme bought you a diamond ring?" Slick asked incredulously.

"He didn't buy it for me," Stephanie said. "He gave it to me. He had bought it for somebody else, but I wasn't supposed to know about that." Slick just shook his head. Strange family. The brother and sister were engaged to each other, the father was a bum, the mother called her only son 'It', and the grandchild's name was Born! How had he gotten mixed up in this clan?

"So why does Supreme make those smacking sounds with his mouth every time he sees us together?" Slick asked.

"He's saying that I'm eating my words," Stephanie said.

"What words?" Slick asked. Stephanie smiled slowly.

"So what happens when brothas turn twenty-one?" Supreme had brought himself to ask his crazy sister one day. He had purposely been avoiding this argument because he thought that it was stupid. Men didn't exist. So where did babies come from?

"Men get older," Stephanie had answered simply. Supreme had just shook his head.

"So what do you classify older brothas as?"

"Adults... hopefully," Stephanie had said simply.

"Why not 'men'?" he had asked, "What's so hard about calling us men?"

"Because 'man' is a title you have to earn," she had said. Supreme shook his head.

"Uh, un," he said flatly. "A dollar is something you hafta earn. How do you earn manhood?"

"First by being responsible," she said. No, she wasn't saying what is sounded like she was saying.

"You mean to tell me that there's no brothas out here being responsible?" Supreme had asked, the offense that he was taking evident in his voice.

"Well that depends on how you define responsible," Stephanie had said.

"Accountable," Supreme had said. "Handling all of your obligations

130

and shit."

"What about all those brothas out here with illegitimate kids?" Stephanie had asked.

"Yeah, what about us?" Supreme had asked hotly. "What about the ones of us that bust our ass to raise our damn kids right?"

"Well the few of you that do are responsible; for you're kids" Stephanie,had began, "but answer me this, would you even have kids if you were being responsible for yourselves?" The sizzle of his sister's point left burn marks across Supreme's powers of rebuttal. He could only say what came to mind; nothing.

"But wait a minute, Sis," he said, after a pause and some thought, "Not that I'm defending myself or other brothas with illegitimate kids, but shouldn't that 'responsibility' thing work both ways? On the Sistas as well as the Brothas?"

"It should but it doesn't," Stephanie had said simply. Supreme shook his head slowly. First mistake. Now she'd be history. Supreme couldn't deny that Stephanie had made some good points, but now it was time to end this insanity.

"So the captain of the 'Niggas Ain't Shit' patrol squad is trying to use a female double standard to win an argument," he said flatly. "I'm a little insulted because I'm you're brother. You shoulda known better than to try to slip some garbage like that past me."

"It's not a double standard; it's a fact. If a woman has an illegitimate kid, she ends up being responsible for it whether she wants to be or not. She can't skip town. She can't just pay some bullshit child support payments. She's stuck with the kid. She is automatically the legal guardian. And who can you thank for that? Lawmakers! And what gender are not most, but all of them? Male! They probably made up that little legality so that they could dodge all their illegitimate kids. And they probably all think they're men too!" See, now she was talking about white people, Supreme was thinking. He didn't know how she expected to win an argument if she had to bring white people into it.

"Still and all Sis, we're talkin' about brothas and you can't say that all brothas are irresponsible."

"I never said I could. I just said that responsibility was first. I got more. Like for instance, all males are dogs." Supreme looked away. Not my own sister, he was thinking. Not with that crap. That line was straight off of a talk show or a female rap song. His sister was in college. She shoulda been able to come up with something better than that.

"First of all, men are not dogs; dogs are dogs. There is no significance to that reference. A dog barks, fetches sticks, and gets slippers. He pees on fire hydrants and chases his tail. The problem is that women who use that reference, use it regarding the way a man has treated them. Is there

131

anything in scientific journals which details the ill treatment female dogs get from their male mates? If not, the reference is unfounded." Then, pausing only to admire his own ability to articulate, Supreme added, "If a man sleeps around a lot, he's not a dog, he's a player. A player's the guy who gets as much ass as he can by playing with women's emotions. Dogs do things based strictly on instinct and training. Players make up their own minds to act like they do. If there's a relationship between the two I'd like you to explain it to me. And one more thing: there wouldn't be so many players if so many women didn't provide the playgrounds." Definitely political office, Supreme was thinking. Mayor, Governor, Secretary of State maybe. Hell, maybe even president. A man who could run down some shit like he had just run down was wasting his time cutting hair.

"So you agree with me," Stephanie had said simply. Supreme looked thoughtful, but decided to remain silent. "Pees on fire hydrants and chases his tail!", she had continued with a laugh, "well we know that players just don't pee on fire hydrants, they'll whip it out and pee anywhere. And about that tail chasing, at least dogs are smart enough to chase their own. Now about that other garbage you was talkin'—about there being no relation to players and dogs—what do all the players call their women? Bitches if I'm not mistaken. Kinda hafta wonder which animal they got that reference from. And what do they do every time they go over to one of their bitches houses? Leave their shit to mark their territory. Coulda picked that trick up from Snoopy! And what do players call that part of a woman's anatomy that they want the most? A pussy, as in a cat! At last check, wasn't it dogs that chased those? Then you said the most ridiculous thing I've ever heard come out of your mouth, and believe me, that's no small achievement. You said that sistas provide too many playgrounds? It wouldn't matter how many playgrounds there were if men existed. Men wouldn't be looking for playgrounds, they'd be looking for a job sites! Somewhere they could build something that would last. But how many brothas do you know who are looking for job sites? Shit, how many brothas do you know are looking for jobs?" Suddenly, it came to him. It took losing an argument that by it's very nature, should lead him to believe that he didn't even exist before it came to him. Nobody argued that hard about men not existing except the sistas who wanted them the most desperately.

"Some day," Supreme had said slowly, "a brotha's gonna come along and make you eat those words."

"I hope so," Stephanie had laughed. "And I hope he looks so good that I don't even mind the taste."

"So, do you still feel that way about men not existing?" Slick asked.

Tony was looking into the hand mirror which was reflecting the bathroom mirror, reflecting the back of his head. He was putting the finishing touches on his edge up. There, that's good. Almost as good as Supreme, he was saying to himself. And it was; good that is, just not nearly on a par with Supreme; yet.

Tony had only begun cutting hair since the incident at Uptown Heads had left him, Tyrone and Steve, barberless. He had been appointed 'barber' because his mother owned a rusty old pair of clippers. The first haircut he gave Tyrone was so bad, it had almost made him quit selling drugs, just so that he could get a decent fade again. The first cut he gave Steve was so terrible, that Steve had to wear a skull cap for two weeks during his summer league basketball games. But the first cut he game himself was the worst. It ended with him cutting all of his hair off and starting over. And it was in this starting over, that Tony decided that he'd get it. He'd actually teach himself to not only cut hair, but to cut hair well. Just coming to this conclusion was a remarkable achievement for Tony, who had never really shown any interest in or initiative for anything. The rest was easy, if not slow. Cutting your own hair was not one of those skills that you could practice every day. You only had so much hair, and it only grew so fast.

THURSDAY NIGHT

Mike was alone. He could tell even in the pitch darkness. He didn't have to reach over. He didn't have to call out. He could just feel it. She wasn't there. She wasn't there and something about her manner, something about the way she had made love to him, something about the look in her eyes, had said she would never be there again.

He didn't want to turn on the light. He didn't want to move. He didn't even want to breath. All he wanted to do was lie there. Lie perfectly still in the blackness, until the light of day made him face a reality he still wanted to believe was not real.

You'd have thought that Sharon had gone crazy. Really.

"Good afternoon, Mr Dunn," she said. "Now let's get down to business." Her face was set so straight she looked almost angry. Her manner was formal to the point of being hostile. Designer frames rested on high cheekbones. An almost-has-the-nerve-to-be-red blazer and skirt complemented flawlessly the perfection of her body and gave her the undeniable aura of authority. She leaned, palms down against the desk, staring Dunn straight in the eye and waiting for a response. He said nothing.

"Well?"

Dunn was still silent.

"I'm waiting Mr Dunn." She was becoming irritated now. But still, he would not speak.

Her face softened.

"Hey," she said softly, smacking him gently on both sides of his face.

"Hey," she said a little louder, smacking him a little harder.

"Hey!" she screamed, knocking him off the chair with a powerful smack. *Jesus!* She had blown it now.

She began to undress. It was the attitude. It had to be the attitude! She knew she'd have to maintain a certain edge, but without losing her cool. She intended to *dominate* Rhineholt Dunn III. By losing her cool, she had just gone from a no-bullshit businesswoman to a whiny bitch.

She looked down at her favourite teddy bear, Mr Stuffins, lying on the floor. Mike had won him for her at an amusement park. He was wearing a suit and tie that she had tailor-made for him. He was standing in for Rhineholt Dunn III.

"I'm sorry," she told teddy earnestly. She picked him up off the floor, hugged him tight and kissed him on the cheek. Then she searched her closets for a better outfit. She wasn't satisfied with any of the alternatives. She shrugged, sighed and went to sit at her desk. She looked at the yellow note pad in front of her. The word 'DOMINATE' was underlined and beneath it were the script for the verbal scenario she had just attempted, and details of the outfit to be worn while attempting it. She looked at it again, shook her head and scratched it out.

The word 'AGGRESSIVE' was next on the list. She studied the script, changed clothes, put Mr Stuffins back in place and went back into action. This outfit, with its toned-down colours, was less threatening than the one she had worn for the previous rehearsal.

"Hello, Mr Dunn. I'm Sharon Moore. I believe you know why I'm here, so let's get right to it." There was a hint of a smile on her face when she finished, but it quickly soured. Not that one either. She scratched her head, then cursed because Mike had done too perfect a job on her hair. "You're gonna meet Rhineholt Dunn III for the first time tomorrow, right?" was the only explanation he had given for styling her hair so perfectly; then he laughed the loudest, strangest laugh she had ever heard.

Sharon went back to the desk. She crossed out 'AGGRESSIVE'. 'BUSINESS-LIKE' was next. The corresponding outfit consisted of boring subtle greys and blues; one of the things she hated most about the prospects of joining the corporate world.

"Mr Dunn?" she asked, as if she was standing in his office, looking in his face. "It's a pleasure to meet you. My name is Sharon Moore." She reached out and shook Mr Stuffins' paw. "I'm happy we're finally getting a chance to meet." *But are you happy?* She knew if she used 'BUSINESSLIKE', she'd be saying one thing and thinking another, and so she decided not to go with it.

It was dangerous enough to tell a man like Dunn what was on your mind; but if you were saying one thing and thinking something else, you could forget it.

Sharon walked back over to the yellow note pad. There was only one option left. 'FRIENDLY' She shrugged. Might as well give it a try! The colours for this outfit were mostly earth tones—colours that implied modesty. She realised that by wearing them she'd be admitting defeat, but at least she'd be beaten by the best.

"Hello! I'm Sharon Moore," she said, extending her hand. "I'm a really big fan of yours!" *Fan?* What was he, a Highrisers forward or something? No, she couldn't be a fan of his, she couldn't be "happy" about anything, and she damn sure couldn't lose her cool. She pulled off the clothes, flopped into an armchair and cracked open a book. She needed to take her mind off her problems, and tomorrow's meeting with Dunn was just one of them.

The problem she *didn't* yet know about sure as hell couldn't have been blanked out by reading a book. But since she wasn't the kind of sista who read a newspaper regularly, or watched the TV news, she had no idea why her *dead* boyfriend hadn't called in two days.

Bang-bang, bang-bang, bang, b-bang-b-bang, banga-banga-bang, bang, bang...bang...bang...

The noise continued until she just couldn't take it anymore. With that fool of a husband of hers in the next room working on what must have been a novel by now, she hadn't been able to get a wink of sleep.

Bang, bang, bang, bang-bang-bang-bang, b-bang, it began again. She got up and walked from the darkness of the bedroom into the glowing light that came from the one, shadeless lamp in the living room.

"Naldo!" she called, coming up behind him. Her voice was drowned out by the banging. "Naldo!" she called again, louder this time. The banging stopped. He was wearing only a robe, shorts and those hideous slippers that her mother had given him as a wedding present.

"What are you doing?"

"Typing."

"I know you're typing. All of Brooklyn knows you're typing. But *what* are you typing?"

"Two things," he said.

"What two things?"

"Well for one, this thesis of yours—which by my thinking shoulda been finished by now, seeing that it's due in next week."

"How'd you know that?" she asked, amazed.

"I read your class syllabus."

This husband of mine! she thought. *Always so thoughtful, loving, and sweet.*

"Naldo, you shouldn't be doing that..."

"Well I've got some real important typing to do after this, so I might as well do my messin' up on your paper," he laughed.

"Renaldo Isaac Franklin Ford, if you mess up my paper I'ma gon' kill you."

"I'ma?" Riff asked, laughing. "Say baby, I'm the poor, black brotha from Fort Greene. You're the bourgie sista from White Plains. You should be sayin' stuff like 'I will most certainly kill you'."

Riff laughed as his wife's rain of soft slaps poured down on top of his head. He grabbed her and pulled her close to him. Her closeness began to arouse him again. "Say baby, whatchu doing up anyway?" he asked rubbing the curve of her hips, an erection beginning to grow in his shorts.

"How could I sleep with James Baldwin at work out here?"

"Yeah, but we got busy once already tonight. You should be asleep," he said, rising from his chair. "And you know what Richard Pryor says. 'If you do it to your woman and she still wanna talk, you got some more fuckin' to do'."

She could only shake her head as her husband picked her up, carried her back to the bedroom and placed her gently down on the bed. He undressed her slowly, then undressed himself. They kissed and caressed gently until finally, he positioned himself above her. He paused before entering her.

"We can still do this again, can't we?" he asked.

She shook her head at her husband's stupidity.

"It'll probably be another two months before I even start to show."

"Good. I wouldn't want the little brotha or sista thinking they were under attack," he laughed.

And for the next hour, Riff thought about nothing but making love to his wife; not finishing her term paper, not the Schwartz brothers' offer to sell him their barbershop in Brooklyn, and not the letter of resignation from Uptown Heads that he still had to type.

The weed made it impossible to concentrate. Every time he thought about something, he thought about it for what seemed like an eternity. He was fixating on the most trivial shit. The notion to get up and do something had been lingering at the back of his mind while he concentrated on more pressing matters—like feeling the buttons on the pillows of his sofa.

After about a half an hour of flipping them over, then back over again, Vince could say for certain that it was the same kind of button on the one side as it was on the other. This was progress. It had taken almost an hour-and-a-half for him to decide that the pillows matched.

There was hair on his knuckles. Vince had never noticed it before. Twenty-three years with the same knuckles and he was only now discovering there was hair on them. Fine hair. Different from the hair on his head and the rest of his body. Its follicles were sparse and it grew like he imagined palm trees grew, swaying in one direction or another, as opposed to straight up like an oak, or curved like branches. Hair, on his knuckles. How long had it been there? Was it hereditary? Did his mother have it? His father? His father... Vince liked him better when he was dead. How can you just step back into somebody's life like that? And then turn out not to be shit neither. To all the kids *he* had fathered—and quite honestly, he had lost count—at least he was something.

If some nappy-headed bastard was to come up to him twenty years later and say: "You're my father, show me something," at least Vince would have something to show. He'd have his own island. His father didn't have nothing. Nothing. Only nerve enough to come back, wanting to be given something.

How you living? How you been?

"Mothafucka how *you* living? *Where* you been? Fuck that jail excuse garbage. Jail ain't no excuse. Jail's where you go when you ain't got a

137

good enough excuse!"

Any man that had fathered him shouldn't have been dumb enough to land in jail. And that's what that bastard calling himself his father was—dumb. Dumb enough to be the type of man with hair on his knuckles. Hair on his knuckles...

There was a quarter kilo of cocaine and a small spoon in front of him. Vince wanted to end his weed high and knew the coke would help, but he couldn't let go of the buttons on the pillows. Every time he went to move his hands, he noticed there was still hair on his knuckles. But he had to sniff the coke. He leaned over to it, pillow in one hand, reaching for the spoon with the other, but lost his balance and fell face first into the coke. Nothing left to do now but inhale.

A sudden jolt of reality made him drop the pillow. Okay now, where was he? Oh yeah, Kenny hadn't called, and that bothered Vince a little. He was sure Breeze was dead by now. He had to be. The police had found blood on the carpet in his apartment, and a gun that had been fired which had Kenny's fingerprints on it. But still, there had been no word from Kenny.

He found this a little disturbing until he figured out that Kenny had probably robbed Breeze's apartment, found something valuable and didn't want to have to share it with Vince. The thought made him laugh. Long ago he had learned from his mentor Reggie Regg to always send a thief to commit a murder and vice versa.

The thief will rob the man he kills and the murderer will kill the man he robs. Either way, murder will be the case, robbery will be the motive, and you won't be implicated.

Words to live by. And that was how he had lived, up until this point. Five years in the drug game without as much as a conviction or a bullet wound to show for it. The only thing that came close to even embarrassing him was the Riff incident. The fact that Riff had smacked him had left him feeling chumped for weeks. Ultimately, he decided against the retaliatory murder his partners were planning. Riff was the type of brotha who—if you tried to kill him and failed—would definitely be successful when he came after you.

And then this Black Experience mumbo jumbo. Breeze had been such a stupid idealist. All that 'black' shit he talked had disturbed Vince, who had been like that once, but had grown up. He didn't try to straddle both sides of the fence. You were either gonna be black or you were gonna be paid. You were never, under any circumstances, gonna be both.

Breeze had surprised him though. He had actually built the underground organisation without Vince's knowledge. That was deep. If Vince hadn't stopped giving a fuck about stuff like that, he would have been impressed. He was still, however, insulted. What would his position be in this new Black Experience thing? If he wasn't gonna run it, he didn't want to be a part of it and if he wasn't gonna be a part of it, it wasn't gonna exist; that simple.

The weak link was always easy to find—look for the one who dresses the flashiest. Reggie Regg had tutored him well. The one who wears the most gold. The one who likes to be seen the most. He'll be the brotha that would turn Judas. Kenny had been perfect. He drove around in a BMW with the windows rolled down in the winter, his wardrobe was nothing-but-brand-name and gold covered his body like lotion. Kenny was definitely the least for the cause and the most for the cash. And now Breeze was dead.

To Vince's surprise the Black Experience had not, as yet, launched a retribution for Breeze's death. Everybody had to know who'd had him killed. Vince had expected a war—but war hadn't come, and the biggest surprise of all was that in just three days, the internationally powerful Black Experience seemed to have dissolved. Vince could only feel pity for Breeze. Hadn't he even read *The Spook Who Sat By the Door*? If he had, he would have learned that each man below a leader in an organisation should be trained two levels above his position in the event that something happens to the people above him. Well something had happened to the leader of the Black Experience. So where were the next two?

Tyrone was cool for a brotha lying on top of a fortune in cocaine. *Cool as hell.* If he emptied all the coke out of its cellophane wrappers, he could've made a cocaine beach. The only thing he would have needed then was some sunglasses, a lawn chair and a glass of 'Sex on the Beach'. He could have had the Caribbean himself, right there on One Hundred and Forty Fifth Street. A Caribbean with no women in bikinis, just roaches in his shoes. Two-hundred-and-fifty-dollar shoes with roaches in them! There was something too ironic about that. These shoes weren't made for some sixteen-year-old black kid on One Hundred and Forty Fifth.

But just because he wasn't supposed to be able to afford them, did that mean that he wasn't supposed to want them? That didn't seem fair. A whole buncha shit didn't seem fair. But brothas wasn't raised to think about fair and unfair. Brothas was raised to think of reality. It was only the occasional brotha who realized that the reality of his existence was unfair.

But Tyrone had been through that. The argument was tired. No more 'ghetto-made-me-do-it' drug dealer. No more 'I'm a sixteen-year-old father, what choice do I have?' No more 'It'll only be for a little while'. No more nothing. The one good thing that had come from seeing Vince fucking his girl was it made him realise that those kind of things were all

139

part of the game. That was just the way things happened. What were most girls to a brotha in that lifestyle, anyway? They were just possessions. They were there for the taking, by the brotha who bid the highest. A girl was just something to show off like a car, to fuck, then get rid of like a whore. And hey, if you got all hooked up into one and got your feelings hurt, well Brah, that was your own fault. No bitch is supposed to be able to hurt your feelings, especially not when you got other shit to worry about like catching a bullet or a bid.

But none of this was any more true to Tyrone than the notion that Elvis was alive. He couldn't play this game. What's more, he didn't even like this game. He wanted girls to himself. Girls he could respect. Not girls who who were with him because it was his turn. He didn't want to have to wear leather in the summer to be the man, or two-hundred-and-fifty-dollar shoes, when the air conditioning in his mother's two-hundred-dollar-a-month apartment in the projects didn't work. He didn't want to duck cops on Eighth Avenue and beef with them niggas on One Hundred and Forty Third and Broadway.

He didn't like the uneasy looks Steve and Tony wore now when they walked the streets with him; like at any moment they could get hit by strays meant for him. He didn't like the looks that brothas—who were supposed to be down with him, since they all worked for Vince—gave him because they thought Vince favoured him while they regarded him as a punk. He didn't wanna keep being too hard, too cool, too smooth, too fly, too wild, too bold, too dope, or too fresh. He just wanted to be Tyrone. The Tyrone he had grown up with. The one he knew.

So what to do now? That was the question. What had been done was a mothafucka. Tyrone was one of the privileged few who knew about Vince's island plan and how he was going to get the money to subsidise it.

It was actually a sweet deal. Vince had discovered where Breeze had hidden the product he had intended to use to set up his own operation. Cocaine; pure and uncut. The value of that much coke was so high that Vince could have bought his own continent! Vince had then offered the coke to the same Colombians who usually supplied him with his shit. The US Coastguard had sunk one of the ships they used to bring coke into the country, off the coast of Florida.

This had sparked an instant four hundred per cent increase in the sale of scuba equipment in Miami—and left the Colombians short on cocaine and long on people to whom they had promised it.

Everything was going down Friday. Vince had stashed the coke in an empty employee locker at the George Washington Bridge bus terminal. Vince was not so foolish as to have it in his apartment or in a car. Tyrone took the A train up to the terminal, with his backpack and made a series of trips back and forth. Each trip, he took out a kilo of cocaine and put back an equal amount of flour.

Would Vince re-check the coke? And if he did, would he figure out who had switched it on him? The answer was 'probably' on both counts. But by the time Vince had checked it and figured out the switch, the Colombians would be after him for not delivering. All Tyrone's hopes were riding on the Colombians killing Vince. And if he got killed in the crossfire himself, at least he'd die as the Tyrone he knew. That brought him the reassurance he needed to get what might be his last night's sleep. There was one question to answer before he dozed off, though.

What was he gonna do with all that coke?

Andrea spat out the mouthful of water, then opened her mouth to take in some more. The rhythm of the water in the shower was constant, her eyes were closed. That way she didn't think so much; and that was her goal—not to think. With her eyes closed, she could be anywhere; a waterfall, a midtown thunderstorm, an African monsoon—did they have monsoons in Africa? *Don't think about it,* she told herself. *Don't think about anything. Don't think.*

Mike was telling her to think, but she wasn't listening. Think about me, he kept saying, but she refused to listen. And she refused to see him running towards her, tearing off his clothes, taking what felt like her entire body into his mouth. Nope, she couldn't see him. Had never seen him. Didn't even know who he was. *Mike who? Oh God...!* Well, she knew it wouldn't be easy. Why had he attacked her like that? She could make sense of everything else but that. Why had he attacked her? She had expected him to question, doubt, maybe even try to talk her out of it, but he didn't. He didn't say a thing. He just rushed up to her like he was dying of thirst and she was the last glass of water on the planet. And oh, how he drank! What they had done could hardly be called making love. They had been fucking. Get-down-to-it, no-bullshittin', bring-ass-to-get-ass fuckin'.

But there was more to it than that. Fucking was supposed to be passionate, but not intimate. Fucking was supposed to be physical, but not spiritual. Fucking was supposed to make you come, but not make you wanna stay. And that was the problem. She'd wanted to stay. Forever. The other problem was, if she stayed in New York, she'd probably try to. And Lord, she didn't want to be one of those sistas, those clingers she'd seen on talk shows who made her want to scream "C'mon girl, get a grip!" because they were all hooked up to some man who couldn't care less about them. And Mike obviously couldn't care less. He had fucked her. Hadn't even tried to make love to her. If he had cared, he would have taken his time, tried to be gentle. But no—he had just seen a free booty

141

opportunity and taken it.

The thing was, at the time she was glad he had at least done that. He coulda dissed her. And then where would she be? Butt-naked in the apartment of a man who didn't even want her? Yuck! The thought was too ugly. It was then that she knew.

She knew it wouldn't be her on the Oprah Winfrey Show having other sistas at home saying "C'mon girl, he's just a man."

She knew she wouldn't stay in the same city with a brotha who would drive her crazy because she couldn't have him but would always want him.

And she knew she wouldn't say no to selling sneakers and boots in Atlanta just because she might be bored every day after work.

The only thing she didn't know was, would she ever get out of the shower?

Breeze got up, looking quite healthy for a dead man, and poured another bucket of ice over the body in the bathtub.

He went into the centre of the one-roomed flat and sat on the rusted metal-bridge chair, the only piece of furniture besides a shadeless lamp on the floor. He was shirtless, wearing only loose-fitting blue jeans and heavy black boots. He rested his elbows on his knees and his chin on his knuckles. The thick muscles of his arms and upper body would have looked strange to anyone used to seeing him dressed, since he always dressed in a way that made him look slim. The peaceful look in his eyes would have looked strange to anyone used to seeing him at all. His eyes usually looked vacant, held nothing—now they held peace.

The heat of the room was unbearable. The temperature outside was ninety even at night. Inside was nearly fifteen degrees hotter—because of the room's small size, poor ventilation and the fact that the heater was broken and always on...except in winter.

Despite the heat, Breeze barely perspired. He sat calmly, occasionally stroking his unshaven face or scratching the back of his head. The room seemed to be sweating in his place. The walls were crumbling; holes and massive paint chippings were everywhere, with layers of old paint visible beneath them. The floor creaked with dry rot. The long busted-out window had been replaced with plastic, which Breeze had removed to let out some of the heat. Three rusted pipes hung directly beneath the ceiling, which was just barely more than six feet high.

The events of the past forty-eight hours hadn't surprised Breeze. He had trained himself never to be surprised. He was, however, disappointed in himself. He had made a poor character judgement. He had taken Vince too lightly. The fact that the Black Experience had been sold out left him indifferent. It made sense.

142

The only way to stop them would be if someone within turned sell-out, as has had been the case with every black movement throughout history. The fact that it had happened to him left him cold. Though he had never been afraid of death itself, the thought of being murdered by a brotha had always made him uneasy. Dying at the hands of a white man would at least have made him a martyr. But dying at the hands of a brotha would just make him another statistic.

Breeze poured another bucket of ice over the body in the tub. The room seemed to be coming apart before his very eyes. So this was how it ended, huh? Seemed fitting. He had begun with nothing—why shouldn't he end the same way?

When Kenny had just 'dropped by' two days earlier, Breeze had been in an off mood. Kenny was the BE's number two man, and if any brotha could bring a chill to a room, it was Kenny. But Breeze knew Kenny as well. So when Breeze pulled his gun out and said "Gimme your gun" Kenny almost blew the whole operation. Looking back, Breeze imagined how Kenny must have sweated. Did Breeze know the plan? And if so, how? Had Vince set him up? Kenny pulled his gun from the front of his pants and tossed it to Breeze.

Breeze inspected it, then looked back at him. "All of 'em," he said evenly.

Kenny reached in the small of his back and produced another—then another from up his pants leg.

Breeze inspected both weapons and looked at Kenny, stroking his chin thoughtfully.

"We ain't using these no more," Breeze said. "Here."

He tossed Kenny the gun he was holding. Kenny inspected it. Breeze was losing it, he figured.

Breeze put all Kenny's guns on the table in front of him and started to talk, with his back to Kenny. Breeze never left his back open to anybody. He was rubbing his face in his hands when Kenny made his move. As Breeze talked on about some brothas in LA who he had met with, Kenny crept up behind him and pointed the gun at the back of his head.

In the explosion that followed, Breeze's chin sunk into his chest. Kenny backed away from the body, then stopped in his tracks. Breeze's head remained hung low, then slowly it began to shake from side-to-side. Then he whirled around to face Kenny. There was nothing in his face, nothing in his eyes. Nothing.

"I didn't wanna do it, man!" Kenny said wildly.

Breeze said nothing.

"It was Vince's idea!"

Still Breeze said nothing.

"You shoulda seen how much fuckin' money he offered me, Yo!"

Breeze shut his eyes tight and shook his head. In one motion, he picked up the nearest gun and emptied it into Kenny's head, chest and torso.

Now he sat through his third day in a 'spare' apartment. Having carried Kenny's dead body five blocks in a garment bag and ordered one hundred pounds of ice, Breeze reconciled himself to his surroundings.

The temperature seemed to have increased by another fifteen degrees. He was at peace. He thought about the friend whose life he had taken, and his ruined plans for a black Utopia, but was at peace. There was nothing but time now, and he could do nothing but wait—and pour another bucket of ice over Kenny in the bathtub. He couldn't even call his lady and wish her luck in that meeting she had the next day.

Atlanta? That fool Andrea wouldn't last a week without The Blue Note, Build Your Own Lunch, shopping on Fifth Avenue, The Shark Bar, and hanging out in SoHo. She was going to up and move sixteen hours away because of some man? You move sixteen hours *closer* to a man, Vanessa told her. But she seemed serious, and Vanessa knew that when Andrea made up her mind to do something, something got done. She said she had to move, so she was moving. But Atlanta? Why couldn't she have started with somewhere simpler like North Jersey. That way she could move back easier when she realised that she was being a fool. And she would realize.

Andrea had brought in a letter. A letter that she herself hadn't seen in the mail slot. She sat, clutching it in her hand, confronting her future, her past and her present all at once. Thanks Andrea.

Rhineholt Dunn III had been perfect for who Vanessa was; the little private-school girl. The little 'white' girl. Dunn seemed the type of man that little 'white' girls married; both the private school-manufactured 'white' girls and the actual ones. His success was part of the ideal he represented. Here he was; young, black, competing and winning in the white man's world. What woman in her right mind wouldn't be attracted to a man like him? This was the type of man that she had wanted to marry, that she should *still* want to marry. He could give her everything.

Supreme had been the thing to try. He was a barber, which she imagined was good for him; it kept him off the streets and out of jail. But other than that, what did he have to offer? No serious woman wanted those street guys. They were thrilling, but too unstable. Any relationship with them would be as unpredictable as they were. That's why smart women got men like that out of their systems when they were young. And that's what Vanessa had been doing.

But Supreme had no right to be more than what he appeared to be. He had no right to be able to hold a decent conversation, with his own point of view and perspective. He had no right to be able to make her laugh just by being himself. He had no right to have a beautiful apartment that looked like a real man lived in it. He had no right to listen to John Coltrane, or have a subscription to *Essence* magazine. He had no right to be so damn beautiful without his hat on. And he had no right to make love to her like they shared one body. He didn't have those rights and he shouldn't have had them. They only made the inevitable more painful and more complicated.

Vanessa let the letter fall from her hand to the floor. She stared blankly off into the far corner of the room. Just when she had almost forgotten about the man. She would have thought he had forgotten about her. It had been over a year since she had sent him her resume for an internship. And now that she was damn near falling in love with the 'try' thing, the 'real' thing comes along. Vanessa picked up the letter again. Its contents hadn't changed.

She had been invited for an interview. It was at four-thirty tomorrow afternoon. And it was with Rhineholt Dunn III.

"I'm tired," Born said to his father, and his father picked him up off the ground, allowing his son to wrap his arms around his head and bury a warm cheek that smelled like baby lotion into the side of his father's neck. The father started on his journey, climbing eleven flights of stairs, luggage and son in tow, feeling no disdain for the broken elevator and smiled.

My boy, the father thought to himself, shaking his head at the colossal responsibility of such a statement. *To actually be able to claim another person as your own...*But there Born was, his boy. And as Supreme yearned for the moment to continue, the opportunity to hold so close that which was his and feel it, smell it, love it, and know that it loved him, made him wish that he could have climbed those stairs forever. Pop Pop had been right. And when, in perhaps the only tribute he would ever pay himself for having forfilled the old man's prophecy, Supreme said in a low tone, "I'ma good mothafuckin' father," his sleeping son nor anyone else in the world for that matter, was in any position to disagree.

RHINEHOLT DUNN III

He folded the paper, and tossed it across his office. The look on his face was serious, almost angry. He sat up straight in his chair, rubbing his hands together anxiously. Anyone would have thought he'd been the loser. But this was his nature, this was his manner. So, he'd pulled off the Wisconsin deal. He was supposed to, wasn't he?

But pulling it off had been hard work. He thought back to how he had found out that an old Wisconsin couple had found oil on their property.

Three months earlier Mrs Staples, a black woman who worked for a Wisconsin phone company, had been doing routine line connection monitoring when she overheard one woman tell another that her husband had 'struck oil' in their backyard. She listened in to the rest of the call, and nearly died laughing when the two women hung up. Oil in Wisconsin? How ridiculous. During her lunchbreak, she called her husband—who worked at the power company—to share the joke with him. He didn't find it funny. He told her to track that day's local call history and get him the numbers of both women. But that could take all afternoon, she argued. Don't argue. Just do it, he told her. After a couple of hours, she had narrowed it down to six possible numbers from three connections. She gave them to her husband, who called them all himself.

Mr Staples found the woman, then went and checked her claim for himself. Yep, it was oil all right! After tapping the ground, he realised there was lots of it. He advised the couple not to tell another soul about their discovery, and made a couple of calls to some brothas he knew in Milwaukee—who then made a couple of calls to some brothas they knew in New York. Rhineholt Dunn III was soon on a plane to Wisconsin.

This was the network he had worked so hard to set up. Black people, if used correctly, could be a more valuable resource than gold. Black people were the janitors, the bus drivers, the subway conductors, the postal workers, the water, gas and power company employees, the phone company workers, the airline attendants and the garbage men. These were people who knew *everything*.

A black man or woman's lowly stature could be turned into profit. Rhineholt Dunn III had realised this and used it to his advantage. The network utilised black people in those positions and rewarded them for useful information—tips, advice, rumours, gossip, anything. This was how Dunn had made it to the top. Now—with more and more people becoming part of the network—it was how he stayed there.

Dunn went to retrieve his newspaper. 'Rhineholt Dunn III Steals Wisconsin Deal!' the headline read. If he was white it would have said 'Rhineholt Dunn III Accomplishes Wisconsin Deal' or 'It's a Dunn Deal'.

But then again, he thought—smiling for the first time in a week—if he were white, he wouldn't have been able to do either.

It was nine o'clock in the morning. The sun had been out for almost three hours. It was too bright in the room for him to deny that she wasn't there anymore. And she would have drowned by now if she'd been in the bathroom all that time. Maybe she was at the store. Or at work. Or at the dry cleaners. Or on the train. Or at the movies. Or in the park. Or at a show. Or anywhere. Anywhere that would allow her to return. And she would return. And until she did, he would not leave that spot.

Mike waited like a man who had no alternative but to wait. He waited silently, barely breathing and without thinking. He didn't look at the clock, because the passing of time would increase the uncertainty of the wait. Of all the things he needed to believe, he most needed to believe that he was not waiting in vain.

When the phone rang, he was ready to tell Andrea that wherever she was, he would be there in less than a minute. He answered the phone with a hello. Supreme's voice startled him.

"She's leaving, Yo," Supreme said. "She's taking a job in Atlanta. She's going down there for a visit today. She ain't coming back, Brah! Her plane leaves Newark International at one. If you take my car, you might catch her—"

Mike hung up without saying goodbye. Supreme was insane. Mike didn't have time for insanity right then. He was busy waiting.

At nine thirty, when the phone rang again, he smiled. He wished he could tell Supreme how wrong he was. That Andrea was right there on the phone, calling to say she was just at the store getting breakfast.

"If you were Ron Sr., you'da left already," Supreme said.

Supreme didn't hear Mike answer, or hang up this time. All he heard was footsteps, running. Then a door opening, and slamming shut.

"Mr Dunn?" His secretary's monotone came over the intercom, breaking the silence that Dunn had worked hard to obtain.

"Mr Dean is here to see you."

Dunn turned his swivel chair to face the window, opposite the door. "Tell him I'll be right with him."

The next thing he heard was his secretary trying to stop Ken Dean as he barged past her and threw open the office door.

Dunn blinked indifferently.

"I woulda thought the President was in here," Dean's voice said from behind him.

"The President just arrived," Dunn said evenly.

"So you'd have your secretary keep the president waiting in your

147

lobby?"

"I had to mentally prepare for your arrival."

"That's very funny. Would you mind turning around?"

Dunn turned slowly in his swivel chair to face him.

"Thank you. I get paranoid that you're making faces or something when you have your back turned to me in that swivel chair of yours," Dean said before adding, "So, how did everything go yesterday?"

"It went."

"The papers say that you shocked Ace's people just by being at that lawyer's office, then when you pulled out that certified check, the whole place went crazy."

"You could call Donald Ace kissing me crazy," Dunn said matter-of-factly.

Dean was incredulous. "He kissed you?"

"Full-on-the-mouth."

Dean shook his head. "Ace is one crazy white man. You know it's probably the first time he's been beat at anything. I mean, truly, decisively beat. And to get his ass kicked by a nigga!" Dean laughed until he noticed the frown on Dunn's face. "Brotha, I meant to say brotha."

"I prefer Rhineholt," Dunn said flatly.

"You would."

Dean shook his head.

"You know, Dunn, you are the whitest black man I have ever known."

"Well, I'm sorry I don't carry a radio on my shoulders, or breakdance, Mr Dean, but I could give it a try if that would please you."

Dean laughed. "No. You couldn't." A wistful look came over him. "Y'know, I worry about you young brothas...I mean, you young Rhineholts nowadays, because y'all never had to work for nothing."

"You're right," Dunn said. "I've always worked for something." Dean shook his head again.

"Now y'see, that's what I mean. Here we are, two black men, just talking. We shouldn't hafta communicate in the language of the corporate world, but with you I feel like I'm talking to a white man."

"In essence what you're saying, Mr Dean, is that I keep you on your toes."

Dean shook his head again. There was a pause. "You know, you wouldn't last a minute in Harlem."

Dunn pondered his words. "Probably not a minute; no."

Dean wasn't sure how to interpret this, so he moved on.

"Is there anything else I need to know, other than what was in that prospectus you gave my lawyers?" he asked

"No, nothing other than that I strongly recommend that you retain the current staff."

Dean nodded.

"I intend to. They made all that money for you, they should be able to do the same for me and my people." He rose to leave, then paused. "You wanna hear something funny?"

"If you'd like to tell me, yes."

Dean frowned. He never imagined he'd encounter a black man with so little soul. "My daughter has the biggest crush on you," Dean said, now wondering why he even continued.

"Your daughter?"

"Yep. But she's seeing some barber now. I think you may be too late."

"Barber?" Dunn asked, as if the word tasted repulsive in his mouth.

"Yeah, some guy named 'Supreme'. Works at the Uptown Hats or Uptown Hedges...Uptown something, anyway...it's uptown. Harlem. The place you wouldn't last a minute in."

"Uptown Heads," Dunn said, after a pause.

Dean studied his expression carefully. It was the first time he had seen him without his trademark look of stiff dignity.

"You know the place?"

"I own it."

"So you get your hair cut up there?"

"I wouldn't last a minute in Harlem, remember?"

His smile took Dean completely by surprise.

"Besides," Dunn continued. "I get my hair cut in my own bathroom. I'm something of a barber myself."

Dean appraised Dunn's cut. "Not bad," he nodded his approval.

"I do know the barber you're referring to, if that's what you're interested..." Dunn said.

"Good brotha?" Dean asked.

"He has his days."

Dean looked only slightly reassured. "I don't know if my daughter would've been your type anyway," he said, as he prepared to leave.

"She's not blond."

Where the hell was Tyrone? That was all that Vince could think. Where the hell was he? A missing right-hand man on the most significant day of his life? This seemed like a very bad omen. All he'd gotten so far was no answer. No answer at his apartment, no answer at his girl's apartment. No answer. Vince put the phone back on the hook. The bitch must have told him I fucked her, he thought. Now he would have to kill him. He could never trust him again. He'd have to kill her too—on general principle. And he would personally oversee these murders. He didn't want things to be 'iffy' three days later, like they'd been about Breeze.

Vince slipped quickly into the back of the car. He had been living on

149

the run for the past few days, fearing retribution from what was left of the Black Experience. Now even that seemed behind him. Over the last two days, most of the Black Experience members had either been killed, thrown in jail, or run out of Harlem. Any who were left were in hiding.

Some interesting news had come earlier that morning: Kenny's body had shown up in the Harlem River down under the bridge. Vince had planned to hit Kenny, but only after he'd reported back about killing Breeze. He was reassured to learn that Kenny had Breeze's wallet on him when he was found.

Vince stood outside the hotel and studied the layout. He stationed two of his people on each of the building's four corners and picked three others to come inside with him. He had everyone check their weapons and ammunition. When he and his men were loaded and checked, they headed inside.

There were three Colombians in the hotel room when Vince and his boys entered carrying suitcases. Vince studied the layout of the room and the Colombians themselves, taking note of where each had his gun hidden. The fat, enforcer-looking one standing near the door had his in a harness beneath his blazer. Vince could tell by the bulge. A young-looking, pony-tailed man stood by the window, with his gun in the small of his back. Vince could tell by how restricted his movements were. The boss—a short, stout man—sat on the sofa with his gun in his sock; a hunch, because he had his legs crossed awkwardly.

Vince's boys went into their 'zone defence'—a strategy that Vince had worked out where, during transactions, his men positioned themselves near men from the other side. Two of Vince's boys stood by the window, near the pony-tailed Colombian, one stood directly in front of the leader and Vince stayed behind the couch, near the enforcer at the door.

There was a closed door in the room. He hated closed doors in drug transactions. There was always likely to be something waiting behind them.

"Where's your bathroom, man?" Vince asked the boss.

"You hafta go now?" The short one asked, sounding just a little too concerned.

"Yeah—I can't talk business with shit on my mind," Vince said, to genuine laughter from his boys, but uneasiness from the Colombians.

"It's out of order," 'pony-tail' told him. "If you really gotta go, use the one in the lobby."

Vince shook his head.

"It can wait," he said, deciding right then that if something went down, the first two shots he fired would go through that door. "Well, we ain't come here to play cards," he said. "You got the money?"

One of the Colombians handed him a suitcase. "You got the goods?"

150

Vince's boys opened up their own suitcases.

Vince counted the money, but kept one eye on 'pony-tail' as he sampled the product. Suddenly he made a bizarre expression and motioned to the enforcer at the door. Vince turned around just as the enforcer pulled his pistol from its harness.

"Yo!" Vince screamed, diving behind the sofa. All guns were pulled simultaneously. One of Vince's boys caught the enforcer with a bullet in the right shoulder, then with another in the face. The Colombians' leader in turn blasted back twice into the brotha's forehead. Vince pumped a hail of bullets through the bathroom door. Seconds later, a bullet-riddled, bloody-faced gang man staggered out, Uzi in hand and crashed to the floor. Meanwhile, another of Vince's boys and the leader killed each other outright with two shots each to the chest. Kaeshon, Vince's other boy, shot, but missed, the pony-tailed Colombian, who returned fire, hitting him in the head and neck.

Vince lay on the floor behind the sofa, breathing heavily but hardly making a sound; he used his entire hand to muffle the sound as he cocked the hammer of his gun. From where he was he couldn't see much, but he knew that his boys hadn't come out of it well. If they had, they would have made a break for the door already. That meant that at least one of the Colombians was still alive. He soon found out which one.

'Pony-tail' was in a low crouch. He had spotted the suitcase full of money lying open on the floor just inches from where Vince was hiding. He crawled towards it, his eyes peeled for danger. As he reached out for it, Vince suddenly slammed it shut and thrust it into his face. The Colombian leapt back and began shooting wildly, spraying the room with bullets.

Down on street level, the sound of breaking glass made the rest of Vince's crew look up from their posts, just in time to see their boss and another man hurtling earthwards from five storeys up. Vince was balled up around his midsection, and as the man crashed to the ground, Vince bounced off him roughly, landing a few feet away on the pavement. Vince was on his feet by the time his boys rushed over with pistols cocked.

"He's dead. Cops are probably already on their way." he said, leading them back into the hotel. They shot through the door to get back into the room and Vince headed right for the product. He sampled it. Flour. He didn't have to ask who. Who else? That nigga was gonna die anyway, but now it was gonna be painful.

Clank!

Another brick. Steve was wondering where he had left his skills, because he definitely hadn't brought them to this game. He hadn't been able to do anything—not even the most basic parts of his repertoire. The first half was almost over and he only had two points. But what really bothered him was that he was trying. He was trying his hardest. Playing textbook basketball and doing everything the way his coaches had shown him. But as hard as he tried, it was tough for him to steady himself, knowing that he was guarding, and being guarded by, the great 'Lawyer'. Steve was amazed by him. The man was hardly past his prime. He could still play and electrify pro basketball if he chose.

The Lawyer had been toying with him, putting on a show for the crowd. Steve just couldn't get it in gear. During a time out, he heard a familiar voice coming from the bleachers.

"Whatcha waitin' on, Steve?"

It was Tony. Next to him was a brotha with the huge hood of a too-large sweatshirt over his head.

"I was waiting for you to get here," Steve yelled back, smiling. "Where you been?"

"I had to kinda stop and pick up a friend."

Tony pointed to the hooded brotha. The brotha removed the hood; it was Tyrone. Steve hadn't seen him since the previous Tuesday, which was like an eternity for them.

"I hope you play like that in two years when you're up against Garvey X," Tyrone laughed. "We could build a new stadium with all those bricks."

Steve walked back on to the court grinning. For the first time in the game, he got into his normal defensive stance and, from it, stole the inbound pass. He shook off two defenders with head fakes and headed full-steam down court. When he noticed the Lawyer at the other end of the court, defending the basket, his instincts took over. In the blink of an eye, he crossed the ball over from his right hand to his left, then back to his right, put it behind his back, and drove hard to the basket with his left hand. When the Lawyer jumped to block the shot, he noticed the ball was missing. Steve had switched it back over to his right hand, and the Lawyer turned just in time to watch an arm moving in a sledge-hammer motion, coming down behind his head and back. B-o-o-o-o-o-o-o-o-m!

A fat dunk. The move had many of the hardcore basketball enthusiasts roaring their appreciation, and even those unimpressed by the sport were in awe.

"But whatchy'all gonna do when I do that?" Steve yelled at Tyrone, who had his buried his head in his hood.

The Lawyer raced back down the court and stood chest to chest with Steve.

"You tryin' to make a fool outta me, boy?" He asked, his face deadpan.

"Naah," Steve grinned. "Just a believer."

"Good afternoon Mr Dunn," Sharon said evenly. "Now let's get down to business." Her manner was formal, almost to the point of being hostile. Designer frames rested on high cheek bones. An almost-has-the-nerve-to-be-red blazer and skirt complementing flawlessly the perfection of her body—she had an the undeniable aura of authority. She was leaning, palms down on his desk, waiting.

Dunn sat in his swivel chair, facing in the opposite direction. "Have a seat, Ms Moore," he said, not bothering to turn around.

"I'd rather stand."

"Why the hostility?" Dunn asked. "We've already come to an agreement."

"Oh, I'm not hostile." Sharon said simply. "I just believe in handling business in a business-like manner."

"And you've come to this conclusion through your years of business experience, no doubt?"

Sharon was silent. *Bastard!*

"To be quite honest with you, Mr Dunn, I haven't had much business experience."

"No-o-o-o!" Dunn said, in a mildly mocking voice.

"Please don't make fun of me," she said.

"I'm not," Dunn said softly.

"I just want to be taken seriously."

"Then be yourself, Ms Moore. Be the woman that discovered a manufacturing compound twice as durable as concrete, yet half as heavy. Don't try to become the distorted image of a corporate woman that you have. Just be yourself. Your credentials speak for themselves."

Hmm, Sharon thought. *Black man's logic, white man's diction.*

"Okay," she said, shrugging. "I'll be myself. You can call me Sharon. What can I call you, Rhinie?"

"Rhineholt is fine."

"Well, Rhineholt, when do I actually get to meet you, now I'm familiar with the back of your chair ?"

Dunn slowly turned the swivel chair to face her.

Sharon nearly fainted.

Dunn just looked at her evenly.

She tried to form words from thoughts that were coming too fast.

"Do you...? Have you...? Because it couldn't be..."

"Ms Moore, is something troubling you?" Dunn asked.

"Yes, your face." Sharon said, flatly.

Dunn looked both surprised and insulted.

153

"I didn't mean it like that," she said, trying to shake some sense into her head. "I'm sorry, you just look like...oh nothing."

"Now will you have a seat?" he asked.

Sharon collapsed in the chair, still staring at him and marvelling.

"Ms Moore, the contract you have with me stipulates that you'll provide large quantities of your product and co-design the proposed office buildings.

"Now it doesn't come into effect until June of next year—and I know you intended to graduate from college before beginning any business ventures. Believe me, I would usually agree that nothing's more important than a young person's education. However, with my recent acquisition of a large amount of territory in Wisconsin, I'll be in need of both your product and your services a lot earlier than I'd anticipated. What it all boils down to is this, Ms Moore: I'm asking you to forego your senior year in college and have your lawyer restructure our original contract to commence at an earlier date."

"Yeah...sure..." Sharon said blankly, neither hearing nor understanding much of what he said. The next thing she knew, Dunn was thanking her very much, wishing her a nice day and escorting her to the door.

Business was business, she thought, as she slowly came out of her trance. Now what had she just agreed to?

Mike's mad-cap romp down the Jersey Turnpike had already gotten him noticed by the Highway Patrol. Problem was, they just couldn't catch him. Travelling in excess of one hundred and fifty miles per hour and using the shoulder of the road as a cushion, Mike proceeded with James Brown-ian abandon. You would have thought he was going to Florida. With Fat Freddie's new single, *'Move on, Black Man, Move On'* pumping from the radio, Mike breezed past a roadblock set up to stop him, wondering why the police would be so stupid as to park in the middle of the highway.

Mike's knowledge of cars was limited to how to drive them, so when he noticed the puffs of smoke rising from his hood, he paid them little attention. He didn't know to check the thermostat, so he didn't realise the car was overheating. And as he sped on, in a state of adrenaline-fuelled bliss, he heard funny noises coming from the engine. He figured he should pull over, but decided against it.

He was approaching the Newark Airport exit on the Turnpike and Andrea's plane would be leaving in under an hour, so on he went until, finally, the car just gave out. As the engine died and he coasted to a stop, he searched for some indication of what had gone wrong. One of the arrows that he'd never looked at was pointed well into the red zone. Red wasn't good, that much he knew.

As the car chugged to a complete stop he leapt out and began banging its scorching hot hood with his fists. Damn this piece of shit! Being stranded in the middle of nowhere, with no ride and no dough, brought new realisations to mind. The cops he had raced by on the highway may have been after him. They might be coming still. He could end up in jail! He banged the hood even harder. And what about Andrea, how was he going to stop her? He kicked the door of the car. Damn this piece-a shit!

"Having difficulties, Brah?" a familiar sounding male voice called out from behind him.

He looked up to see Slick and Stephanie had parked right behind him and were now eyeing him curiously. He didn't ask any questions, just jumped into the back seat. "Yo, I got to get to Newark. Fast!"

"You're in Newark." Slick said cautiously. Anybody in such a hurry to get to where he already was was in a dangerous frame of mind.

"I mean the airport."

"Why are you going to the airport, Michael?" Stephanie asked.

"To catch Andrea. She thinks I'm gay. Or at least she thought that I was gay; now she thinks that I'm not, but that I just don't want her, which I do...but she doesn't...look, can we talk about this on the way?"

Slick, who was still no wiser, nodded and started the car. "So you only think you want her?"

"Naah, I know I want her. I just think she thinks I don't."

Stephanie, confused by all this thinking and wanting, asked the only question that made any sense to her.

"Why are you going to the airport, Michael?"

"I need to tell her how I feel."

"Is this Vanessa's friend Andrea?" Stephanie asked.

He nodded.

"Where's she going?" Slick asked.

"Atlanta." Mike said.

"So why don't you just wait 'til she comes back?"

"Because she isn't. She took a job down in Atlanta."

"Why?" Stephanie asked.

Mike shrugged. "To get away from me."

"Damn brotha! You chasing women outta town with it!" Slick asked in amazement. "You must have some good..."

"Slick!" Stephanie yelled, slapping him on the back of the head. He doubled over laughing.

"What time's the flight, Mike?" Stephanie asked.

"One."

She looked at the clock on the dashboard. "Don't worry. We'll get you there in good time."

Her smile made him relax a little. "Where were you two off to anyway?"

"To deliver this car to a customer," Slick told him.

Mike noticed the car he was in for the first time. It had an interior such as he had never seen: butter-soft, cream-coloured leather, except for the area between the front and back windows, which was of re-finished wood grain. The instrument panel looked like the cockpit of a rocket—as if the driver would be able to control just about everything but the way other people on the road were driving. Mike felt like he was melting slowly into the interior.

"So, the designer of the Slick Silhouette is also the delivery man?" Mike laughed.

"Yep. And I'm also the proprietor of Slick's Taxi—so when I drop your ass off don't forget the fare!"

Mike noticed the car had a phone. "Steph, you'd better call Supreme and tell him to report his car stolen. If he doesn't, he'll be arrested for shit he never even heard of."

"It's a clinic!" screamed the announcer's voice over the loudspeaker. Steve had just made another one of those moves. The Lawyer would answer undoubtedly. The two had been going tick for tack, move for move, shot for shot, for what seemed to be hours. The fans were exhausted. They had been on a roller-coaster ride—watching the most incredible physical poetry they'd ever seen. They were too tired to watch any more, but too afraid they'd miss something to leave. The other members of Steve's and the Lawyer's teams had all but quit themselves. They were still on the court, but were content just to give the ball to either Steve or the Lawyer and watch, with as much awe as the rest of the crowd, lest they be the recipient of some funky pass thrown by one of the two.

Steve and the Lawyer were having fun. Each had risen to the challenge of the other, and decided to take it higher. Steve had proven to be a few steps quicker than the ageing Lawyer, while the Lawyer was considerably stronger than the not-yet-fully-developed Steve. Both men were using their advantages whenever possible. When Steve danced, the Lawyer pushed, when Steve glided, the Lawyer bullied. Steve was amazed to see how the Lawyer—a finesse player in his day—could adapt to play a physical game against him. The Lawyer was just amazed that he was still moving around out there. He was exhausted!

It was only during the last time-out that Steve remembered that this was a game, not a show—and that his team was behind by one point with only seven seconds left.

They were so close to the first-ever victory for a summer league team against the Lawyer. His team had the ball. There was no question who it

156

would go to. There was no question who the defence would key on. Steve walked back onto the court, casually rubbing his right tricep, imagining that some people would actually feel pressure in situations like that. He noticed the Lawyer eyeing him from the other end of the court. Steve stood idly and let the four members of the defence surround him. The Lawyer stayed back to protect the basket. Steve's team in-bounded the ball to its point guard, who started walking it up court.

When two of the Lawyer's team-mates turned to press him, the point guard lobbed the ball far into the air, in the general direction of the opposing team's basket. Two seconds had elapsed.

Steve, who had been acting like he wasn't even involved in the play, took off. No one in attendance could believe the incredible burst with which he breezed up court. The Lawyer—who had been caught off guard—reacted just a second too late to make the steal, and instead positioned himself right in front of where the ball would land. Steve caught the ball, which had been lobbed to the right side of the court some ten yards ahead of him, in stride and on his first dribble, crossed over to his left hand, shifted his entire body and drove with it on an angle towards the left corner of the foul line. Two more seconds had elapsed.

The Lawyer, who had been frozen in place by Steve's quickness, watched him head to the basket for what he was sure would be another one of those moves. Using all the pride, all the love for the game and all the competitive spirit left in him, he charged. Judging from the angle Steve was taking to the basket, The Lawyer figured he could beat him to it if he headed straight for it. The two were on a collision course.

Steve knew what the Lawyer had in mind. He was going to let Steve drive all the way to the basket, put up a shot, then use his incredible vertical leap to block Steve's shot—a tactic his fans used to call 'contempt of court'.

Today, Steve was determined to be found innocent.

He drove closer to the spot on the floor where he was sure that the Lawyer would make his move, stopped just short and watched the Lawyer go sailing by, his arms outstretched, and crash into a heap out of bounds.

Two more seconds had elapsed.

Steve had intended to pull up for a soft, ten-foot jumper, but the force of his momentum was still carrying him forward. Having no choice but to jump or be called for travelling, he allowed his feet to leave the ground. Holding the ball out in front of him in his right hand, while trying to position his body for a decent shot, he spun sideways, doing an almost complete three-sixty, before the fact that he was about to land made him flick up an off-balance desperation shot with one second left on the clock. As he turned to watch the ball in flight, Steve toppled over, landing on his back, but never taking his eye off the ball. The crowd gasped. All eyes followed the ball, as mass telepathy seemed to guide it towards the basket.

The Lawyer watched helplessly from a kneeling position, almost hoping it would go in himself. The ball kissed the front end of the rim and bounced backwards toward the goal. The crowd gasped again.

The ball kicked off the back off the rim on an odd spin and flew a few inches to the right. Another gasp.

The ball bounced off the right side of the rim. Another bounce. The crowd held their breath.

The ball settled, balancing perfectly on the left side of the rim. Steve's eyes burned through the ball as if sheer will would make it fall.

It did.

It was the most beautiful miss anybody had ever seen.

"A-a-a-a-a-a-a-a-ah," the crowd exhaled in unison.

"Damn!" Steve screamed. He climbed to his feet, then stomped off the court—pissed. He didn't even notice the Lawyer, who had walked up next to him.

"Relax," he said, smiling. "You take losing that personal, you won't do it too often."

But Steve had just lost, and he couldn't be consoled.

The Lawyer understood.

"Hey," he said, turning to leave. "You'll be all right. You took the shot. The game was on the line and the ball came to you. You controlled whether your team won or lost. You took the shot. A lotta people never know what that means, or what it feels like. They always wait for somebody else to take the shot for them. You'll be all right. My man, you're the Real."

'The Real', Steve wondered as the Lawyer walked off. Could this be the beginning of one of those great NBA nicknames like the Lawyer, the Doctor, the Iceman or Magic? 'The Real!' Steve thought to himself. 'The Real'.

"Hey!" Steve called out to the Lawyer.

The Lawyer turned.

Able to find nothing better to offer, Steve settled on:

"Thanks."

The Lawyer smiled and continued on his way.

Steve went through his duffle bag and pulled out his heavy sweat pants and hooded sweatshirt, which he put on right over his sweaty game clothes. Tony came down to greet him.

"You shoulda drew the foul, man."

"I know," Steve said shaking his head. "I started thinking about that after I missed."

"Well, you had time to think about it then. You got the rest of the summer to think about it now."

"Thanks for the love," Steve said sarcastically.

"You ready to get outta here?"

"Yeah. Where's Tyrone?"

Tony frowned.

"He broke out earlier. Said something about it not being safe for him on the streets right now."

Steve was confused. If it wasn't safe for him on the streets, why would he go back out there alone?

"Thanks," Mike said, as he emerged smiling from the back seat. "You folks have been..."

"Yeah, yeah," Slick interrupted. "Just get the fuck out."

Mike walked up to the driver's side and leaned into Slick's open window, his arms folded across the roof. "Is it me, or have I experienced nothing but negativity from this man ever since this trip began?"

"Trip?" Slick asked, incredulously. "We haven't gone ten miles."

"It isn't you, Mike. Slick's being a brat," Stephanie said, unsure whether Mike was really offended or not.

"Yeah, but you know I still love you," Slick told him, in a deep, meaningful tone.

Mike became suddenly serious.

"Look, I work at Ensembles, all right?" he began slowly. "I don't wanna hear a mothafuckin' thing about men *loving* each other." Both Slick and Stephanie looked concerned fearing they might have offended him before Mike added, "I just wanna hear about the *sex!*"

"You're nuts!" Slick said, gave Mike the 'peace' sign and then drove off.

"All right y'all," Mike said in his normal voice.

"Be safe!" Stephanie screamed from the moving car.

"Yeah brotha," Slick added. "And good luck!"

Mike nodded his thanks.

He made his way through the entanglement which was Newark International Airport. He stopped at the information booth to ask what was leaving for Atlanta at one.

"An airplane," was the sarcastic reply. He decided not to ask again. He looked at the departure monitors. There were two airlines with flights leaving for Atlanta at one. He'd have to run back and forth between them. He moved in a pattern, checking and re-checking places as if following a script.

He checked the departure gates, the magazine stores, the book stores and the coffee shops. Time was not on his side. Turning to leave one of the departure gates he spotted her, about a hundred yards away, sitting reading a magazine.

"Andrea!" he screamed at the top of his voice.

She sat staring blankly at him for a moment, then got up and started running in the opposite direction. Mike took off after her, slipping in and out of the crowd—dodging security guards, hopping over and between people and things. Each time she looked over her shoulder, Mike had made ground. He was right behind her when he saw a fat, white, security guard coming in the opposite direction. The guard straightened his right arm to clothesline Mike, who almost ducked it completely. The guard still managed to bump him, and Mike had to spin to keep his balance. He heard a pop.

Then, when he was so close he could reach out and touch her, he grabbed his knee and went down in a heap.

"Andreaaaaaaa!!!!"

The rest of the security guards pounced on him, while the fat white guard swaggered with pride at having captured him.

"He's clean, sir," another guard said to the fat one after he had searched Mike. The fat guard didn't seem satisfied.

He stood over Mike, his hands on his hips. "You ain't no Muslim tryin' to blow up the joint now, is ya?"

"Andrea!" Mike screamed. She was standing at the foot of an escalator, looking over at him face-down, helpless, in obvious pain and probably about to be arrested. She broke down, and started to approach him.

"Why are you leaving me?"

The guards had handcuffed him and were about to drag him off, but the fat one motioned for them to stay put. He wanted to hear this.

"Leaving you?" Andrea asked incredulously. "I never had a you to leave."

People in the airport lounge began to peer curiously at the spreadeagled black man, writhing in pain.

Mike shook his head. "You always had a me," he said. "You had me the first day I saw you at Build Your Own Lunch and every day after that."

"Then why did you say you were gay?"

"Gay?" the fat guard asked incredulously, then added to the security guards, "Back up fellahs. Don't anybody get too close!"

"I never actually said I was gay."

"You said Supreme was your boyfriend. Isn't that enough?"

"Sure, it's enough!" the fat, white guard laughed. "He's fruity."

"I said that because I thought that if I didn't say I already had a boyfriend, you might try to introduce me to some other brotha you knew

160

who was really gay."

"So why didn't you just tell me the truth?" she asked.

"Would you believe a man in butt-tight jeans, make-up and a blouse who said he wasn't gay?"

"What's wrong with that?" the fat guard asked earnestly as the other guards slowly began to back away from *him*.

"I guess not," Andrea said. "But why didn't you *ever* get around to telling me?"

"I wanted to, but then I said that stupid shit about you always looking good on Mondays, and I just knew that you would think I was gay because I had seen you in the same place, every Monday, for a year and a half, and didn't say a word to you."

"I remember when you said that," Andrea said. "But I just thought that you didn't want me, that's why you had never said anything."

"Didn't want you?" Mike asked incredulous. "Girl, for the past year-and-a-half you're all I've been able to think about! I couldn't wait for Monday to come so I could go to Build Your Own Lunch and look at you for an hour. Why else would I have been there? The food ain't that damn good.

"You were always with brothas. I didn't know who they were. I didn't know if you were a United Nations ambassador or a high-priced prostitute.

"Anyway," Mike continued, "What could I have said? 'Hi, my name is Mike Edwards, you don't know me but I've loved you since the first day I saw you. That's why I come into this dumb restaurant every Monday afternoon, so I can sit in the next booth over and stare at you'?"

The fat security guard nodded unevenly. Sounded good to *him*.

"Well, for starters," Andrea said. "I would have thought you were so cute!"

"You'da thought I was a psycopath!" Mike laughed. Andrea visualized just such a scenario.

"Yeah, I probably would've," she said after some thought. "But you could've said something else, Mike."

"Something else like what?" he asked.

"Anything. Just to let me know that a brotha like you was here."

"Okay, that's enough. Let's go," the fat guard said, motioning to Mike.

"Wait a minute," Andrea said, concerned. "It's all right now."

"The hell it is!" the fat guard shouted. "That man damn near started a riot."

"But I'll take him back!" she contested.

"You mean you'll bail him out. He's going to jail."

Andrea scowled at him. "I'll bet if he was white he wouldn't be going to jail."

The fat security guard paused a moment and looked thoughtful.

"I bet if he was white he couldn't have dodged my tackle."

Rhineholt Dunn III's upper body hung loosely from his swivel chair. His day was almost finished. In all his time spent as a businessman, he had never had a day so exhausting. Nor one he'd enjoyed as much. He looked at his agenda, wishing he could cancel his last appointment, but he couldn't. It was his destiny. He looked at his watch. It was four-fifteen. The appointment was in fifteen minutes.

He fingered the small name plaque on his desk. RHINEHOLT DUNN III, EXECUTIVE it read. He remembered the time when older, more experienced, men said that name in mockery. Now they said said it in fear.

He remembered the time when people indifferently asked, "Who?" Now his name was greeted with reverence. He remembered the time when he didn't appreciate his name. Now he did.

Dunn shrugged. He had nothing left to accomplish; nothing to prove. He had started with nothing. The fact that he now had more than nothing should have been sufficient. But it wasn't. What was it that drove him? Was it ego? Was it a burning desire to succeed? Was it the fact that Rhineholt Dunn I had been right; there is only one 'best' and he had to be it? Not the black best. Not the male best. But *the* best. Would it ever end? If it did, where?

Dunn breathed hot air into his fist. His finger tips were cold. His finger tips usually got cold right before an important deal, but what was about to happen in the next fifteen minutes wasn't going to be a deal. *What is it going to be and why do I have to be here?* he asked himself. He was rubbing his hands together furiously now. His finger tips were numb.

Right on time, Dunn's secretary's voice came over the intercom.

"Mr Dunn, your four-thirty appointment has arrived."

"Send her in." He dimmed all of his office lights, partially closed the blinds and got into position as the door opened.

Vanessa walked into Rhineholt Dunn's dimly-lit office with nervous trepidation. She took a hasty look around. The man had remarkable taste. The office was huge. The carpet was an impeccably clean, pearl white and so were the walls. There were two matching sets of black leather furniture which were positioned as independent work stations and rest areas. His desk was a fine polished mahogany. There was a Coltrane print on the wall. The *Love Supreme* album cover. Why did it have to be 'Love *Supreme*'? Supreme was the last person she wanted to be thinking of right now. She had reached her destiny. Supreme had been part of the journey.

Her visual tour ended when a voice said:

"Have a seat." It was a clipped, proper, even tone; the only thing betraying its racial origin was its depth. Vanessa smiled, remembering Supreme's heavily Harlem-accented voice saying "Sit down girl, this ain't no subway," during her second visit to Uptown Heads.

"Congratulations on the Wisconsin deal, Mr Dunn," Vanessa said humbly.

"Thank you," he said. "I'm impressed that you keep abreast of such issues."

"I like your art," she said. "Are you a big Coltrane fan?"

"Perhaps the biggest. He died a year before I was born and I can only imagine the body of work he would have produced had he lived."

Vanessa imagined Supreme saying: "Yeah, he made some dope shit!" She frowned. *No more thoughts of Supreme. No more.*

"Well Ms Dean, let's get down to business. First I'd like to apologise for not responding to your resume earlier."

"I assumed that you were busy," Vanessa said, beginning to wonder if she was going to have to look at the back of his chair for the whole meeting. What was so interesting out the window anyway?

"Yes, I was deeply engrossed at that time," Dunn said.

Supreme was chasing the mischievous Born, who had purposely put his shoes on the wrong feet to see if he could run faster. Vanessa had laughed and laughed...

"Well, I'm just glad that you hadn't forgotten me."

"Oh, absolutely not, Ms Dean. In fact, I was so impressed by your resume that I almost called you the day I received it; as it was, I made a mental note of it."

Supreme was brushing the back of Fat Freddie's neck with quick, even strokes, once he'd finished the cut. It was the only time during any haircut that he looked serious, earnest...

"Well, in a way Mr Dunn I'm almost glad you didn't. I've had a chance to grow more as a person. I believe that now I might possibly be more of an asset than I was when I first submitted my resume."

"That's interesting. I've never heard a person express happiness because they weren't hired immediately."

Supreme, at the movies, asking "do you remember him in...?" or "do you remember her in...?" knowing all the black actors and actresses by name. She wanted to kick him for ruining the movie. Then he'd look at her, just look at her, and say softly, "I'm really glad you came with me..."

"Well that's why you hire people. Because they do things that nobody else would have thought to do," she pointed out.

"Good point."

"Thank you."

Supreme slapping her hands away, again and again, as she reached for whatever it was that he'd just stuffed into his back pocket. And her pretending she had forgotten about it—then picking his pocket as they waited for the train, only to find it was her favourite book, Tar Baby by Toni Morrison, which he'd been reading because she'd said it was her favourite...

"I like the way you think, Ms Dean. I've always thought that most employers hire people for the wrong reasons. Experience, education and professional history are all good determinants of what someone has done, where they have gone to school, and where they've worked, but they don't show how that person thinks."

Supreme, the night they made love, telling her softly: "I'm here, I'm here, I'm here," over and over as he held her. He was there. Now where the hell was she? "I can't go through with this." she whispered to herself.

"Ms Dean, I like to conduct interviews with my back to the interviewee so that what I see doesn't prejudice my decision—"

"Mr Dunn, I have a confession to make," Vanessa interrupted.

"Confessions are for Catholic priests, Ms Dean—" Dunn said whimsically. "—not your future boss."

"Not that kind of confession, Mr Dunn." Vanessa said calmly. She had either missed or ignored the fact that Dunn had just hired her.

"I want to tell you the real reason that I sent you my resume."

"To be considered for a position, I would hope."

"Yes Mr Dunn, but not with your company—with you," she said, with as much composure as she could manage. "You see, I first heard about you about two years ago. It was in some newspaper article describing names to watch in business in the future. The article said that you were the 'new kid on the block'. I remember it saying that your 'young, ruggedly handsome, black face seems more suited to a modelling career than the cut-throat world of free enterprise'."

"I remember the article."

"Soon there were more articles published about you. Each one projected you bigger, brighter and bolder than the last. They made you seem like a god."

"You can't have read all of them," he laughed.

"Oh—I thought the less flattering ones were even more impressive than the ones that fawned all over you!"

"How so?"

"They showed the ruthless side you'd need to be successful."

"You manage to see a great many things, Ms Dean."

"I started cutting out all the articles about you and taping them to the wall near my bed. I'd watch the news every night, hoping for another account of something you had done, something you had said. I faxed you my resume at least fifteen times; I guess the time you got it was the time it finally reached your desk. I practiced what I'd say if I ever got an interview."

"Why did you do all this?" Vanessa paused.

"Because I loved you..."

Her voice tapered off as she heard herself say the words. Dunn was silent. "I knew I had to. You see, you represented everything I ever wanted. I'd always dreamed of the perfect man for me, even before I'd ever heard of you. He'd be intelligent, successful, beautiful and mysterious. For years he seemed like he would always be just a dream. And then you came along. You're brilliant, successful, from all accounts attractive, and so very mysterious. You were my perfect dream man."

"When did your feelings change?"

"How do you know they have?" she asked.

"You used a series of past tenses, I represented...you dreamed.. you loved..."

"Well a couple of months ago I met a man. I thought he was gay at first, actually, but that's another story. He was attractive enough, tall enough, and built nicely enough, but I knew—or at least I *thought* I knew—that we could never have anything that would last. I mean, aside from the classic 'good girl's attraction to a bad boy', there was nothing. He was loud, rude, arrogant, chauvinistic, sexist, had terrible grammar and was a downright pain in the ass! He didn't seem to be too intelligent at first and didn't look like he'd ever be successful at anything other than his job which wasn't much. But then, I fell in love with him."

There was a short silence. "Well, how could you not?" Dunn asked sarcastically.

"To top it off," Vanessa continued, "he's an employee of yours."

"An employee of mine?"

"Yes. He works as a barber at Uptown Heads. His name is Supreme. You see Mr Dunn, my problem was that I wanted a mystery man to come and sweep me off my feet. I wanted a love like you read about in romance novels; like you see in the movies. I wanted a man that already had everything, a man that was perfect, who would include me in his perfect life, make me his perfect wife and we'd live perfectly ever after."

"And now?"

"Now I want what I've got," she said thoughtfully. "A man who isn't perfect. A man who has next to nothing. A man who quite often pisses me off with his know-it-all, Mr Trivia, Encyclopedia Brown philosophies on every subject under the sun! A man who makes me laugh. I mean, laugh 'til I ache. A man who makes me smile because he's smiling and when he's smiling everything feels all right. A man who I think loves me, and who I know I love."

Dunn was silent.

"So, I'm sorry, but I couldn't accept the position. I attempted to obtain it for fraudulent reasons."

"But looking beyond that Ms Dean, I still think that you would make an excellent employee..."

"Perhaps; but just not for you," Vanessa concluded.

"I'm sorry you feel that way. But it has been a pleasure talking with you..." Dunn said, and as the swivel chair turned slowly, Vanessa strained her eyes to see through the dimness. When she was able to fully make out Dunn's profile, Vanessa's eyes widened as if witnessing the impossible. Supreme had cut his hair! It looked like it had been chiseled onto his head. It didn't make him look mean though. Just beautiful in an altogether different way. Of all the things she could possibly have thought of, Vanessa wondered why it was right then that she thought of Stephanie's last name.

"Why didn't you tell me your father was Ken Dean?" he asked, his face even, with only the slightest hint of mockery in his eyes.

"I didn't know that it made any difference," Vanessa heard herself say. The next thing she heard was the purring motor of a running car.

When you're driving along the Palisades heading north, you can see the city across the river, to your right, over the tree tops.

You have to follow the passing buildings closely and almost have to study geography to know exactly where Manhattan Island ends and where the Bronx begins. That is, if you care in the first place. Westchester is looming just north of where you're focusing and—even if you are from the New York area—if this is your first time travelling on the Palisades, you're probably wondering just where in the world you're going, heading north, on a highway, on the wrong side of the Hudson.

When you see the sign that says 'Welcome to New York State' you really get paranoid. Where in the hell are you being welcomed *from?* You just saw Manhattan five minutes ago. If you weren't in New York then, where were you?

If you hadn't just awakened from having fainted in Rhineholt Dunn III's office, you might realise that you most probably just left Jersey. If you had just woken up from having fainted in Rhineholt Dunn III's office, you would probably have more important things to think about.

"Where are we going?"

"To my house," he said.

"But the apartment in Harlem..."

"Supreme has an apartment in Harlem," he said.

"But aren't you Supreme?"

He laughed. They made the rest of their journey in silence. Vanessa was amazed at the difference in the scenery. The whole area they drove through looked like one big Central Park. She saw exit ramps for places that she had never even remotely heard of; Orangeburg, Pearl River, Nanuet, Spring Valley.

"What is this place?" she asked, after he took one of those oddly named exits, drove for a while and pulled up to a quaint-looking house.

"Rockland County," he said.

"A cheesy writer friend of mine grew up here."

She followed him inside. For once, she didn't look around. She wasn't interested in the decor. She was interested in the truth. She had waited long enough, so now chaise longues and antique bureaus could wait.

He led her through a narrow hallway into a huge, opening room she figured to be the living room, offered her a chair and sat down beside her. He sat there smiling for almost a full minute. She waited patiently.

"I have a confession to make to you, Ms Dean."

"Confessions are for Catholic priests, not your ex-girlfriend Mr...whoever you are."

"I guess I deserved that."

"You deserve a lot more than that."

"Well then I guess I have some explaining to do."

"*Some* is an understatement."

"Would you like something to drink, or...?"

"Just start talking," she said, cutting him off.

"The name on my birth certificate is Rhineholt Dunn III," he began finally. "And wearing a tailor-made suit and four-hundred-dollar shoes, I get called by that name between nine in the morning and five in the afternoon every weekday, down on Wall Street.

"Wearing big jeans, boots—regardless of the weather—a hoodie, a button-down, or, if push comes to shove, a T-shirt; thirty minutes later on weekdays and all day on weekends, I get called Supreme up in Harlem.

"A lot more than my clothes change in that half an hour though. I have to change from the one persona to the other."

"So you're telling you have an alter ego?"

"No, just two sides to the one. It was something my grandfather taught me. He said that all Dunns have two sides—one side for 'messing up', one for 'taking care of business'. He also said that in most of the Dunns, the two sides were out of synch. So that when you needed one, the other would arrive.

"I just decided to get my act together. See the positive aspects in both sides and use them when I needed them. Dunn was for handling business..." He paused, smiling: "...and you've already met Supreme."

Vanessa just sat there, rubbing her index finger across her bottom lip, waiting for the end of the story.

"I was born in Co-Op City in the Bronx and moved to Harlem when

I was seven. I met Mike and this brotha named Vince on my first day of school up there. That's when Mike hit me with that damned mud-pie—which, if you remember, he was just getting around to apologizing for when I met you! Fifteen years—"

"Finish the story."

"Okay. When I was seventeen, my grandfather, Pop Pop, also know as Rhineholt Dunn I, died. A week before, I had found out that my girl-friend Denise, was pregnant. My grandfather's death seemed to initiate some inner war between the 'taking care of business' side of me and the 'messin' up', psycho hoodlum Supreme; the main focus of which was Denise.

"Rhineholt Dunn III hated her; Supreme was in love with her. We'd both hate her ass soon enough, though. About a month after Pop Pop died, I caught her screwing Vince."

Vanessa frowned. "When she was pregnant?"

He nodded.

"That's nasty!"

He nodded again.

"Naturally I drank more and messed around with more women, but what was bugged-out was, I also started getting good grades in school, and I also started cutting hair.

"Pop Pop had been a barber and he gave me a pair of clippers for my seventeenth birthday, so after I practiced on Mike and he practiced on me, we started our own travelling hair-cutting business. I was making big dough, too. My mother had never worked and my father lost his job, so I was paying the rent, buying the food—everything.

"No man can be second man in his own house, so when my Supreme side started speaking up for his rights, my father kicked his side—and every other side—out.

"That night Rhineholt Dunn III and Supreme formally split. Rhineholt setting off to start his career in business and Supreme doing something he was already becoming relatively great at—cutting hair. That way I could earn good money and still get to spend some uptown quality time."

"Where did you get the money to start in business?" Vanessa asked. The story was becoming more fantastic by the minute.

"Mike gave it to me," he said casually. "I had given all the money I had to Stephanie. So Mike gave me a loan. The first thing I did with it was buy an old disco that the city was damn near giving away. Remember that spot Infernos?"

"The one in Harlem that burned down?" she asked.

He nodded. "It was home for Born and I for about six months before it became Uptown Heads."

"So let me get this clear. Straight out of high school you bought your own barbershop, then went right to Wall Street?"

"Not exactly. Mike had gotten a basketball scholarship to Adam Clayton Powell University, and as part of his deal he insisted that I come along as his personal masseur. Mike was such a hot recruit that he could get away with that sort of thing. I would work at the shop during the day and take mostly night courses. I went straight through school, summers and everything, and graduated with honours in three years with a major in Finance and a minor in Economics.

"Mike probably could have done too, but playing ball he missed a lot of classes. And when he got injured in his sophomore year he damn near had to take off a semester. Of course, with me supposedly being his masseur, the guy wanted knee rubs and all kinds of craziness but one night I told him he had some real pretty legs and I never had to touch that brotha again."

"So after college you just got a job on Wall Street and stayed there?" Vanessa asked.

"No. I never had to work for anybody. Aside from becoming a certified broker and licensed commodities trader, I just kept my ear to the ground. Found out who and what was hot. I had been getting such good grades during school that I was awarded a post-entry academic scholarship, and working at Uptown Heads I had saved a lot of money—so I started looking for ways and places to invest it. I loaned Hot Rod the money for his first studio equipment. I was a majority shareholder in the movie studio that signed Jungle Jim, and I loaned him the money for his first video camera. I'm sponsoring Gary through med school. I co-owned the record label that Fat Freddie, Natalie Austin and King James all record on. I gave Kookin' Keisha and Cee Jay grants to finish their work. I loaned Vic Juliano the money to open up Ensembles.

"I loaned Slick Shawn Sanders the money to research, develop and patent his idea for a new automobile—the car we just came home in as a matter of fact. They had the talent and the initiative to go places and I had the capital to compensate them for the trip. A lot of times, I used Supreme's 'ghetto' popularity and made deals as Supreme, working for Rhineholt Dunn III."

"And this is how you've come to run New York?" Vanessa asked, impressed.

"I run next to nothing in New York now—all I own is a huge clump of oil-rich land in Wisconsin. I sold all of my New York holdings except one."

"Why did you buy all that land in Wisconsin?"

It was something she had wondered about for a while.

"'Cause I'm on some ole Marcus Garvey shit," he said—and for the

169

first time during the entire conversation, Vanessa clearly, distinctively, heard Supreme. She also noticed a shift. A very small, but very notable shift in his attitude, demeanour and personality.

"So you want to take black people back to Wisconsin instead of back to Africa?" she teased.

"What in the world is there for a brotha left to do in New York? You can't farm. You can't grow your own food. You can't live off the land because there is no land. You can't build anything because everything's already been built. You can just live with what was here before you. That's not cool.

"The majority of black people in this country who don't think they can get anywhere in life, don't think they can because they don't see contributions by anybody that looks like them. They just think, *'hey, the white man's been in charge—he's gonna be in charge. Ain't nothing anybody can do about it, so fuck it.'*

"They know that brothas are never gonna run things here and don't see why they should. The only thing most people know about black history is that Martin Luther King had a dream. They don't even know that he woke up. So when I show 'em a young brotha way out in Wisconsin, building his own cities, and redesigning his own state and local governments and—pretty soon—fixing up this screwed-up government, they'll come out to Wisconsin with clothes, cars and Afro Sheen in hand."

"So that's what you want?" Vanessa asked, a little sceptically. "Black separatism?"

"Naah." He shook his head. "Black alternatives. We'll see how many blacks will stay in New York, Philly, Boston, Chicago, LA, Atlanta, DC and Detroit—with their rats and roaches, poverty and crime, slums and slumlords and ready-made ghettoes—when they can come out to Wisconsin and build a new life. We'll see how many brothas and sistas will stay places where they're still discriminated against and abused because of their race, when—in Wisconsin—black will be the colour of choice.

"We'll see how many of them will stay in places where Black History Month in school is in February—when in Wisconsin it's all year round. We'll see how many niggas will wanna stay niggas."

Vanessa sat there staring. This guy was talking about building a new world! Was he crazy? You couldn't do that type of thing. Nobody would allow it. Absolutely nobody would follow it. He seemed to be reading her mind.

"You know, not everybody in the colonies thought that America should be independent of England," he said matter-of-factly. "The fact is, the American Revolution was an act of treason." He paused there to let his point sink in. The colonists who rebelled felt that they were justified though. They felt mistreated. So they decided to build their own government. The colonists, for the most part a group of criminals and misfits."

A history lesson. A barber was giving her a history lesson! Now she'd heard it all. But there was more.

"If the colonists thought that they were being treated unfairly, what the hell do you call what's happened to us for the past four hundred years?"

"And if they can build a government and their smartest dude was Thomas Jefferson—the slave owner—then I know I can, when I got people like Mike, Riff, Gary, Jim, Keisha, Slick, April, Freddie, King James, Rod, Nicole, Cee Jay, Sharon, my sister, Andrea and you."

Vanessa shrugged. Why not? He was right about one thing; white people had already done it, why *couldn't* brothas and sistas do it? Here she was with a barber who said his friends were smarter than the people who drafted the Declaration of Independence and the Constitution.

And he was probably right!

"How did you get all the money to buy that land in Wisconsin, anyway?" She recalled reading that he had been struggling to do just that.

"Well, your father organised a group of black businessmen and women to buy every asset that I liquidated."

"That was nice of him," Vanessa said with a smile.

"Nice? Hell, that was business. I don't have no garbage assets, so everything I sold had major profit potential. Them folks didn't buy my stuff to be nice, they bought it to make money."

"But I read somewhere that even if you sold everything you owned you'd still be short."

"I was," he said.

"Then where'd you get the rest of the money?"

"I borrowed it."

"From who?"

"From Rhineholt Dunn IV."

"Born?" she asked, amazed.

He nodded. "Rhineholt Dunn IV. Born Supreme. See, both names are on his birth certificate. Born Supreme's in parenthesis. I didn't wanna name him Rhineholt Dunn IV, but it was the last thing Pop Pop asked me to do before he died."

"How did Born get that kind of money?"

"From selling my grandfather's old farm in North Carolina to a company called Big Money Realty," he said. He looked thoughtful before adding: "He's got other money that I'm not sure where it came from."

"Well that was nice of Born," Vanessa said cheerily.

"Nice? That rat is charging his own father eight-and-a-half per cent interest!"

"So that's how you beat Don Ace?"

The story was coming together like pieces of a puzzle.

"Damn, you really had your eye on Rhineholt Dunn III, didntcha? Yeah, that's how I beat him. You know what the funny thing was, though? I had always pictured Ace as some 'good ole boy' racist who was just harassing me because he hated to see negroes succeed in the world of business. When Born and I walked into that meeting yesterday and presented that old Wisconsin family with the cashier's check, Ace kissed me! And I mean dead, smack, in the middle of my mouth. I didn't know what to do. I mean, it wasn't like some gay kiss or something. It was a kiss like a father would give a son.

"I felt like Chicken George and Massa Tom in *Roots*. But when Ace kissed me, it made me wonder if the only reason he's been sweating me so hard all this time was because he's a competition freak and I was the only one who could give him any."

Vanessa nodded. Seemed plausible.

"You took Born with you to Wisconsin?"

"You think he would have let me leave him? He wanted to see how his money was being spent!"

Vanessa laughed.

"How did you avoid being photographed all those years?"

He laughed.

"Photographers were never allowed in my office. If you notice, all the pictures of me are outside of my office."

"But I never saw you in any pictures."

"If you look closely, you'll notice me standing in the background of almost every crowd picture that a photographer took trying to get Dunn. All I did was put on on my 'Supreme' clothes and flip my hat backwards at the end of the day's business. When a photographer heard I was in the area and went to take a picture, he would just run right over me—never even considering that I could be Rhineholt Dunn III."

"So it was sort of a reverse stereotype thing?"

He nodded.

She paused a while. "So what would I have found if I had looked in that locked closet in your apartment in Harlem?"

"Suits. Rows and rows of business suits."

She nodded. His story was nearly complete. She knew the 'who', the 'what', the 'where' and the 'when'. The only question left was...

"Why didn't you tell me any of this before?"

"I had to see if you loved me," he said simply. "Rhineholt Dunn III would be easy for a woman to fall in love with—being rich, successful and intelligent. Supreme would be much harder for a woman to fall in love with. Firstly he's poor, then add 'loud, rude, arrogant, chauvinistic, sexist, has terrible grammar and is a downright pain in the ass'..."

Vanessa laughed—his ability to quote her was remarkable.

"But the woman who loved me would have to love us both."

"So if I had come into Dunn's office today and said I was still in love with Dunn, I'd have been..."

"Outta here, ghost, gone, later!" he said decisively.

"So that's the reason you kept Rhineholt Dunn III's identity a mystery?"

"Mostly. The other reason was, Supreme had too much of a reputation as a clown. Rhineholt Dunn III needed to be taken seriously as a no-nonsense businessman. If the entire city knew that Rhineholt Dunn III, New York's leading businessman, was actually Supreme, the barber from Uptown Heads, I might have some of my less patient, less articulate customers interrupting a merger deal with: 'Yo, whassup, God? Am I gonna get this cut or what?'"

Vanessa burst out laughing as she pictured that.

"By the way," she began, smiling: "How come Supreme, speaks 'ghetto' English, yet today your English has been flawless?"

He shook his head disappointedly.

"Vanessa, don't you know that every black man has to be bilingual? I speak normally when I'm in Uptown Heads. But I can also throw down that tighty-whitey bullshit when I hafta. Most brothas can. Look very carefully at that brotha with his hat turned backwards, bopping to the sounds of his headphones the next time you get on the train. He could be the C.E.O. at IBM."

Vanessa shook her head in amazement at the truly remarkable individual sitting in front of her.

"So you mean to tell me—" she began in her 'so let me get this straight' tone, "—you actually flip-flopped back and forth between personas every day?"

"Not only that," he laughed. "These two sides really didn't like each other! I had even convinced Mike, Born, Stephanie and Vince to view them as two different people."

Vanessa looked deeply into his eyes as she adjusted herself in her seat. "So who are you now?" she asked coyly.

"Who do I look like?" he returned the serve.

"The man I fell in love with."

"Well, there you have it." he said smiling.

"One thing, though..."

"What's that?"

"I think you need some serious therapy!" she said, only half-joking.

"Maybe so," he shrugged. "But I'm feeling much better now." He turned off the lights and they made love over and over and over again.

Supreme awoke slowly, still in the half-dream of Vanessa. When he looked around he found that she was gone. In her place was a note. Mike had called while he was asleep. There was something going down at his apartment in Harlem. She had caught a cab and he should head that way too. Supreme shook his head. It couldn't have been an emergency, if Vanessa hadn't even bothered to wake him. He needed to go back into the city that night anyway. He had to go by Uptown Heads and pick up its financial records. Then he'd go straighten out whatever Mike had fucked up over at his apartment.

The drive seemed to take forever. It was only about ten-thirty, but he was exhausted. The day at the office had been demanding, and making love to Vanessa for another two hours hadn't helped any either. It was after eleven when he arrived at the dark, empty barbershop.

Supreme stomped tiredly through the shop to the back room where the books were kept and turned on the light. As he gathered up all the records and journals he'd kept since he purchased Uptown Heads, he noticed some slips of paper under one of the kids' toy building blocks in the corner. He moved the blocks and picked up the pieces of paper. There was a series of numbers in some odd configuration written on all of them, with a portion of the *Wall Street Journal* taped to each one. The portion of the paper had the same stock circled on each page. Supreme scratched his head as he tried to figure out what the numbers meant. Slowly, a sinking feeling began to get the better of him.

He remembered that Born and some of the older kids were doing something suspicious in that room every Saturday morning—they were too young and far too impatient to actually be investing, even if they had been forecasting. He realised the only other thing they could have possibly been doing was playing the numbers! How? Or better yet, who?

Who knew enough about numbers to teach kids how to predict them? Who knew what stock to follow and could show kids how to follow it? Who had been around that environment and had the experience too?

The image slammed into his mind with the force of a locomotive. Who else? *Bumpy!* Supreme shook his head, remembering the legendary history of that old man. The old player was now trying to turn Supreme's son into a young one. He'd kill that senile old fool. And as for Born...

Supreme stood stoically, thinking of a way to punish him, and yet wishing he had thought of doing the same thing at Born's age. He turned out the light and walked out of the room, forgetting to close the door. When he had walked about five feet, he heard the strangest creaking sound coming from the next room. He paused, and glanced around the pitch-black Uptown Heads before retracing his steps. He heard the creak again. Now he saw how Born had always known whenever he tried to catch them in the back room; a loose floor board!

Supreme continued walking towards the front door. As he was about to open it and leave, he heard a commotion outside—the sound of men fighting. Not being a big fan of stray bullets, Supreme decided to peep through the blinds before venturing out. The block was abandoned save for the two figures going at it. It was Vince and Tyrone; Tyrone was clearly getting the better of Vince.

Tyrone had tried to go straight home after he had left Steve's game, but spotted two of Vince's boys outside his apartment building from a block away. He headed back to the park to meet up with Steve and Tony, but by the time he got there the game had ended and everyone had left.

His next stop was Tony's apartment, where his mother told him that Tony and Steve had just left on their way to Steve's. At Steve's he found out that Steve and Tony had just left on their way to Supreme's. Facing either certain death on the streets, or a chance that Supreme might forgive him, he had decided to head over to Supreme's. That was when Vince drove up beside him.

Vince had been driving around the city for hours looking for Tyrone. Perhaps foolishly, he had sent all of his boys in different directions and was in the car alone. When he finally caught up with Tyrone, his first instinct was to shoot him on sight, but he decided that he wanted to do some more personal damage first.

He decided to kick Tyrone's ass, underestimating both the seriousness of his injuries from his five storey fall, and Tyrone's skill with his hands.

Supreme watched the brawl with interest. There they were, two 'dead' people out in the street fighting. Should he call somebody? The police? Or the morgue? Vince was getting badly beaten.

After one particularly damaging combination from Tyrone, Vince stumbled backwards into a wall and pulled out a gun. Supreme had seen enough. He rushed across the street to where the murder was about to take place. Both the murderer and the potential victim were surprised to see him. Supreme grabbed Tyrone and, using his left arm, wrapped him behind his back, shielding him from Vince.

"All right, yo. That's enough!" he told Vince.

"So it speaks."

"That's *enough*, Vince," Supreme repeated.

"How's it enough? I don't see nobody dead."

"And you won't either. You're not a murderer."

Vince nodded. "You know this would be a fucked-up time to find out that you was wrong."

"I don't plan to," Supreme said, evenly.

Vince studied him, with deadly intent. "Neither did Reggie Regg."

175

"So you killed Reggie. I know you killed Reggie. Everybody knows you killed Reggie. I also know that Reggie's the only person you ever killed. Killing wasn't for you, so you made sure you never had to do that shit again."

Supreme paused, and watched the murderous look in Vince's eyes dissolve.

"So you killed Reggie. You ain't no killer. Just like one drink don't make you a drunk and having sex once don't make you a ho—killing one dude don't make you a killer."

Vince seemed momentarily convinced, then confused, then sure again.

"Yeah," he said, nodding.

"Killing one dude don't make you no killer. But killing the *right* dude does. I killed Reggie Regg because he was the right dude to kill. I'll only kill a nigga myself if he's the right dude to kill. And that's what the man hiding behind your back like a little bitch is. The right dude. He tried to have me killed and, even worse, he tried to fuck up my money. Now what could make him more *right* than that?"

Supreme shook his head wearily.

"Look man, put the gun down and go home. This shit is stupid."

"You always think you can tell people what to do, don't you?" Vince spat.

"That's your fuckin' problem! Ever since I've known you, you always thought you could boss people around. Well, this ain't high school, man. And you ain't got the first gun! So I suggest you take your stupid-name-havin'-bastard-son-lovin' ass home and forget you was even here tonight."

So that's where this was heading, Supreme thought. Vince needed to hype himself up to kill Tyrone. All the fake bravado and street talk was bullshit. Vince wasn't using it to convince Supreme and Tyrone. He was using it to convince himself.

"You know how stupid you sound?" Supreme asked, almost laughing.

"How stupid *I* sound?" Vince asked incredulously. "*I'm* the nigga with the gun. *You're* the nigga out here with just your shirt on arguing with an armed man!"

Supreme laughed.

"Man, if I wanted a gun, I'd take yours."

There was a look of confused hurt in Vince's eye.

Supreme knew he was calling Vince's bluff, but he also worried about what Vince would feel he had to do because of it.

"Man, you always thought you was a bad nigga, didn'tcha?" Vince said. He sounded like he was on the brink of murder, or tears.

"Man, I never thought I was bad," Supreme said, a little uneasily. The look in Vince's eyes was the last look a lot of brothas had seen before somebody—somebody as emotionally unstable as Vince—had killed them.

"Yeah, you did," Vince continued, gearing more towards murder than tears. "All safe in your school, and barbershop and office building down on Wall Street, thinkin' you was bad..."

Supreme could only shake his head.

"You never knew the truth, didcha?" Vince continued.

"You never knew all that 'good nigga' bullshit you was doing wasn't nothin'. That fuckin' making-it-in-the-system, faggoty-white-shit was only gonna get you more and more white asses to kiss and that's whatcha been doing."

Supreme felt a tightness. A hot tightness. His whole body seemed like it was connected to one thick, pulsing nerve. A nerve that, if Vince said one more thing, might—

"But you've done it now I guess. Yeah, Wisconsin and the whole shit. But tell me one thing...Is that your face, or the last white man's ass you kissed?"

Supreme reached out with two arms; one for the gun in Vince's hand and one for Vince's neck. Supreme heard the shot, and felt the jolt send his body reeling. Tyrone looked down the barrel of the gun in terror—sure that he would be next to die. Sure, until he looked into Vince's eyes.

As Supreme's body tumbled, then spread across the concrete, Vince looked like a man who was watching his own brother die. His mouth hung open, his eyes wide. Tyrone turned to look at Supreme's almost lifeless body, for that moment unconcerned about his own fate.

He saw a circle of blood form on the back of Supreme's shirt, that seemed to be coming from his neck. Then he heard the sound of laughter...Supreme's laughter.

There was something about the sound of it. It was genuinely joyous. It transcended place and time. You didn't have to hear the joke—or even know what was funny—to want to join in. Supreme arose from the concrete with a smile that lit up the night. He walked back to where Vince was still standing, gun in hand. "Look at this," Supreme said, motioning to his bloody shoulder.

Vince looked cautious.

"You know this is the same shoulder that Denise's Pops shot me in."

Slowly, Vince began to smile. His whole demeanour changed. Suddenly, he wasn't a twenty-three-year-old drug dealer about to kill a barber any more; he was the seventeen-year–old-kid with the academic scholarship to Garvey X, just rapping to his best friend.

"Word?" Vince asked, still grinning.

"Yeah, I was holding his grandson and the man shot me." Supreme shook his head at the memory. Vince shook his head as well.

"Yo, that's how the man was. He was a nut. I remember when I was still messin' with Denise..." he paused.

Supreme looked startled. The spell was broken. The mention of Denise—the reason that their friendship had ended—brought the two men back to reality.

"It's too bad we're havin' this conversation right now, man," Vince said flatly, wistfully. Supreme nodded slowly. His life was about to end. He was sure of it.

"Yeah, it's too bad, now that it's too late," Vince continued. Supreme was silent. Tyrone was still rooted to the spot, terrified.

"Well, I guess I'll see you in the next life," Vince said.

"Vince, if you're gonna shoot me, shoot me. Don't talk me to death!" Vince laughed a humourless chuckle.

"That Supreme," he said. "Always the funny man."

He raised the barrel of his gun toward Supreme's head. Supreme's mind filled with questions. Should he run? Lunge? Duck? Reach for the gun? Beg for his life?

The sound of the shot was so distant—and its impact so painless— that Supreme smiled in thanks to Allah, the merciful, who had spared him any discomfort and suffering.

As he made his ascent and prepared to enter the gates of heaven, he heard loud cursing behind the clouds. He wondered who the offending angel could be... he would have to let the Creator know what went on in the ranks when his almighty back was turned...

The cursing grew louder as Supreme grew closer to the gates. Unable to locate its source, he opened his eyes.

Vince was standing crouched over, still cursing, blood pouring from the hand that had held the gun. Supreme saw it on the floor, and kicked it out of his reach.

He was still alive. How come? One Hundred and Twenty Sixth Street was empty—except for a couple of parked cars, a stray cat, and litter. But way off in the direction of Lenox Avenue he saw the silhouette of a tall, slim figure. Supreme watched the figure approach.

In the middle of his struggle to finalise the Wisconsin deal, Supreme had heard the story of Breeze's demise, and had stored it—and the emotions it brought—in the back of his mind. Now, as he watched Breeze approach, he went through the full cycle of emotions. He couldn't hide his smile as Breeze drew nearer. Tyrone, who now believed he had seen the dead rise twice in one night, passed out.

Supreme revived him with a gentle kick in the midsection and a, "Get up you fuckin' jackass!" Tyrone stood up quickly and took shelter behind

Supreme, peering over his bleeding shoulder in panic. Vince was now hopping and spinning in pain. He noticed Breeze in mid-spin and froze. Breeze aimed his gun at Vince.

"Nice shot," Supreme said with a smile.

Breeze nodded.

"I heard you was dead."

"I am," Breeze said flatly. "To everybody it matters to."

"Well, it matters to me—and you ain't dead, mothafucka!" Vince cried, between gasps of pain.

"Shut up!" Breeze and Supreme said simultaneously.

"Whatcha gonna do now?" Supreme asked Breeze.

"Lay low. Reconsider my options, figure out my next move."

"You know my offer of work still stands."

Breeze shook his head.

"Didcha at least think about it?"

"I still am," Breeze said earnestly. "But my life ain't worth the bullet it would take to kill me right now. You think that, if I worked for you, that would change? Or it would stop at me? You and everybody else that worked for you would be in danger...It's not worth it."

Breeze shook his head. Supreme nodded solemnly.

"You think you're gonna make it?"

Breeze shrugged indifferently.

"Whaddaya think's gonna happen to you?" Supreme asked.

Breeze shrugged again. "What happened to Malcolm?" he asked rhetorically. Malcolm X had been shot and killed, everyone knew that. But Supreme knew that it wasn't the fact that Malcolm had been killed, or even how, that Breeze was referring to—but by whom.

"An inside job, Yo?" Supreme asked.

"Was it *really* an inside job when Malcolm was killed, Yo?" Breeze asked.

Supreme looked thoughtful. If what Breeze was implying was true, then his destiny was already determined. The only thing that wasn't set was his date with it.

A brand new, jet black Slick Silhouette with two men in the front seat, raced up on the curb beside them. Breeze motioned for them to hold on for a moment.

"It's a funny thing when you can't trust anybody," he said to Supreme. "I've lived my whole life that way. My main goal right now is to make it through the night and if I see a tomorrow, do the same thing."

He cast a furtive glance at the men waiting for him in the car.

"Let's hope those two brothas in there have the same intention."

Supreme nodded.

"You know," Breeze began again, reflectively: "I don't have any

179

regrets. I never did a thing in my life that I wouldn't do again. If most people were born in the kind of situation that I was, when they became a criminal, they'd be complaining that the world had owed them something. I would never even waste the breath." He paused.

"But if I coulda changed one thing about my life, I woulda known you back when he did," he said, nodding to Vince. "Things mighta ended up different."

"A lotta good it did him," Supreme said.

"Yeah, but he's stupid."

They laughed. There was too much to be said between the two of them to say anything more. Both were sure of only one thing: they would never see each other again. Breeze turned, grabbed Vince roughly by the arm, opened the back door of the car and shoved him in. Breeze moved to follow him in, then paused and looked back at Supreme.

"By the way...congratulations on the Wisconsin deal."

"You knew from the beginning, didntcha?"

Breeze nodded.

"How?" Supreme asked. Breeze smiled.

"Couldn't be two mothafuckas like you in the same city."

He got into the car and closed the door and soon it had disappeared around the corner. Before it had gone fifty yards, Supreme heard a single shot ring out. He closed his eyes—unsure whether to mourn for the friend of his youth, or the one he had just made moments ago.

Semi-recovered, Tyrone was now staring at him wildly. "What did he mean by 'congratulations on the Wisconsin deal'?"

Supreme began to walk towards Lenox Avenue.

"Didn't Rhineholt Dunn III make the Wisconsin Deal?"

"Come on!" Supreme said angrily.

Tyrone shrugged and followed obediently.

FRIDAY'S FAREWELL

Nothing really changes on Lenox Avenue when it rains. Everybody's already so into whatever they're doing or going to be doing, that the rain doesn't do anything but make them wet and they've all been wet before. If you looked around on a rainy day, you'd notice that nobody seemed particularly disturbed by it. The rain soothed the pain of Supreme's gunshot wound. The walk was familiar. The time of night was also familiar. The day was just different, that's all. And his partner of course. His partner was different. This walk, which usually came on Saturday nights, was usually with Mike. With Mike, Supreme could talk during the whole walk, or remain silent the whole twelve blocks, it would make no difference. He and Mike were like an old, married couple. They knew each other so well, they didn't have to make up something to talk about just to kill the silence. But Supreme couldn't deny the uneasiness he felt walking silently next to Tyrone. Tyrone who had been dead for the last couple of months, was now undeniably alive and what could Supreme talk to him about? What could Supreme ask him? How was his trip?

"I'm sorry about everything, man," Tyrone said, breaking the silence and saving Supreme the necessity.

"You should be," Supreme said flatly.

"It's just...my girl was pregnant and it didn't seem like I had any other choice," Tyrone said.

"See, but that's the thing," Supreme began, "if you didn't have any other choice, I could almost understand. If you had looked in all the want ads, if you had walked up One Hundred and Twenty Fifth Street looking for work until you dropped, if you had tried to sell T-shirts, oils, incense, anything, if you had begged and borrowed, if you had asked your mother, your grandmother, your grandfather, me, Mike, Riff...anybody! If you had done everything else you possibly could have first, then got involved with that bullshit, I could almost understand. And notice I said 'almost'."

Tyrone nodded evenly.

"The easy way out," Supreme said. "How come it's you brothas headed to Garvey X that are always looking for the easy way out?" Tyrone shook his head, although he knew that the question hadn't been intended for him to answer.

"What was all that shit back there with Vince about anyway?" Supreme asked.

"I set him up to get killed," Tyrone said casually.

"How d'ya do that?"

"I stole about five million dollars worth of coke he was about to use

181

in a big deal and substituted it with flour."

"Five million dollars?" Supreme asked, trying to mask the extent of his interest.

Tyrone nodded.

"What d'ya do with the coke?" Supreme asked.

"I flushed it down the toilet," Tyrone said.

Supreme made an odd face.

Noticing, Tyrone asked, "You woulda done the same thing, right?"

"Five million dollars worth?" Supreme pondered the question a while. "Down the toilet, huh?"

Tyrone thought he detected disappointment. Supreme shrugged, but Tyrone noted that he didn't actually answer the question.

Supreme looked over at him and for the first time noticed the hair cut that was very different from his own, or any other than he had seen. It was a new work, from a fresh, new perspective.

"Who's been cuttin' your hair?" Supreme asked Tyrone.

"Tony."

"I didn't know he could cut!"

"He couldn't, but after you threw me out, I needed a barber. I didn't wanna go to Kool Moe or anybody like that, so I let Tony experiment on me. This is the best one yet. The first few were horrible."

"Well he's a fast learner," Supreme said, nodding. Maybe he had solved another problem.

The two walked on in silence for another few blocks, before Tyrone could gather up enough courage to ask him the question he'd been dying to ask since they had started walking.

"Are you Rhineholt Dunn III?"

"No," Supreme said, shaking his head. "He's me."

Tyrone's eyes widened, amazed. Without missing a beat his tone of voice became almost Dunnish as he asked: "Do you think a loan might be in order for a prospective Garvey X University student, sir?"

Supreme looked at him, and laughed. "I'll think about it."

When they finally arrived at his apartment, Supreme became suspicious of the pitch blackness he could see under the door, in a room that was supposed to contain at least four people by now. He opened the door slowly, reached in from behind it and turned on the lights.

"Surprise!"

He walked in to find the faces of everyone he knew. Faces that shone with happiness. Happiness for him and happiness for some new belief they all seemed to have in themselves. Among them were: Born who up until that point had been heading for a spanking; Vanessa who still was; Stephanie and Slick; Mike and Andrea, Steve and Tony; Riff and his wife Stacey; Fat Freddie, King James, Jungle Jim, Hot Rod, Gary, Nate Allen,

Natalie, Kookin' Keisha, Cee Jay, Angie, April, Rock Killer, Pat Erving, Mike's sister Shirley and his brother Ronnie, Dave; 'Big Money Larry, Cool Antoine, True Lee, Pretty Ass Jamal, Strong Stan, Sexy Suzy, Dee Dee, Lori, Veronica, Anita; Bumpy—wearing a brand new suit—;Dr Charlie Andrews, Nelson Gibbs, Willie T Williams, Crazy Injun; and Sharon, who had the same dazed look on her face now, that she'd had hours ago when she agreed to work for him. Supreme felt a pull in his chest when he looked at her. He'd have to pull her aside later, he told himself. He'd have to pull her aside and tell her that her boyfriend was dead. That even if he was still alive tonight, he was dead. He would have to, he told himself.

"Guess what y'all?!" Tyrone cried loudly, becoming his old self once again. "Supreme is Rhineholt Dunn III!" The quiet that followed was thicker than solid metal. Tyrone looked from face to face and each face returned the same look of bored tolerance for an idiot. Tyrone was confused. Vanessa, who had been amongst the last to know, held up the day's paper. There, right under the headline 'Rhineholt Dunn III Steals Wisconsin Deal', was a picture of Supreme, with a surprised look on his face, being kissed by Donald Ace.

"Oh!" was all Tyrone could say. "So everybody already knew?"

"Everybody but you," Steve said coming forward to slap his friend affectionately on the back. The majority of the people in the room joined him. It was good to have Tyrone back from the dead.

Supreme had a drink in his hand and was making his way over to Vanessa when he remembered his bloody shoulder. He called Dr Andrews over. "Gotcha medical bag on you?" he asked.

"Of course."

"Now's your chance to prove yourself again," he said, motioning for the doctor to follow him as he walked towards the terrace. "Yo, Vanessa, Mike, Andrea, Riff, Tony and Tyrone! Y'all come with me for a sec."

They all followed.

The group went out on to the terrace, the half-roof protecting them from the rain. They watched as Dr Andrews worked on Supreme's shoulder, it seeming so absurd that Supreme of all people, could turn out to be Rhineholt Dunn III, that no one could even think to ask him why his shoulder was bleeding.

Dr Andrews cut through the shirt and took Supreme's drink out of his hand.

"What is this?" he asked.

"Vodka."

"You mix it?"

"Naah."

Before Supreme could continue, Dr Andrews had poured it over his naked shoulder.

"Aaaawww! Damn Doc! You and Gary are the sneakiest medical mothafuckas I've ever seen!"

Dr Andrews laughed. He had already dislodged the bullet. The rest would be easy.

"All right, now." Supreme's voice took on a distinctively Rhineholt Dunn III vein, "anyone who's read today's newspaper article knows something about my plans for Wisconsin...The bottom line is, Born and I are leaving for Wisconsin tomorrow. The first thing we're going to do when we get there is decide how we want things arranged. It will be a short trip and I should be back soon to discuss it with all of you. Now, Mike and I have already gone over what his end of everything is. He's going to use that architecture degree that's been sitting in his closet collecting dust, to co-design some of the structural implementations we plan to undertake with Sharon. He'll be flying out sometime this week to get a look at things for himself. Andrea, if you could fly out with Mike, I'll need you to get an idea of how you could devise your own black business phone book. Or, for that matter, start a phone company. There's no time to think small. It's time to build."

Andrea nodded. Was this really the same gay barber she'd met at Zimbabwe's?

"Riff," Dunn said, "are you still interested in owning a barbershop?"

Riff nodded slowly. He looked away from Dunn, away from the others and off into the direction of the park in the distance. He pulled a typed resignation out of his pocket and handed it to Dunn.

Dunn read the letter and ripped it up. Riff looked at him, startled. He would have punched Supreme in the mouth for the same thing. But he wasn't looking at Supreme.

"Uptown Heads is for sale," Dunn said simply. "You know the location, you're familiar with the clientele and the owner is willing to give you a deal."

"But with Mike and Supreme leaving, I'd still be one barber short, even with Kool Moe," Riff said.

"No you won't," Dunn said, shaking his head. "Hire Tony."

"Tony?"

"Yeah, he cut Tyrone's hair."

Riff took a look at Tyrone's cut. He studied it with all the attention to detail of a diamond cutter. Then nodding, he said:

"Could work."

"Tony, would you like to work in Uptown Heads?" Dunn asked.

"Naah, I wouldn't mind," Tony said, a bit shocked. "I just can't tell jokes like you, or beat people up like Riff. Maybe I could be Mike."

Everyone laughed.

"Just be yourself," Dunn said simply. Then he turned to Tyrone.

"In answer to your question Tyrone, no, I won't give you a loan. But I will give you a job. You can sweep up hair for your friend Tony at Uptown Heads." He turned to Riff, and added, "I'll pay his salary myself."

"You'd better," Riff joked.

"What did you need me out here for?" Vanessa whispered in his ear.

"I just wanted to tell you that I love you," he whispered back. "I know I've never told you before."

Vanessa was overcome by emotion until he added, "And now, since Riff's psychiatrist wife is here, I'm gonna seek that help that you suggested."

She burst out laughing and kissed him. Dr Andrew finished his shoulder, warning him to seek a second opinion immediately.

"Yo, Gary, come check my shoulder out!" Supreme called into the crowded room. Everyone on the terrace laughed.

"Let's go back inside."

Supreme pushed everybody back through the terrace door, except Mike, who he grabbed by the arm. "So you got her back, huh?"

"Yeah," Mike said.

"You happy or sad?" Supreme asked, a wide smile on his face.

"Both," Mike said, with a smile that matched his.

"Aaaah! You might as well die right now then!" Supreme joked.

"Might as well," Mike laughed. "How'd you know she was planning to leave anyway?" he continued.

"Vanessa told me."

"How did you know that I even dug her like that?"

"It was written all over your face, Brah!"

Mike smiled broadly. "You played a homo for me, man. Carried me home when my leg was fucked-up. Let me borrow your car any time I needed it. Loaned me money. Saved me from losing my girl." He paused. "There's only one thing I can think of saying to a brotha who did all that for me...I really am sorry I hit you with that mud-pie in the third grade."

"Well it's about time you *really* apologised! Supreme shrieked. "You didn't think I took that bullshit at Zimbabwe's seriously, did you? And even if I did, that wouldn't mitigate the fact that you hit me in the face with a mud-pie! A god-damned mud-pie!"

Mike could only laugh as Supreme continued his tirade. It was a small price to pay for a friendship as good as theirs. There was a lot more to tell him that night, though. He'd been thrown in jail and only released because the judge was a romantic. He hoped that Supreme wouldn't be needing his old car any time soon, because it was being held as evidence. And after only three months of actually knowing her, but a year and three-months of loving her, he and Andrea were engaged.

All this would have to wait until later, though, Mike thought as he and Supreme re-entered the party with their arms around each other's shoulders; Mike leaving his arm on Supreme's shoulder despite the fact that Supreme's blood was fucking up one of his favorite shirts. All this would have to wait until later. After all, there was a party going on and Supreme, shot, bloody, and exhausted, would have to be the life of it.

End

NEW!

Black Classics

NEW from The X Press— an exciting collection of the world's great forgotten black classic novels. Many brilliant works of writing lie in dusty corners of libraries across the globe. Now thanks to Britain's foremost publisher of black fiction, you can discover some of these fantastic novels. Over the coming months we will be publishing many more of these masterpieces which every lover of classic fiction will want to collect.

TRADITION by Charles W Chesnutt

In the years after the American Civil War, a small town in the Deep South struggles to come to terms with the new order. Ex-slaves are now respected doctors, lawyers and powerbrokers—And the white residents don't like it one bit! When a black man is wrongly accused of murdering a white woman, the black population, proud and determined, strike back.For a gifted black doctor, the events pose a huge dilemma. Should he take on the mantle of leading the black struggle, or does his first responsibility lie with his wife and children?

THE BLACKER THE BERRY by Wallace Thurman

Emma Lou was born black. Too black for her own comfort and that of her social-climbing wannabe family. Resented by those closest to her, she runs from her small hometown to Los Angeles and then to Harlem of the 1920's, seeking her identity and an escape from the pressures of the black community. She drifts from one loveless relationship to another in the search for herself and a place in society where prejudice towards her comes not only from whites, but from her own race!

IOLA by Frances E.W. Harper

The beautiful Iola Leroy is duped into slavery after the death of her father but manages to snatch her freedom back and start the long search for the mother whom she was separated from on the slave trader's block. She rejects the advances of a white man, who offers to relieve her from the "burden of blackness" by marrying her and eventually finds love and pride in her race.

THE CONJURE MAN DIES by Rudolph Fisher

Originally published in 1932, *The Conjure Man Dies* is the first known mystery novel written by an African-American. Rudolph Fisher, one of the principal writers of the Harlem Renaissance, weaves an intricate story of a native African king, who after receiving a degree from Harvard settles into Harlem of the 1930's. He becomes a fortune teller or 'Conjure Man' and quickly becomes a much talked about local figure. When the old man is found dead the rumours start spreading. Things are made even more confusing when he turns up very much alive!

THE AUTOBIOGRAPHY OF AN EX-COLORED MAN
by James Weldon Johnson

Until his school teacher points out to him in no uncertain terms that he's a "nigger", the anonymous narrator of *The Autobiography of an Ex-Colored Man*, believed that his fair skin granted him the privileges of his white class mates.

The realisation of what life holds for him is at first devastating, but as he grows into adulthood, he discovers a pride in his blackness and the noble race from which he is descended. However a disturbing family secret is soon to shake up his world.

THE HOUSE BEHIND THE CEDARS
by Charles W. Chesnutt

A few years after the American Civil War, two siblings, Rena and John Walden, 'pass' for white in the Deep South as their only means of obtaining a share of the American dream.

With a change of name and a fictitious biography, John starts a new life. But for Rena, the deception poses a bigger dilemma when she meets and falls in love with a wealthy young white man.

Can love transcend racial barriers, or will the dashing George Tryon reject her the moment he discovers her black roots?

Also Available *Black Classics*

Three more forgotten greats of black writing will be available from December 1995. Check out: *A LOVE SUPREME* by Pauline Hopkins, *THE WALLS OF JERICHO* by Rudolph Fisher and *THE PRESIDENT'S DAUGHTER* by William Wells Brown. Ask for details in any good bookshop. Only from **The X Press**.

Books with ATTITUDE

THE RAGGA & THE ROYAL by Monica Grant Streetwise Leroy Massop and The Princess of Wales get it together in this light-hearted romp.   £5.99

JAMAICA INC. by Tony Sewell   Jamaican Prime Minister, David Cooper, is shot down as he addresses the crowd at a reggae 'peace' concert. But who pulled the trigger and why?   £5.99

LICK SHOT by Peter Kalu   When neo-nazis plan to attack Manchester's black community they didn't reckon on one thing...A black cop who doesn't give a fuck about the rules!   £5.99

SINGLE BLACK FEMALE by Yvette Richards   Three career women end up sharing a house together and discover they all share the same problem-MEN! £5.99

MOSS SIDE MASSIVE by Karline Smith   When the brother of a local gangster is shot dead on a busy Manchester street, the city is turned into a war zone as the drugs gangs battle it out.   £5.99

OPP by Naomi King   How deep does friendship go when you fancy your best friend's man? Find out in this hot bestseller!   £5.99

COP KILLER by Donald Gorgon   When his mother is shot dead by the police, taxi driver Lloyd Baker becomes a one man cop-killing machine. Hugely controversial but compulsive reading.   £4.99

BABY FATHER/ BABY FATHER 2 by Patrick Augustus Four men come to terms with parenthood but it's a rough journey they travel before discovering the joys in this smash hit and its sequel.   £5.99

WICKED IN BED by Sheri Campbell   Michael Hughes believes in 'loving and leaving 'em' when it comes to women. But if you play with fire you're gonna get burnt!   £5.99

FETISH by Victor Headley   The acclaimed author of 'Yardie', 'Excess', and 'Yush!' serves another gripping thriller where appearances can be very deceiving!   £5.99

PROFESSOR X by Peter Kalu   When a black American radical visits the UK to expose a major corruption scandal, only a black cop can save him from the assasin's bullet.   £5.99